LETTERS FROM KATE

Realizing what she'd found, Allison scooped up the letters. She was stuffing them back into the manila envelope when she was seized by a thought so stunning that it stopped her hands in midmotion.

Maybe she was meant to find these letters.

Maybe, in this time of shattering crisis, there was something here that would help her understand the proud, impossibly stubborn man she'd married.

Or maybe not. The letters were private and precious. She had no business touching them.

Still vacillating, she gazed down at the scattered envelopes, trying to decipher the blurred postmarks. The latest one was dated a few months before Kate's death.

One envelope, this one plain, white, business size, and thicker than the others, bore no postmark, stamp, or address, only a single line, written in an unsteady hand.

For Burke, to be opened after my death.

Don't miss any of Janet Dailey's bestsellers

JANET DAILEY

LETTERS FROM PEACEFUL LANE

ZEBRA BOOKS
KENSINGTON PUBLISHING CORP.
www.kensingtonbooks.com

ZEBRA BOOKS are published by

Kensington Publishing Corp.
119 West 40th Street
New York, NY 10018

Copyright © 2019 by Revocable Trust Created by Jimmy Dean Dailey and Mary Sue Dailey Dated December 22, 2016

All rights reserved. No part of this book may be reproduced in any form or by any means without the prior written consent of the Publisher, excepting brief quotes used in reviews.

To the extent that the image or images on the cover of this book depict a person or persons, such person or persons are merely models, and are not intended to portray any character or characters featured in the book.

If you purchased this book without a cover you should be aware that this book is stolen property. It was reported as "unsold and destroyed" to the Publisher and neither the Author nor the Publisher has received any payment for this "stripped book."

All Kensington titles, imprints, and distributed lines are available at special quantity discounts for bulk purchases for sales promotion, premiums, fund-raising, educational, or institutional use.

Special book excerpts or customized printings can also be created to fit specific needs. For details, write or phone the office of the Kensington Sales Manager: Attn.: Sales Department. Kensington Publishing Corp., 119 West 40th Street, New York, NY 10018. Phone: 1-800-221-2647.

Zebra and the Z logo Reg. U.S. Pat. & TM Off.

First Kensington Books Hardcover Printing: February 2019
First Zebra Books Mass-Market Paperback Printing: April 2019
ISBN-13: 978-1-4201-4491-8
ISBN-10: 1-4201-4491-X

ISBN-13: 978-1-4201-4493-2 (eBook)
ISBN-10: 1-4201-4493-6 (eBook)

10 9 8 7 6 5 4 3 2 1

Printed in the United States of America

This book is dedicated to Mary and Jim

ACKNOWLEDGMENTS

For Elizabeth Lane, whose invaluable help is always appreciated.

CHAPTER 1

Branson, Missouri
October

Alone on the balcony, Allison Caldwell watched the shadows deepen across Table Rock Lake. Even in the fading daylight, the hills that framed the water burned with autumn color—the flames and crimsons of black gum and bittersweet, the scarlets and golds of maple, ash, oak, and hickory, all at the peak of their fall glory.

In the darkening twilight, lights glowed from the distant boat marina, blurring into mist as a bank of fog moved in over the lake. A gull winged its way shoreward. A sport fishing boat, trailing a wake like a silver ribbon, passed and vanished from sight.

Below the trail that passed the house, a fresh breeze rippled the water. It tugged at Allison's long diamond earrings and loosened tendrils from her upswept honey-blond hair. She raised a manicured hand to control the damage but made no move to go back inside to the party.

Behind her, on the other side of the French doors, her guests were sampling pâté with truffles, caviar, tiny Bavarian sausages, and a rich selection of vintage wines. Fifteen minutes from now they'd be sitting down to a dinner of black bass on cabbage, caramelized plantation shrimp, pea tendrils, and walnut toffee tartlets. Allison had put weeks of work and planning into this forty-seventh birthday dinner for her husband, to say nothing of the small fortune the caterer had cost. But the result had been worth the effort. From the food to the décor, from the mellow piano jazz CDs that Burke liked, to her own chic little black Armani dress—everything was perfect.

So why did the thought of going back inside make her want to lean out past the rail and puke all over the hydrangeas?

Filling her lungs with the moist air, Allison struggled to calm her nerves. She would have to rejoin the party soon or there'd be even more talk. But every time she turned toward the doors, the snippets of conversation she'd overheard returned to stab her in the back.

"So, Burke's got himself a little trophy wife. How old is she? Thirty, maybe thirty-five? Lord, what would Kate say? The poor dear must be turning over in her grave!"

"And just look at this place! That leather couch alone must have cost three thousand dollars. The woman's going through his money like a cat through a tin of sardines. Let's hope Burke had the sense to draw up a prenup."

"I'll wager he's going to need one. They got married last year—you remember that fairy-tale wedding at Top of the Rock. How much longer do you give it before they're talking through their lawyers? Six months?"

"A year, tops. Care to lay a little bet?"

"Fifty bucks? You're on!"

Allison willed herself not to cry. Tears were hell on mascara, and the last thing she wanted was to walk back into the party with raccoon eyes. But she'd tried so hard to make Burke's friends like her. All that effort, and now this. She might as well have spat in their judgmental faces!

"Here you are." The strains of "My Funny Valentine," from the Ahmad Jamal Trio CD, drifted through the French doors as Burke came out onto the balcony. At the sight of her rigid back, he turned and closed the latch softly behind him. The music fell to a hush that blended with the clink of crystal and the muffled sound of voices.

"Is everything all right, honey?" She felt his big, strong hands slide around her waist. Allison had fallen in love with those hands, just as she'd fallen in love with his cobalt eyes, his close-clipped platinum hair and the dimple in his jutting chin. She hadn't been looking for an older man, let alone a wealthy one; but from the moment he'd stepped into her small California gift gallery to buy a silver mermaid charm for his daughter, she'd felt as if they were meant to be together.

What had gone wrong?

"Allison?" He drew her back against him, his lips brushing her shoulder. "Are you okay?"

"Fine." She nodded, not wanting to spoil things for him. "Just getting a breath of air."

"Tired?"

"It's been a long day."

"Quite a shindig you've put together. The gang's impressed, I can tell."

Sure, they are. Just ask them about your little trophy wife. "I wanted your birthday to be special," she said.

"Any night with you is special." He pulled her closer, his arms moving to cloak her shoulders. The scent of the expensive men's cologne she'd bought stole into her senses. She knew he'd only worn it to please her, but she still liked it. "I'd have settled for burgers at Stumpy's and an early bedtime," he murmured against her hair. "You know that, don't you, Kate?"

Allison went cold in his arms. It had been six years since Burke's first wife had died of cancer. Still, when he was distracted, hers was the name that popped out of his mouth. Allison knew it wasn't intentional. Often, like now, he didn't even seem aware of what he'd said. But one would think, after so much time . . .

She pulled away from him. "We'd better go back inside. Dinner should be ready in a few minutes."

"I can't stay for dinner." He blocked her path to the doorway. "That's what I came out here to tell you. I just got a call from Max at the theater. The Mayweather Family Gospel Singers are opening tonight. Two hours before the show, Mrs. Mayweather found out her husband was cheating. They had a big blowup. She blacked his eye, and now she's refusing to perform with him. The audience is getting restless. If there's no show, they'll be wanting their money back. I've got to drive into town and straighten out the mess."

"But surely it can wait till after dinner! It's your birthday! There'll be a cake—"

"It'll have to keep, Allison. I've got to go now. Tell

our friends I said to enjoy my birthday party. They'll understand."

"But will your wife?" The words burst out before Allison could stop them, gushing like blood from a ruptured artery. "When you proposed, you talked about all the good times we'd have together. But all you seem to think about is that blasted theater business of yours! Lately I feel as if I don't even exist for you!" She blinked away a scalding tear. "Damn it, Burke, sometimes you don't even remember to call me by the right name!"

He stepped backward, his mouth a grim, flat line. "I don't have time for this, Allison. Not now."

"So when *will* you have time?" she demanded, catching the sleeve of his dinner jacket. "Tomorrow? Next month? How about never?"

"Don't be a child." Jerking loose, he turned and walked away. As he opened the door, the lush piano notes of "The Second Time Around" drifted into the twilight.

For an instant Burke seemed to hesitate. Then he strode across the threshold and closed the door with a click, leaving her alone.

Allison's stomach clenched as she heard the garage door opening and, seconds later, the growl of Burke's 1988 Porsche Carrera backing down the driveway onto Peaceful Lane. He drove that old car like a testosterone-charged teenager, especially when he was upset; and that twisting highway between here and downtown Branson could be dangerous at night, especially in bad weather.

She should have told him to be careful. But then, what difference would it have made? Burke never paid any heed to her concerns. She could only pray he wouldn't slide off the road or cut too close around a blind curve and meet a truck coming the other way.

Smoothing her hair, she turned back toward the lighted French doors. She had no choice except to go back inside and put on a cheerful face for Burke's friends. But she knew there'd be talk, especially after the way he'd gone roaring off.

Burke had said they'd understand, and maybe they would. He'd worked for decades, first as a theatrical agent, scouting the country for talent, and then as CEO of a company that included the agency, some real estate holdings, and the American Heartland Theater, which had earned a solid reputation in Branson, a town whose lifeblood was wholesome family entertainment. Guarding that reputation was all-important to him. But would it have killed the man to wait an hour before racing to defuse a crisis—especially when his presence at dinner meant so much to her?

Forcing a brittle smile, she opened the door and stepped back into the great room. Heads swiveled toward her, then jerked self-consciously away. Conversations that had stalled at her appearance resumed on a stilted note. Most of the couples at the party had known Burke for more than twenty years. They'd known Kate as well. Some of them, especially the women, behaved as if Kate were still alive and Allison was an interloper who'd broken up Burke's first marriage.

Sprinkled among these old friends, however, were a few younger people who worked for Burke's theatrical agency. Garrett Miles, the partner who managed the financial and legal end of the business, caught her eye across the room and cut his way through the crowd toward her.

Garrett had been hired out of Harvard with an MBA and had stayed on to become Burke's right-hand man. His affable manner and movie star smile masked a mind like a steel trap. Allison couldn't say she liked him. He struck her as too smooth, too sure of himself. But right now Garrett was the only port in a storm of hostility.

"You look like the Goddess of Angst," he muttered in her ear. "Are you all right?"

"I'm dandy," she lied. "Did Burke happen to tell you he was leaving?"

"He did. Don't worry, everything's under control here. I've spread the word that he had an emergency and couldn't stay. You won't need to explain a thing."

"Thank you, Garrett." Her tone carried an edge. "I don't suppose you offered to go in his place, did you?"

"Actually, I did." He gripped her elbow and propelled her out into the dimly lit foyer. "Burke insisted on going himself. The problem was a personnel issue, not a finance issue, and he didn't trust anyone else to smooth things over."

"I see." Allison exhaled, willing herself to relax. She had nothing to gain by alienating this man, especially tonight, when she needed his support. "Sorry about that," she said with a raw laugh. "It's just that I was hoping Burke could relax and enjoy his friends tonight. He's been so preoccupied lately—working till all hours, coming home exhausted and then lying awake the rest of the night . . ." She glanced up to see Garrett's gold-flecked eyes watching her intently. "If Burke were involved with another woman, I'd have something to fight. But my rival is that damned business. Short of burning the American Heartland Theater to the ground, there's nothing I can do!"

Realizing she'd said too much, Allison glanced back toward the brightly lit great room. "Sorry again," she said, forcing a smile. "I do tend to get carried away. Isn't your wife here tonight, Garrett? I don't recall seeing her."

"Burke didn't tell you?" One brown eyebrow lifted. "Julie and I separated last month. I've moved into one of the company condos. She's filed for divorce."

"That's too bad—and no, he didn't tell me." Allison licked her lips, a nervous habit she'd been trying to break. "Burke doesn't discuss company business, let alone the personal lives of his colleagues, with me. After all, I'm only his wife."

"God, then you don't even know, do you?" He was gazing down at her like a doctor about to deliver a terminal diagnosis.

"Don't know what?" A sense of foreboding hovered over her head, as if a vulture had flapped down to perch on the chandelier. "Tell me what's going on, Garrett. Now."

"The American Heartland's been losing money for the past year—and now, with the fall season on, it's like the dam's broken," he said. "Last spring we took out a short-term bank loan just to get the place up to code. We fixed the roof, replaced the old seats, and got a new lighting system. But it wasn't enough to improve our ticket sales."

"But why?" Allison had always assumed Burke's business was doing fine. "What's wrong?"

Garret shook his head. "The building's old and still doesn't have the technical setup for the spectacular shows that audiences want these days. And even with the agency reps scouting for talent, the top acts are out of our price range. Bottom line—most of our old customers are going for the big names, the flashy displays and aerial acts, or the dinner theater shows. We're having to discount the tickets just to fill the seats."

"But there must be something you can do." Allison struggled against disbelief. This was real, and she needed to pay attention.

"The only way to compete with the newer, bigger places would be to shut down for six months, do a complete remodeling job, and reopen in the spring with a big-name act."

"That sounds like a good plan. But what about the money?" Allison had run her own small gallery in Capitola. She was no financial wizard, but she knew the basics of what it took to operate a business. At the top of the list was capital.

"Burke and I are still weighing the options," Garrett said. "Aside from just shutting down, we've got two choices. While our credit's still decent, we can refinance the business for enough to cover the existing loan and make the updates. But it would leave us over our heads in debt. Worse, if we couldn't make the payments, we'd lose everything."

By *we*, Garrett meant Burke, who would take the risk and stand the loss—that much, Allison knew, was a given. Garrett had been made a partner for his expertise, but his financial stake was little more than a token. "And the other choice?" she asked.

"We could take on a new partner, an investor with deep pockets who could revamp the American Heartland and make it everything it should be—a partner with connections to some of the biggest names in the entertainment business."

"That sounds like an easy choice. Do you have an investor in mind?"

"I do—someone who's very interested and has the

resources we need. But Burke's dragging his heels—
doesn't want anybody else to have a say in his business. I think he's in denial. The original bank loan's
due at the first of the year. If we just let things slide,
we'll be in foreclosure."

Allison stared up at him, feeling as if the blood in
her body had drained into the floor, leaving nothing
for her heart to pump but thin, dry air. She must have
swayed on her high heels because Garrett reached
out and laid a hand on her shoulder.

"We're trying to keep it under wraps," he said,
"but you need to understand. Burke's been under
one hell of a strain."

"But why didn't he tell me?" she whispered. "I'm
his wife, for God's sake, not some child who needs to
be coddled and protected!"

Garrett's fingers were smooth and hard against
her bare skin. "Knowing Burke, I'm sure he had his
reasons. Right now, the best thing you can do for
him is go back to the party. Be nice to his friends.
Act as if nothing has happened."

"They don't know?"

"Nobody here knows except you and me. For now,
consider it our little secret." His hand lingered on
her shoulder, his touch suddenly too intimate. Allison stepped away.

"I'm going back by way of the kitchen," she said.
"If dinner's ready, maybe you can help me seat the
guests. And don't worry about my giving anything
away. I'm a good actress."

But as she thought about the coming ordeal of a
five-course dinner, she wondered how the glassy smile
on her face could fool anyone who cared enough to
look. She'd counted on Burke to keep the conver-

sation lively. Alone, surrounded by people who despised her, how could she possibly hold her own?

Why hadn't Burke told her the American Heartland was in trouble? How could he have let her spend money on herself, on refurbishing the house, and on this god-awful charade of a birthday party, when he was facing financial meltdown? And how could he have let her say the things she'd said to him tonight? If she'd known about the trouble, she would have understood. She would have stood by him, supported him, sacrificed anything to help him save his dream.

If Burke had shared his concerns with her, she could have been a real wife to him. Instead, in her innocence, she'd behaved like a spoiled child! Burke's headstrong nineteen-year-old daughter, Brianna, would've shown more maturity than she had, Allison chided herself. But this latest clash wasn't all her fault. When Burke came home, the two of them would need to have a long, serious talk.

Evanston, Illinois

The vintage Harley-Davidson cruiser roared northward along Sheridan Road, past the Grosse Point Lighthouse and onto the side road into Evanston's Lawson Park. Brianna clung to the driver's leather jacket, her jeans-clad legs nestled behind his. Until six weeks ago, she had never ridden on a motorcycle. And she had never in her life known a man like Liam Shaughnessy.

Liam Shaughnessy was twenty-three years old. He was six feet tall with tawny, shoulder-length hair, piercing blue eyes and an Irish cross tattooed on his upper left arm. He was soft-spoken and polite, but with a subtle manner about him that whispered of controlled danger. Being close to him made Brianna's blood simmer with womanly urges.

Not that he'd tried to sleep with her. In her time attending Northwestern, she'd survived more wrestling matches with entitled frat boys than she cared to remember. But so far, Liam hadn't crossed the line with her. It was driving her crazy.

Now he pulled into a near-empty row of parking spaces between the green swath of the park and the long strip of sandy beach that edged the shore of Lake Michigan. At this hour, with the last rays of the sun setting behind them, the beach was all but deserted.

Brianna removed her helmet and shook out her russet curls. Then they yanked off their boots and socks, and raced, barefoot and laughing, across the sand. The water was cold. They stood at the edge, letting the small waves lap at their toes. When Brianna began to shiver, Liam took off his jacket and wrapped it around her, holding it in place with his arms. "Warm enough now?" he asked, nuzzling her hairline.

"Warm enough," she murmured, closing her eyes and leaning back against him.

"What is it with you, Brianna Caldwell?" he asked. "Here you are, a fancy college girl with big career dreams, hanging out with a man who sleeps over a garage and had to drop out of high school to get a job. What would your father say if he knew about you and me?"

"My father's a fair man. He wouldn't judge you for that."

"But you haven't told him about us, have you?"

Brianna didn't reply. The truth was, her father would want her to find a man with an education and a future that would promise the kind of life she'd enjoyed growing up. But Liam was a good man who cared about her, and she'd fallen in love with him. How could she explain that to Burke Caldwell, who believed it was a man's first duty to provide a bountiful life for his family?

"I knew you hadn't told him," Liam answered her silence. "Don't worry, I understand. You might want to hold off until you get the key to that new car he promised you. A BMW convertible—that'll be one hot set of wheels."

"Stop it, Liam." She pulled away and turned to face him. "You're making me sound like a conniving, materialistic little bitch. It's not about the car. The car is just a thing. I'm waiting for the right time, that's all." She glanced at her watch. "And speaking of the right time, I need to get back to the dorm. It's my roommate's birthday, and we're going out for pizza. It's my dad's birthday too. I want to call him before we leave."

Brianna had her phone with her and could've called Burke from here. But Liam had never liked the idea of dating her behind her father's back. That old-fashioned attitude was one of the things she loved about him. But it was also an ongoing source of friction. Making him wait while she made the call would sour the good time they'd enjoyed this afternoon.

He caught her close and gave her a quick, hard kiss. "All right, let's go," he said. "Wish your old man a happy birthday for me."

As they rode back toward the campus, Brianna clung to his back, holding on tight. She could feel his rigid muscles through the leather jacket. Liam was poor but proud; and the thought that she might be ashamed of him would be enough to drive a wedge between them.

She couldn't stand the thought of losing him. But if she wanted to keep him, changing things would be up to her.

Branson,
The same night

By eight fifteen, the meal was over and the guests were making excuses to leave. Allison stood at the door and spoke to each couple, her smile frozen on her face. They thanked her politely and trooped down to their cars—Ron and Debbie Ellis, who'd been friends of Burke's since high school; Tricia Kenwood, Kate's cousin, with her husband, Rich; Burke's long-time fishing buddy, Hoagie Atkinson, with his wife, Cindy, and the others who'd known Burke over the years. They were probably as relieved to see the evening end as she was.

Garrett was the last to leave. He lingered at the door as the other guests vanished into the night. "Will you be all right?" he asked, taking her hand. "If you need any help or just want to talk, I'd be happy to stay."

Allison shook her head. "The caterers will clean up, and I'll be fine. If you want to help, go find Burke. Try to see that he gets some rest."

"I'll do that." His handclasp lasted an instant longer than necessary. "Get some rest yourself. You look as if you could use it."

"Don't worry about me," she said, still smiling as if

her lips had been glued into place. "I just need time for all this to sink in."

And it would have to sink in fast, Allison told herself as she watched him jog down the front steps to the drive. If the worst happened, she could certainly handle being poor—she'd been poor most of her life. But how would Burke survive the collapse of his company? And apart from everything else, how could she ignore the fact that her husband had kept a terrible secret from her?

Fragments of conversation drifted up to her from the cars that were parked along the curb—laughter, bits of gossip, promises to get together in the weeks ahead; then, booming above the rest, she heard the bullhorn voice of Hoagie Atkinson.

"Remember how we used to come back from a day on the water and Kate would toss our fish on the grill and haul the cold beer out of the fridge, and we'd sit around that old picnic table laughing our damn-fool heads off? Now *there* was a woman who knew how to throw a party!"

The phone was ringing as Allison re-entered the house. She plunged across the foyer to answer it, twisting her ankle as one stiletto heel caught the edge of the mat.

On the fourth ring she fell against the wall, grabbed for the phone, and snatched the receiver off the hook. "Burke?" she gasped.

"No, it's Brianna. Where's my dad?" Burke's only child had not been home since the wedding. On the phone, she treated Allison more like an answering service than a member of the family.

"Your father's on his way back to work," Allison said. "You might be able to reach him on his cell phone."

"Work? You let him go to *work* on his *birthday*?"

"It's not as if I had a choice, Brianna. It was an emergency."

There was a long silence on the line. "Well, I'll try to call his cell," Brianna said. "But I can't believe he's working tonight. Good grief, what are his managers for?"

Allison's left eyelid had begun to twitch, heralding what was apt to be a murderous headache. "Just in case you can't get through, is there anything you'd like me to tell him?"

"Just happy birthday. I sent him a present—he should be getting it in the next couple of days. Oh, and I found a car I like. I'll have the dealer call him tomorrow." There was a pause. Allison could hear girls' voices in the background. "All right, I'm coming! Just hang on!" Brianna shouted, muffling the receiver. Then her voice came back. "Gotta go. You *will* tell him I called, won't you?"

"Of course." Allison's twitch had migrated into her temple and begun to throb. "Take care of yourself, Brianna."

The only answer was a click. Allison sagged against the wall. From the kitchen, she could hear the caterer and his crew cleaning up the dishes. How much would Anthony's bill be? A thousand dollars? Two thousand? She'd paid scant attention when she'd ordered the food and service. Until now, a few hundred dollars either way hadn't mattered.

Limping on her twisted ankle, she made it to the couch and collapsed on the black leather upholstery. Her eyes roamed the splendid great room, from the cathedral ceiling with its hand-hewn beams to the tall flagstone fireplace.

After their wedding, Burke had given her carte blanche to decorate the two-story frame house on Peaceful Lane, with its stunning view of the lake. He had bought the property sixteen years ago and kept it after Kate's death. When Allison had moved in, the inside was much as her predecessor had left it.

Kate had favored homey florals, ginghams, quilted wall hangings, and framed Thomas Kinkade prints. Allison had replaced the sun-faded curtains and sheers with plantation shutters. The timeworn flowered chintz furniture and baby-blue carpet had been hauled off to Goodwill. Polished hardwood now gleamed on the floors. The black sofa and earth-tone chairs, decorated with bright red and gold cushions, were arranged around a glass coffee table in a conversational group that seemed to drift on the thick, white flokati rug.

The walls had been stripped of their patterned paper and refinished in cool tones of ivory, pewter, and latte. Around the room, Allison had hung her precious collection of Australian Aboriginal paintings—the one thing she'd lavished money on in her single days. The Kathleen Petyarre above the fireplace—a five-foot expanse of tiny dots that looked like the surface of a rough granite slab—had cost more than her old car. These days the painting was worth three times what she'd paid. Maybe she could sell it. She would sell the whole lot of them if it would help Burke. What did it matter?

The sound of closing doors told her the caterers were leaving by way of the kitchen. They would send her the bill in the morning. She would pay it in full, of course, along with a generous tip for the servers.

Deep in her chest, a tangled thread of annoyance jerked into a hard knot of anger. Why hadn't Burke told her about his problems? Why had he let her blunder ahead, spending money like a drunken sailor while his friends sneered at her extravagance?

Why in heaven's name hadn't he stopped her?

More to the point, why hadn't she stopped herself?

The pain in her temple had mushroomed into a blinding headache. Trying to read or watch TV until Burke came home would only make her feel worse. For now, there was nothing to do but gulp down some ibuprofen, go to bed, and try to sleep it off.

Rousing herself from the sofa, she dragged herself up the stairs to the second-floor landing. The guest bathroom was on her right. She opened the medicine cabinet, dumped two extra-strength ibuprofen tablets into her palm, and tossed them down with a glass of water. The pills would help the pain. Too bad they couldn't help anything else.

Across the hall was the one room Allison had known better than to redecorate. From the stuffed animals and ruffled cushions on the bed to the old *Lord of the Rings* Orlando Bloom poster on the ceiling, Brianna's bedroom remained exactly as she'd left it when she went off to college. Allison rarely ventured into her stepdaughter's territory, but tonight, with her mind in turmoil, it seemed like a natural place to wander.

Or maybe she craved some deeper punishment to take her mind off the pain in her head.

The door was ajar, probably left that way by the cleaning woman when she'd finished dusting. Allison slipped into the alien space and switched on a dresser lamp with a ruby glass shade. The reddish glow cast Brianna's childhood collection of stuffed unicorns, dragons, and other mythical creatures into monster shadows on the walls.

It was a child's room, a teenager's room, a young woman's room, every corner crammed with the memorabilia of growing up. Allison had never known such a room. Her own single mother had dragged her from job to job, from town to town. Life had been a string of dingy furnished apartments and motel rooms, her childhood treasures whatever could be crammed into a cardboard box and tossed into the back seat of a rusty Chevrolet Impala.

She would have died for a room like this, a place to keep and call her own.

Brianna was nineteen now, a striking young woman with her mother's red hair and her father's chiseled features and long-limbed stature. She'd been accepted into a prestigious journalism program at Northwestern University, where she was working toward a career as a TV reporter.

Allison's eyes roamed over the shelves of books and CDs, the photo albums, the school yearbooks—finally coming to rest where they always did, on the eight-by-ten leather-framed photograph that sat on top of the bookcase.

Brianna, she suspected, had left the photo out as a gesture, to remind her new stepmother that *this* was, and always would be, her family. The three figures in the informal portrait were standing on a dock with a boat behind them and a huge, black Newfoundland dog at their feet. A younger Burke, ruggedly handsome in jeans and a faded polo, stood with one arm around his carrot-topped twelve-year-old daughter and the other arm around his wife.

Kate.

In recent months, Allison had begun to identify with the heroine of Daphne du Maurier's *Rebecca*— the young second wife, overshadowed by her glamorous predecessor. But Katherine O'Malley Caldwell was no Rebecca. Her photographic image showed a short, almost dumpy-looking woman whose baggy blue CHIEFS sweatshirt hung over a waist that had already begun to thicken with early middle age. Her wind-tossed cinnamon hair was touched with gray at the temples, her skin spattered with freckles and etched with laugh lines. Her generous, unpainted mouth had been caught in an impish grin.

Now there *was a woman who knew how to throw a party!*

Head still pounding, Allison turned away from the photo, switched off the lamp, and wandered down the hall toward the master bedroom. When she'd married Burke—the ceremony a romantic dream in the hilltop chapel at Big Cedar—her friends had told her she was fortunate to be getting a widower. No ex-wife to deal with. Wasn't she lucky? But there were times, like tonight, when she wished she could call Kate on the phone and invite her to a long, chatty, insightful lunch. Maybe it would help her understand why Burke had shut her out of his life.

The silent phone mocked her from the nightstand as she struggled to unzip the back of her dress— a job she'd planned for Burke. Her skimpy new black lace teddy, along with the black satin sheets on the bed, were to be part of his birthday gift. She'd imagined letting him unwrap her like a present, then pulling him down onto the pillows for a night of slow, sensuous loving.

Not tonight, dear, I have a headache . . . After wiping off her makeup, Allison let the dress collapse around her ankles, stepped out of her shoes, unpinned her hair, and slipped between the watery layers of satin. Burke might not be home until tomorrow—there was a room above the agency office for when he had to stay in town. But, damn it, the least he could do was call and give her a chance to make things right—if they could ever be right again.

She slept fitfully, distracted by the rain outside, the slithering sheets on the bed, and her own warring emotions. What should she do when Burke came home? Confront him and demand an explanation? Apologize and melt in his arms? Play innocent and hope he'd decide to be honest with her? There was no good resolution to this kind of betrayal.

At eleven fifteen, with her nerves in tatters, she reached for the phone, punched in the first six digits of his cell number, hesitated, then changed her mind and hung up. Trying to talk with Burke at a bad time would only make things worse. Wait for his call; that would be the smart thing to do. Sooner or later it would come. He almost always phoned her when he was going to be late.

But then, they'd never parted the way they'd parted tonight.

It was almost midnight, and Allison was beginning to drift, when the ringing phone shattered the silence. Her eyes shot open. She groped wildly, catching the receiver as the phone went crashing off the nightstand.

"Burke?"

"No, Allison, it's Garrett." His voice was calm. Too calm. Allison went clammy with fear.

"What is it? Is something wrong?" she croaked into the phone.

"The ambulance just took Burke to the hospital.

I'm on the road now. I'll be by to pick you up in about twenty minutes."

She fought the creeping numbness of denial. "What—happened?"

"He rolled the Porsche on the way to town," Garrett said. "After I left your place I went to the American Heartland. Nobody there had seen him. When he wasn't at the agency, and his cell didn't answer, I got worried and called the highway patrol. The troopers finally found him down the slope from the road, pinned under his car."

"Oh, God, is he—?"

"He's alive. But he was still unconscious when the paramedics arrived. We'll know more when we get to the hospital."

Allison battled waves of nausea. "I'm coming now," she said.

"Now, Allison, you're in no condition to—"

She disconnected the call.

CHAPTER 2

Allison walked into the hospital room at Cox Medical Center, her eyes bloodshot, her hair falling in strings around her face. She had flung on the first things that came out of the closet—her jogging shoes, a pair of jeans, and one of Burke's old gray sweatshirts. Her headache lingered like a dusty cobweb in her brain, but she'd forgotten it in the rush to reach her husband's side.

Refusing to wait for Garrett, she'd driven the mountain highway herself, screeching around the hairpin curves in the white Lexus Burke had given her. This couldn't be happening. Not to Burke. He was so strong, so vital. Surely she would arrive at the hospital to find him sitting up in bed, joking about the brief scare. They would collect his belongings and she would drive him home. Everything would be all right.

But it wasn't all right. The truth struck Allison as soon as she caught sight of her husband through a maze of plastic tubes and blinking monitors in the

ICU. There could be no going back. Burke's life, and hers, would never be the same.

The polite young Indian doctor had tried to prepare her. Burke was semiconscious now, but he'd suffered a concussion and some spinal injuries, which would need surgery. It was too soon to know whether the damage would be permanent.

Allison walked toward the bed, feeling the liquid resistance of the air as if she were moving through water. Burke lay between blinding white sheets, the neck of the faded green hospital gown falling loose around his throat. An IV needle connected to a saline drip was taped to the back of his left hand. Above his head, monitors blinked and hummed like a committee of cold-eyed robots.

Struggling for self-control, she stood looking down at him. His sunken eyes were closed above the plastic oxygen mask. His skin was grayish and mottled with bruises. A white bandage wrapped his head. He looked worn-out, vulnerable, and wounded. The urge to bend down, gather him close, and rock him in her arms was so overwhelming that it brought a freshet of tears. How could she not have noticed the exhaustion, the strain in him? How could she have been so wrapped up in her glamorous new life as Mrs. Burke Caldwell that she'd allowed this to happen?

Her eyes traced the outline of his body beneath the thin cotton blanket—the taut belly and lean hips, the muscular legs, lying slightly apart with the feet making a little tent beneath the covers. Denial surged through her brain like a drug. Permanent damage? What nonsense! Tomorrow morning Burke would be fine. He'd wake up, bound out of bed, and life would go on as if this nightmare had never happened. There was nothing wrong with him that a good night's sleep wouldn't cure!

It was the urine bag that finally undid her—the sight of it dangling like a flat yellow moon from under the sheet near the foot of the bed. Allison stared at the fluid that dripped out of the catheter tube, flowing from the body of a man so helpless he couldn't even get up to relieve himself. Her knees went weak.

Sagging against the bed, she groped for his hand, found it and held on tight. His eyelids fluttered but failed to open.

"It's all right, my love," Allison murmured. "I'm here. We're going to get through this together."

His dry lips moved ever so slightly. "Kate . . ." he murmured. "Don't leave me, Kate . . ."

Overwhelmed, she sank into a bedside chair and pressed her face against the sheet.

She didn't realize she'd fallen asleep until she heard his voice.

"Allison."

Her eyes shot open. Gray light filtered through the half-closed blinds. Burke had pulled off the oxygen mask and was watching her with alert blue eyes. Emotion welled in her throat. He was awake. He knew her.

"How . . . are you doing?" she asked idiotically.

"I've seen better days." He gave her a twisted smile. "How about you?"

She leaned over him, raised his hand, and kissed it. His fingers were cold against her lips. "I'm so sorry," she said. "I didn't know, Burke—about the company problems, the strain you were under. How could you have let me make such a fool of myself?"

His only reply was a brief tightening of his hand around hers.

"Why didn't you tell me?" She gulped back a sob. "Why did I have to learn the truth from Garrett? I would have understood. I would have stood by you."

"It doesn't matter anymore. We need to talk, Allison."

Still gripping his hand, she sank back onto the clammy metal chair. "What you need right now is rest. Anything you have to say to me can wait till you're feeling stronger."

"This can't wait." With effort, he twisted his neck to turn his face toward her. "Just keep still and hear me out."

His voice had dropped to a whisper. Allison leaned closer, a knot of apprehension tightening in her stomach. She kept her grip on his hand, refusing to let go.

"Everything you said to me at the house was true." His voice rasped in his throat. "When I asked you to marry me, I made you a lot of promises—promises I meant to keep. I wanted to lay the world at your feet, girl. I wanted to spend every minute of the time God gave us just making you happy. If I'd known what a rough ride this was going to be, I'd have walked away and kept right on walking."

"Hush!" Allison laid a finger against his chapped lips. "Don't you dare talk like that. I behaved like a fool. I said stupid things, ugly things I didn't mean. But that's all in the past. Right now, all I want to do is help you get—"

"I said hear me out," he snapped. "Damn it, Allison, this is hard enough to say without you interrupting!"

She stared at him, shocked by his vehemence.

"I thought there was a chance to save the business. But now that this has happened, it's all going down," he said. "The American Heartland, the money, me, the whole damn-blasted house of cards! A year from now, if I'm still alive, I'll be lucky to have a roof over my head. This isn't what you signed on for, girl. It's not what I promised you."

"Burke, it doesn't mat—"

"*Listen* to me! There's nothing you can do here but sit around and wring your hands. As soon as it's light outside, I want you to drive back home. When you get there, call a lawyer, the best one you can find. Tell him you want to file for divorce."

Garrett stepped into Allison's path, halting her as she fled blindly across the waiting room.

"Are you all right?" His hands clasped her shoulders, forcing her to face him. "Lord, what's wrong? Is Burke—?"

Allison willed herself to speak calmly. "Burke's awake and talking. I'm just a little . . . unraveled, that's all. I'll be fine."

He shook his head. His eyes were bloodshot, but his thick brown hair was neatly combed. He'd changed from his dinner clothes into khakis and a fresh navy polo shirt. "You look like you could use some coffee," he said, steering her toward the cafeteria. "Come on. We need to talk."

We need to talk. Burke's words came back to haunt her as Garrett steered her past the nurses' desk and down a tiled hallway that smelled of coffee and disinfectant. It was important that she file at once, Burke had told her. Missouri wasn't a community property state like California. Only assets acquired after the marriage were considered marital property, which in this case was next to nothing. But with Burke's help, a sharp lawyer should be able to secure her a share of his assets before hungry creditors closed in and took everything. The American Heartland was likely beyond saving, but Burke had promised to hold off the vultures long enough for her to get her cut of his financial accounts, as well as the house and the cars.

"I owe you that much for the pain I've caused," he'd said. "You're a smart, beautiful woman, Allison. You'll get along fine without me."

Allison had risen slowly to her feet, feeling as if the floor were crumbling away underneath her. "I'm your wife, Burke," she'd said, forcing each syllable out of her constricted throat. "I married you for better or for worse. If you want a divorce, you can bloody well get one yourself!"

Without waiting for his response, she had turned away and walked out of the room.

"Here you are." Garrett guided the steaming Styrofoam cup into her hands. He had seated her at a table next to the window. Allison realized she had no memory of walking into the cafeteria or sitting down in the chair.

"Anything else? A Danish?"

She shook her head and took a sip of the scalding black coffee. It burned her tongue but the sudden caffeine jolt jump-started her brain. "What about the American Heartland and the agency?" she asked, astonished by her own self-possession. "Burke seems to think they'll go under without him."

He gazed at her intently over his coffee cup. "I'll be running things in Burke's absence," he said. "I'll do everything I can to keep the business going. But I'm going to need your help."

"Why, for heaven's sake? Burke was lucid when I left him just now. He seems perfectly capable of making decisions." Allison winced inwardly as she remembered the scene in the ICU.

"True. But he's had a concussion. Even if he's sharp, he's going to need weeks of rest, especially if he has back surgery. While he's recovering, you can act as a go-between and keep me informed about his condition." Garrett took a sip of his coffee. "But that's down the road a bit. Right now I need a favor."

He waited for her to respond. When she remained silent, he continued. "We have three contracts pending for future acts. There's a woman who does a great Patsy Cline cover and a couple of others. Burke took them home for a final read-through a couple of nights ago. I need them by tomorrow in case we have to renegotiate. Can you find them and get them to me by then?"

"You're sure Burke didn't bring the papers back? Have you checked his briefcase? His car?"

Garrett nodded. "I'm certain they're still at your house. If it isn't too much of an imposition—"

"No, it's fine. The papers should be somewhere in his study, most likely his desk. I'll look for them when I go home to shower and change."

"It might save time if we asked him where he put them."

"No. Leave him be. He needs his rest."

When Garrett shot her an odd glance, Allison realized she'd spoken too quickly. He was probably wondering what was going on. Well, let him wonder.

She was going to need some time before she faced Burke again.

"Once you've found the contracts I can send somebody to pick them up," Garrett said. "That way you won't need to hurry back."

"Don't bother. In any case, I don't plan to be at the house long. I can bring them here or to your office."

"The office, then, if you don't mind. The sooner I get back to work, the better. For now, I'll be doing two jobs. I'm depending on you to keep me informed about Burke."

You can't just pick up the phone and call him? Allison bit back the words as she slid her chair out and rose to her feet. "What do the contracts look like?" she asked.

"About five pages each, together in a plain manila envelope. The margins should have Burke's notes on them in red. You'll know them when you see them."

"Fine. I'll drop the envelope off on my way back here." Allison rose wearily to her feet. "If you have any questions, you can ask Burke. He's still the man with the answers. Thanks for the coffee." She turned to go.

"Are you sure you're all right?" he asked. "I'd be happy to drive you back to the house."

"You have a business to run, remember?" She strode away, willing her unsteady legs not to betray her. Right now, Garrett Miles was the only person who could save Burke's business. But he was an ambitious man, and he was clearly looking out for his own interests. She would have no choice except to cooperate with him. But she could not afford to lean on him.

As she stepped into the parking garage, the truth struck her like the flash of sunrise coming up over the hills. It wasn't just Garrett. In her small circle of people who mattered, there was no one she could count on for support. Burke was wounded and defiant. Brianna hated her. She had no family, and her single friends, even the close ones, had moved on after her marriage. There was no one she could confide in, no one who would offer so much as a comforting shoulder when she felt beaten and bloodied.

Her safe, pretty little world was falling apart, and there was no one to help her pick up the pieces.

Allison rolled the windows down and opened the sunroof for the drive back to Peaceful Lane. She drove with the wind in her burning eyes and Mick Jagger's raunchy baritone blasted "You Can't Always Get What You Want" from the stereo. Fighting the black undertow that threatened to drag her down, she sang along at the top of her lungs.

By the time she'd parked the car in the driveway, left a message on Brianna's cell phone, showered, dressed in gray slacks and a black T, and twisted her hair up with a silver clip, it was after 7:00 A.M. She would find the missing contracts, then force down a bite of breakfast. After that it would be back to the war zone that Burke's hospital room had become. The day was bound to be hellish, but no matter how much he tried to hurt her, she would be there for him.

Burke's study had not been greatly changed by the remodeling. He'd allowed Allison to replace the curtains with shutters and the worn-out carpet with colorful kilim rugs over hardwood flooring, but he'd refused to part with the battered walnut veneer desk, the shabby leather chair, or the outdated brass reading lamp that hunkered beside it. The bookshelves lining the inner walls were stocked with a lifetime of treasures—books, photos, travel souvenirs, and models of boats and planes. These Allison had known better than to touch.

Burke had tactfully boxed up the pictures in which Kate appeared. Still it was here, in this very masculine room, that Allison most strongly felt the woman's presence.

Walking to the desk, she glanced around its cluttered surface for the manila envelope containing the contracts. There was no sign of it, nor could she find any loose pages that matched Garrett's description. Allison sighed. She had hoped this task would be simple. She was in no mood for a long search.

One by one, she opened the desk drawers and pawed through their contents. Common sense told her she was wasting her time. Burke would never have stowed a vital contract in the center drawer with its clutter of pens, pencils, sticky notes, string, tape, and paper clips. Nor would he have put it in the drawer that contained nothing but household bills, receipts, and unused checkbooks, or the drawer that held the instruction books and spare cables for his computer. But at least, if she failed to find it, she'd be able to tell Garrett she'd gone through the desk.

The large file drawer was next. Allison riffled through the folders, knowing that the missing envelope wouldn't be there. Why would Burke file away the documents he'd planned to take back to work? Maybe he'd left the envelope in the foyer, the kitchen, or even the garage on his way out of the house. She should have checked there first.

Only one drawer—the small lower right one—remained. Sliding it partway open, Allison saw a box of powder-blue linen stationery with matching envelopes, an assortment of flowery all-occasion note cards, several pens, and a roll of unused 33-cent postage stamps. Kate's things, most likely. They looked as if they hadn't been touched in years.

Pushing on the drawer to close it, she felt a slight but stubborn resistance. Something in the rear had caught on the inner frame of the desk. Not wanting to do any damage, she worked the drawer the rest of the way open. There in the very back, crumpled at one corner, lay a large, plain manila envelope.

As soon as she lifted it out of the drawer, Allison knew it wasn't the envelope she was looking for. The contents, whatever they were, felt too thick and lumpy to be flat legal documents. She was debating whether to return the envelope, unopened, to the drawer when the phone jangled. She answered on the second ring.

"Allison? Garrett again."

Her pulse slammed. "What is it? Burke—?"

"Relax. That's not why I'm calling. I'm at work, and I just found the contracts under some papers in Burke's office."

"So I can stop looking."

"Right. Sorry, I hope you didn't spend too much time."

"Only a little. I'm glad you found them."

"Are you holding up OK?"

"Fine," she lied.

"You'll call me if there's any change in Burke's condition?"

"Of course." Allison hung up the phone without

saying goodbye and sank back into the worn leather chair, feeling as if every ounce of energy had been sucked from her body. With the contracts in Garrett's hands, there was nothing to keep her from returning to the hospital. But she lacked the strength to face the war of wills that would erupt as soon as she stepped into Burke's room.

The manila envelope lay on the desk in front of her. In her present condition, the mere thought of putting it back in the drawer made her feel tired. But given the chance that Brianna might come rushing home and see that her stepmother had been snooping, Allison knew it would be prudent to leave things as she'd found them.

Willing her hand to move, she picked the envelope up by its nearest end—the bottom. As she lifted it, the flap at the top fell open, spilling the contents onto the desk.

Allison stared at the scattered heap of letters, folded into pretty envelopes that made a rainbow of pastel shades on the desktop. Except for one that was sealed, they'd been torn off at one end, the way Burke tended to open his letters. They were addressed to him, at the far-flung locations where his work as a talent agent had taken him.

The labels in the upper left corners bore the return address of this house—6314 PEACEFUL LANE. And above the address, the name on each one was KATE CALDWELL.

Realizing what she'd found, Allison scooped up the letters. She was stuffing them back into the manila envelope when she was seized by a thought so stunning that it stopped her hands in midmotion.

Maybe she was meant to find these letters.

Maybe, in this time of shattering crisis, there was

something here that would help her understand the proud, impossibly stubborn man she'd married.

Or maybe not. The letters were private and precious. She had no business touching them.

Still vacillating, she gazed down at the scattered envelopes, trying to decipher the blurred postmarks. The latest one was dated a few months before Kate's death.

One envelope, this one plain, white, business size, and thicker than the others, bore no postmark, stamp, or address, only a single line, written in an unsteady hand.

For Burke, to be opened after my death

Allison's throat tightened as she held it. This letter, if that's what it was, had almost certainly been written last. And it appeared that it had never been opened.

But never mind that. Today, with her life crumbling like a sandcastle, the last thing she needed was to read the intimate thoughts of the woman Burke had loved.

Hastily, as if fearing she might change her mind, she began scooping the letters into a pile. One letter slipped loose and dropped to the floor, spilling its folded pages—sunny yellow sheets bordered with daisies—onto the carpet.

She reached down to gather them up. The first page had fallen open, lying faceup, inviting her—almost daring her—to read it.

As her fingers brushed the paper, Allison felt a shiver of anticipation. She would read only one letter, she vowed. Then she would put them all back in the drawer and forget she'd ever seen them.

Her pulse quickened as she put the three pages in order, smoothed out the creases, and began to read.

My Darling Burke,

The rains have come early. This afternoon, while I was mulching the hydrangeas, I noticed a cloud bank creeping in over the lake. Now it's lying out there like a big, shaggy, wet dog, with no plans to leave. I've opened the French doors to let in the breeze. A few minutes ago, when I looked out beyond the balcony, I saw the first flash of lightning.

Earlier tonight I tried to sleep. But the house is too quiet, the bed too wide and empty without you, so I'm curled in your big leather chair, wearing your ratty old plaid bathrobe over my pajamas. The robe smells like you, which is why I stop myself every time I get the urge to throw it in the laundry. Wearing it is the closest I can come to feeling your arms around me.

Brianna's off at a slumber party and Captain is snoozing in his favorite spot under your desk. From the way his arthritic old legs keep twitching, I'd say he's dreaming about chasing seagulls on the wharf, or maybe treeing that snooty Siamese next door.

A few minutes ago I almost picked up the phone and dialed your hotel. Don't worry, I came to my senses in time. It's after midnight here and God knows how late it is in Miami—sorry, you know I never bother to keep track of such trivialities as time zones. Whatever the hour, I'm aware that you've had a hectic day and need your rest. Besides, the ringing of a phone in the dark hours is a nightmare sound. Even when it's a wrong number, your pulse doesn't stop jerking till dawn. I wouldn't inflict that on you for the world. But I wish I could hear your voice right now—or better yet, I wish I could fly across the country on the wings of night and creep between your sheets.

We wouldn't even have to make love. Just holding you would be enough.

Since that isn't possible, I've decided to write you a letter. Oh, yes, I know it's the twenty-first century, and email is the way to go. It's fast and efficient and won't wake you up in the night. But I hate the sterile look of those words on the screen. A letter is more intimate—the paper I've touched, the curves, dots, and lines of words that I've formed with my own hand, the envelope I've sealed with my tongue, to be opened by no one but you. I realize I'm hopelessly out of date. But I've always enjoyed writing letters to people I love.

Wondering . . . How much time have we spent apart in the past twenty years? I've never tried to add up the days, weeks, and months, the missed holidays and anniversaries, the crises I had to survive without you. But then, why should I? It's the time we've spent together that counts—you, me, Brianna, the dogs, the boat, our friends. We've had a rich life, Burke. And the rough times have only made the good times sweeter.

Which brings me to a bit of news. It's nothing you need to be alarmed about, and certainly no cause for you to come flying home. If it were, you'd have gotten one of those awful late-night phone calls. And you haven't. So don't worry, OK?

Here it is. Last week, when I was showering after a run to the landing and back, I found a pea-sized lump in my left armpit. The doctor took a biopsy, and the results came back today. The picture isn't pretty, my sweet. But the specialist is hopeful that we've caught the cancer in time to stop it (there, I've used it, that nasty old C word).

I start chemo (another of those ugly C words) next

week. *The doctors say I'll lose my hair, which will probably make me look like Patrick Stewart in drag. But you and Brianna always did like* Star Trek, *didn't you? And my hair will grow back thick and curly when the treatment's over, or so they tell me. I should even lose some weight in the bargain. Think how sexy I'll look on the boat next summer!*

I know my news will worry you, Burke, but please don't let it change anything between us. I'm a strong woman, and I'm going to fight this thing like a tigress. I plan to be around for years to come—to dance at Brianna's wedding and rock her babies in my arms, to celebrate our fiftieth anniversary, and maybe our sixtieth! Not only am I not going down without a fight—I am not going down, period!

So put this letter aside and be at peace. In two weeks, when you fly home, I'll be waiting at the airport to welcome you with open arms. Until then, stay well, be safe, and know that I'll always be here for you.

All my love,
Your Kate

CHAPTER 3

Racked with grief and worry, Brianna sobbed against Liam's jacket. The call about her father's accident had come early that morning. Allison had delivered the news, her voice so calm that Brianna had wanted to scream at her. *What's wrong with you? This is my father! He could be paralyzed! He could even be dying!*

But she hadn't screamed. With amazing self-control, she had asked a few questions, promised to come as soon as she could get a flight, and then phoned Liam, who'd picked her up and driven to a nearby park where they could talk. Only now that she was in his arms did she give full vent to her emotions.

"I can't lose him, Liam," she said between sobs. "I already lost my mom. I can't even imagine losing my dad, too."

His arms tightened around her, cradling her close. "From what you've told me, it sounds like he's going to be all right."

"All right?" She gulped back a sob. "He has two

shattered vertebrae in his back. They're operating on him this morning. What if he doesn't wake up? You've seen those TV shows where the lines on the monitor go flat. Anything can go wrong during surgery." She pushed away, far enough to look up at him. "I need to go. I need to be there."

"I know," he said.

"Thank you," she said, loving him, needing him. "What about school?"

"I'll take my laptop and try to keep up. But if my dad is in a bad way, or if he's going to need me for a long time, I may have to drop out of the program."

His azure eyes searched the depths of hers. She knew what he must be thinking. If she stayed in Branson, they would be forced apart, maybe for good. If things went badly, they could be seeing each other for the last time.

"I love you, Brianna," he said. "And I want you to know that whatever happens, I'll be here for you."

Fresh tears sprang to Brianna's eyes. Liam had never said those words to her before. She knew he meant them from the bottom of his heart. But right now they couldn't be allowed to matter.

Drifting on a pain-edged opioid cloud, Burke groaned and opened his eyes. A jumble of cords, tubes, and blinking monitors swam in his vision. *The hospital*—at least he knew where he was. That was a start. Closing his eyes again, he struggled to remember more. Slowly, like pieces in a jigsaw puzzle, the fragments of his memory began coming together.

He remembered driving the Porsche down the rain-slicked highway, hitting a curve too fast, and sliding toward the edge. Then there'd been nothing until he woke up with Allison's worried face hovering over him. He'd told her to get a lawyer and file for divorce while she could still claim some of his assets. He hoped to hell she'd taken his advice. By the time he was on his feet again—if ever—there'd be nothing left.

After that, he recalled the coffin-like confinement of the MRI and later, the young Indian doctor coming into the room to talk to him. The concussion was moderate and should heal with time and rest. His spine was another, more frightening matter.

The accident had shattered two vertebrae in his lower back. The fractures needed to be stabilized with a metal cage as soon as possible to prevent nerve damage to his legs as well as incontinence and impotence—words that Burke couldn't say even to himself. He'd scrawled his consent on the form. They'd wheeled him into surgery; and that was the last thing he remembered until now.

Bracing against fear, he willed his legs to move. They stirred beneath the sheet—feet flexing just enough to reassure him, thank God. But right now there was no way to know about the other critical parts. Would he be in diapers for the rest of his life? Would he ever make love to his wife again?

As if the thought could summon her, he heard Allison's voice from the hall outside his room. "But will he be all right, Doctor?" she was asking.

"The surgery went as well as could be expected." The doctor spoke with a slight accent. "But the recovery's going to take time. He'll need rest and care."

"And the end prognosis?"

"All we can do is hope for the best, Mrs. Caldwell. You can go in now, but he's still under sedation for the pain. He might not be quite himself yet."

Not quite myself? What the hell is that supposed to mean? My body might be broken, and my head hurts, but my mind is fine!

"Thank you." Burke heard the familiar cadence of Allison's footsteps coming closer. Then she was leaning over the bed, a lock of her honey-blond hair tumbling over her stunning violet eyes. Lord, he loved her so much. But she didn't deserve any of this. Why couldn't she just walk away with whatever she could take and let him deal with this new hellishness like a man?

"Hello, Burke." She brushed her lips with a fingertip and touched his mouth in a semblance of a kiss. "How are you feeling?"

"Like shit," he growled. "What are you doing here? Did you get hold of a good lawyer?"

"The doctor warned me that you might not be yourself yet." She pulled up a chair and sat down next to the bed. Dressed in jeans, a black sweater, and a tan raincoat, she looked as if she hadn't slept since the accident. Her face was bare of makeup and there were shadows under her eyes. This experience had to be hell on her. All his fault. If he hadn't gone storming off after putting her down, then driving like a maniac on that road in the rain . . .

"The lawyer?" he demanded, pressing the question.

Her weary expression didn't change. "I told you, if you want a divorce, you can get one yourself. I'm not calling a lawyer, and I'm not going anywhere."

"Then you don't understand what you're looking at. Think about it. This is no time to be a sentimental fool." He shifted in the bed, biting back a whimper as he felt the lumpy bulk of the dressing, the drainage tube, and the ice bag that lay against his lower back. Right now, all he wanted to do was rip out all the clamps, stitches, tubes, and needles, swing his feet to the floor, and walk out of this place a whole man. But that wasn't his reality. Not anymore.

His gaze shifted to the window, dark night through the slats of venetian blinds. The sound of an incoming helicopter penetrated the glass. Only now did he remember that, before the surgery, he'd been transferred from the ICU to Cox Medical's new orthopedic/neurological building on Cahill Road behind the main hospital. "What time is it?" he asked.

She glanced at the wall clock. "It's five minutes after eight. You were in surgery and recovery most of the afternoon. The nurse says you can have some juice anytime you want. And you can have solid food in the morning."

"Never mind that. Does Brianna know about the surgery?"

"I called her early this morning and again while you were in recovery. She'll be here as soon as she can get a flight."

"You should've told her to stay in school. What can she do here except make a fuss and get in the way?"

"You know better than that. She's your daughter, Burke. She'll want to be with you. I can call her now, on my cell, if you want to talk to her. She'll be relieved to hear your voice."

"Never mind." Burke loved his daughter, but she was young and tended to react strongly to both joy and pain. And seeing him like this was bound to bring back memories of losing her mother. He wasn't ready to deal with the emotion—or his guilt over what this accident would do to her life. There'd be time for that later.

"Have you spoken with Garrett?" he asked.

Did her eyes flicker away, or had he only imagined it? "He's in the waiting room now, wanting to see you. I can put him off if you're not up to talking business."

"I might as well know what's going on. Send him in."

"Do you want me to stay?"

"No. Go get some coffee. Or better yet, go home. I don't need you to sit here wringing your hands. There's not a damned thing you can do."

For an instant she looked as if he'd slapped her. Then she forced a smile. "I'll get myself some coffee," she said. "And I'll tell Garrett he can come in."

She walked out without looking back. Burke knew he'd wounded her. Maybe now she'd come to her senses and call that lawyer.

The door opened again, but it wasn't Garrett who came into the room. It was a perky blond nurse who looked young enough to be his daughter. "Up to the bathroom," she said. "We've got to get you moving so you won't form blood clots."

Burke willed himself not to swear at her as she helped him slide off the bed and totter across the floor, trailing tubes, lines, and his IV hanging off a metal rack. Everything hurt. A blasted dog would get more dignified treatment than this, he thought as the door closed behind him.

When he was back in bed, the nurse cranked him into a half-sitting position, brought him some orange juice with a straw and turned to leave. "If you need anything else, just push the call button, honey," she said.

Honey? Good God! Get me out of here!

Burke was sipping the juice, wishing it was scotch on the rocks, when Garrett walked in without knocking and closed the door behind him. Dressed in a black polo and tweed blazer, and carrying a briefcase, he looked like an ad from *GQ*. But then he always did.

"How are you feeling?" Garrett asked. "Is the staff treating you right?"

"Don't even ask," Burke grumbled. "What's happening with the American Heartland? Did the Mayweathers go on, or did you have to refund everybody's tickets?"

"By the time I got there, everything was fine," Garrett said. "After Max reminded them that they'd signed a contract, and if they didn't perform, they wouldn't get paid, they came around. As the old saying goes, the show must go on. But because of the late start, we had to give out discount vouchers for future tickets."

"Well, thanks for that, at least." Burke placed his paper cup on the bedside table. "But we both know it's only a Band-Aid."

Garrett nodded. "That's why I'm here. There'll be some needed changes going down before you're on your feet again. I'll be negotiating with the bank and scouting for new investors in the theater, things that can't wait for your recovery."

"I'm laid up, not dead, Garrett. I'm counting on you to keep me informed and involved in everything."

Garrett frowned and glanced at the briefcase,

which he'd placed on the empty chair by the bed. "I'll do my best," he said. "But your top priority has to be healing and getting your strength back. Meanwhile, I need the authority to bargain and make on-the-spot decisions for the company. Agreed?"

"That depends." Burke didn't like the turn this conversation had taken.

Garrett opened the briefcase and took out a manila folder. "I've taken the liberty of having this power of attorney drawn up. Once you've signed it, I'll be able to negotiate contracts and make deals for the company. You'll be able to take it easy and focus on getting well." He opened the folder to reveal a single-page document with a blank for a signature and another for a witness. He thrust it toward Burke. "Read it over. I've got a pen. I can call one of the nurses to witness your signature."

"Put that away." Burke shook his head. "Hell, I'd be crazy to sign anything while I'm up to my ears in painkillers. Whether you like it or not, Garrett, no decision is going to be made without my say-so."

"Then you've just tied my hands." Garrett replaced the folder and snapped the briefcase shut.

"So be it," Burke said. "I'm still the senior partner, and any decisions will have to go through me. Understood?"

"Understood. I'll stop by tomorrow." Garrett was clearly displeased. He strode out of the room without another word.

Burke lay back on the pillow. The pain was a thick, tightening knot at the root of his spine. He shifted in the bed, worsening the pressure. *Damn!* He had never felt so helpless in his life. The worst of it was having Allison see him like this.

The perky blond nurse walked into the room with

a small paper cup. "Time for your pain meds, honey," she said.

Honey. If she said that word one more time, he would leap out of bed and strangle her, Burke thought. But he sat partway up, took the pills in the cup, and swallowed them with a sip of water. From somewhere above his head, he could hear an annoying, repetitive beep.

"That's it." The nurse gave him a smile. "Lie back and rest. Those beeps you hear are your oxygen monitor, telling you to take deep breaths. You need to clear your lungs after surgery."

Burke took several deep breaths, and the beeping sound stopped.

"Keep it up," the nurse said. "Once the meds start working, you'll probably go back to sleep."

Sleep sounded like a grand idea, since being awake was nothing but sheer misery. "If my wife comes back, tell her to go home and get some rest," he said.

"Will do. Sleep tight."

Burke lay back and kept breathing in and out, in and out. Slowly, as the pain medication seeped through his system, he began to drift.

Allison was just finishing her coffee when Garrett walked into the cafeteria. He didn't look happy.

Without asking, he laid his briefcase on the table, pulled out the chair across from her, and sank onto it with a sigh.

"I'm afraid the accident has affected your husband's mind," he said.

"Of course it has. He's angry, frustrated, and lashing out at the world. Can you blame him?"

"Not for that. But he's in denial. He thinks he's

capable of running the business and dealing with all the issues from his hospital bed. But he's not a well man, Allison. I'm worried about him, and you should be, too. He needs to focus his energy on healing."

"Is that what you told him?" Allison asked.

"Yes. I even offered to take over the business while he's on the mend."

"Let me guess. He wouldn't hear of it."

"He was downright irrational. If he'd been on his feet, he might've tried to throw me out of the room." Garrett reached across the table and laid a hand on Allison's arm. "It's up to us—his wife and his partner—to protect Burke from himself. If we fail . . ." His gaze narrowed. "If we fail, the stress could kill him."

Garrett had an agenda. Any fool could see that, Allison told herself. But his words had planted a seed of guilt and worry. She could feel it sprouting, growing, in the depths of her conscience. She was his wife. It would be up to her to see that he got the rest and care he needed.

"Promise me you'll take care of him." Garrett's clasp tightened on her arm. "And that you'll encourage him to let me carry the burdens while he heals. If anybody can make him see the light, it's you."

Good luck with that. Right now, all he wants from me is a divorce. Allison knew better than to give voice to her thoughts.

Feeling cornered, she rose from her chair and picked up her purse. In a way, Garrett was making sense. Burke needed to rest. But getting him to let go of his responsibilities would be like trying to force a lion off its kill—even a wounded lion.

"Promise you'll keep me posted," Garrett said as she prepared to leave.

"Only if you'll promise me the same," she said. "Until now I haven't paid much attention to Burke's business. I need to start."

"Yes, Burke's told me about your little gallery and how well you managed it. I'll be happy to keep you in the loop."

Sincerity wasn't Garrett's strong point, Allison thought. But for now she had nothing to lose by giving him the benefit of the doubt. "Thanks," she said. "I'm sure we'll be in touch."

After leaving the cafeteria, she took the elevator back up to Burke's room. Was Garrett right? Would Burke be in danger if he didn't back away from his responsibilities to the theater, the agency, and his other holdings?

As Burke's wife, it would be up to her to answer that question and to maintain the balance between what her husband wanted and what he needed— even while he was trying to push her away. She would have to be strong—stronger than she had ever been in her life.

Could she do it? Could she put up with his pain, his rage, his frustration, even when it was directed at her?

The door to Burke's room was ajar. Allison slipped inside and found him fast asleep. Standing next to the bed, she gazed down at her husband. Love welled in her, so strong that it brought tears to her eyes. He looked so tired and vulnerable. It was all she could do to keep from brushing her hand over his cheek, or leaning down to kiss his closed eyelids. He was her warrior, wounded, yes, but still fighting.

"The oxycodone will probably knock him out till the middle of the night." The nurse spoke from the open doorway. "He told me he wanted you to go home and get some rest."

Allison turned to face her. "Are you sure he'll be all right?"

"Don't worry, he's stable and doing fine, aside from the pain. But that's to be expected. We'll call you if there's any need to come back." The blond woman studied Allison's tired face. "Go on home, honey. You've got a long road ahead of you. If you don't take care of yourself, you'll end up in here, too."

"Thanks for the good advice. For now I'll take it. But tell him I was here, and that I'll see him first thing in the morning." Allison stepped through the doorway, then paused. "If his business partner, Mr. Miles, shows up, tell him to come back later, all right?"

"I'll be off shift at ten, but I'll pass on the message."

"Thank you." Allison walked back down the hall and out to the parking lot. Only as she stepped outside, and the cold, misting rain struck her face, did she realize how exhausted she was. She hoped the coffee she'd drunk in the cafeteria would keep her alert on the drive home.

Her Lexus was chilly inside. Before pulling away, she turned on the lights and wipers and dialed up the heat. The radio would help keep her awake. She reached for the button to turn it on, then changed her mind. What she needed was silence. She needed to calm her mind and think.

As she took the on-ramp to Highway 65, the night lights of Branson spread westward like a glittering carpet. Theaters, restaurants, malls, and other family attractions swarmed with the visitors who were the lifeblood of the town. Headlights streamed along the main artery that led through the entertainment district.

Branson was like no place Allison had ever known. Cradled by the Ozark Mountains, in an idyllic setting that made it a mecca for fishing and golf, the town had much to offer. But as a transplanted Californian, even after a year of living here, she still felt like an alien visitor—a visitor living in a house with another woman's ghost.

Only her love for Burke had anchored her to this place and strengthened her resolve to make a home here. Now the world she'd built around that love was rocking on its axis. Holding it in place would be up to her.

Soon the powerful car had carried Allison beyond the bright lights. As she drove through the rainy darkness, the words of Kate's letter echoed in her memory.

I'm a strong woman, and I'm going to fight this thing like a tigress . . .

Kate had lost her battle with cancer. She would not be here to see Brianna's wedding, to snuggle her grandchildren, or to celebrate a golden anniversary with Burke. But what a fighter the woman must have been.

Now it was Allison's turn to be a fighter—this time for Burke. But she'd never faced a challenge like this one. Did she have the courage to be a tigress—to pit her will against his when it was in his best interest? Did she have the wisdom and patience to get him, and their marriage, through this crisis?

What if she failed? What if she couldn't measure up to the woman Kate had been?

The storm was clearing now. As she turned onto

Peaceful Lane, she glimpsed patches of sky through the parting clouds. The house was dark, but the garage lights came on as she raised the door and drove inside. Seeing the empty spot where Burke had parked his Porsche, she felt a tightening in her chest. Resting her forehead against the steering wheel, she closed her eyes and let acceptance sink in. Nothing here, she told herself, would ever be the same again.

In the house, she turned on the kitchen light and checked the voicemail on the landline phone. There was a curt message from Brianna. She'd be arriving at the Branson Airport tomorrow at two fifteen. Allison didn't look forward to picking up her stepdaughter. The conversation was bound to be awkward, if not downright hostile. But somebody had to be there to meet her flight and drive her to the hospital.

Brianna could be difficult. But the girl had already lost her mother, Allison reminded herself. She was bound to be upset. At the very least, she deserved kindness and understanding.

The fridge was stocked with leftovers from the ill-fated dinner party. And Brianna's room was always kept in readiness, with clean sheets on the bed and towels in the bathroom across the hall. As for the master bedroom . . .

With a sigh, Allison headed for the stairs. Those black silk sheets on the king-size bed would give Brianna one more reason to pass judgment on her stepmother. Now, while there was time to change them, the sheets would have to go.

By the time she'd stripped the bed and replaced the scandalous silk sheets with some pastel-flowered cottons, Allison's long night and stressful day had caught up with her. This morning, just after reading Kate's letter, she'd gotten the word from Cox Medical that Burke had signed the consent form and was on his way to the O.R. for spinal surgery to stabilize his broken vertebrae. Ten minutes later she'd been in the car, breaking speed limits to get back to the hospital, where she'd spent the rest of the day.

Tonight she was dead on her feet. All she wanted to do was fall across the bed and pass out. But then she remembered Kate's letters. She had no memory of having put them back in the drawer.

Downstairs in Burke's study, she saw the letters scattered on the desk, where she'd left them. They lay like a broken rainbow of spring colors—pinks, blues, greens, and yellows on the polished walnut surface, waiting for her to collect them and put them away.

Too tired to stand, she sank into Burke's big leather chair. It was an old chair, so well used that the worn cushions had conformed to the shape of Burke's body. She settled into its contours, seeking comfort but not finding it.

Kate had been sitting in this chair when she'd written to Burke about the discovery of her cancer. She'd been wearing his old flannel bathrobe—the one Allison had stuffed into a donation box after replacing it with a $350 cashmere robe from a high-end catalog. If Burke had missed the old robe, he'd never said a word.

The letter she'd read earlier lay open where she'd left it to answer the call from the hospital. Although she should've known better, Allison found herself rereading the first few lines, then the first page, then the second and third.

She could feel the tenderness in every line of Kate's neatly rounded, schoolgirl script. She could feel the longing, the love, and the little intimacies of a shared twenty-year marriage. No wonder Burke still missed his first wife. And no wonder Brianna resented the younger woman who could never replace her mother.

Allison refolded the pages and slipped them back into their daffodil-colored envelope. What had possessed her to read that letter? Whatever she'd been looking for, she hadn't found it. Those heartfelt lines had only shown her how poorly Burke's second marriage compared to what he'd lost.

Gathering up the rest of the letters, she stuffed them back into the manila envelope. The temptation to read more of them was there—but no, the letters were private and personal, meant for no one's eyes but Burke's. Reading them would only deepen her own hurt. She should never have taken them out of the drawer.

Opening the file drawer all the way, she stuffed the large envelope into the very back. There, it was done, she told herself as she closed the drawer. She would never touch those letters again.

Rising, she wandered back into the kitchen and opened the fridge to look for something to drink. There was wine from the party, a couple of diet colas, some orange juice, and a quart of milk past its expiration date. Nothing looked good. But seeing the party leftovers reminded her of the need to call Burke's friends and tell them about the accident.

Could she do it? Their numbers were in the outdated Rolodex on Burke's desk. Allison had used it to find their addresses when she'd sent the party invitations—written invitations with an RSVP, from Burke's trophy wife. They'd probably hooted about that behind her back.

Calling them could wait till morning, she decided. Or better yet, she could ask Garrett to do it. Right now, what she needed was rest.

In the chilly bedroom, she stripped down, pulled on her sweats, plugged in her phone on the night-stand, and crawled between the sheets.

She'd hoped to fall asleep as soon as her head touched the pillow. Instead she lay staring up into the darkness, her thoughts racing like runaway horses on a carousel.

What about Burke's car? Where was it now? She would need to call the insurance company—she didn't even know which one. And where was Burke's phone? Maybe Garrett knew. After all, he was the one who'd called the police. But she couldn't become depen-dent on the man, Allison reminded herself. He would be all too quick to take advantage of what he perceived as her weakness. Now was the time to take charge and be strong.

First thing tomorrow she would be at the hospital, whether Burke wanted her there are not. She would be patient and understanding with Brianna. But when it came to her husband's welfare, she would not be put off by anybody—including Burke him-self.

Like Kate, she would have to be a tigress.

Reading Kate's letter the second time had burned words and phrases into Allison's memory. She re-called what Kate had said about Burke's being away so much in his work as a talent agent, missing birth-days, holidays, anniversaries, and family crises. But through all that, they'd managed to hold their mar-riage together.

We've had a rich life, Burke. And the rough times have only made the good times sweeter.

Rough times. So the marriage hadn't been perfect

after all. But what kind of rough times had Kate and Burke survived? What had given them the strength to move on together?

Now, with her secure world shattering around her and Burke demanding a divorce, Allison ached with the need to know.

Too restless to sleep, she flung back the covers and walked across the bedroom to the French doors that opened onto a small second-floor balcony. The damp night breeze stirred her hair as she leaned on the rail, gazing out across the lake toward the distant lights of the marina.

Burke still kept his boat there, stored in dry dock. Not once since his marriage to Allison had he even mentioned taking it out on the water. Allison had assumed he was too busy with work or had lost interest. But maybe his reasons went deeper than that. Maybe the vintage twenty-foot Cobalt 200 Bowrider held too many memories.

She had memories, too, Allison reminded herself. She'd been married at nineteen, to her high school sweetheart, a dazzling boy named Kevin who'd dreamed of becoming an actor. She'd followed him to Hollywood and waited tables to pay rent while he found an agent, landed occasional bit parts, and partied with friends she didn't like or trust. The dream of stardom had ended after three years, when she'd lost him to a drug overdose. But before that, there'd been moments of sweet craziness when she'd almost believed things would work out for them.

Allison had picked up the pieces of her life and moved on. But she'd been wary of involvements with men—until, years later, Burke had walked into her little gift gallery, and the magic had happened.

Where was the magic now?

Had it ever been real? Or had it been that sweet, fleeting craziness all over again?

Shivering as the chill penetrated, Allison turned away from the railing and drifted back into the bedroom. Downstairs, Kate's letters waited for her like a Pandora's box that she feared to open. She had vowed not to touch them again. But what if Kate and Burke's loving marriage held some insight into surviving this crisis and saving her own? How could she turn her back on that chance?

She would read one more letter—just one—tonight. After that, she would weigh the wisdom of reading the rest.

Decision made, she wrapped herself in the cashmere robe she'd given Burke, left the bedroom, and walked down the hallway to the stairs.

CHAPTER 4

Allison switched on the desk lamp, settled into Burke's chair, and opened the bottom left-hand file drawer. She wasn't proud of herself for what she was about to do, but desperate times called for desperate measures.

Was that true, or was she just rationalizing the urge to snoop?

She found the manila envelope she'd stuffed into the back of the drawer. Pulling it out, she laid it on the desktop.

Just one letter—that was all she would read. And she'd made up her mind on the way downstairs that she would make a random choice, taking a chance on what she'd find.

Focusing her gaze into the darkness beyond the desk, she reached into the manila envelope and groped among the letters. Choosing one, she tightened the clasp of her fingers and pulled it free.

The small envelope was pink, addressed to a motor lodge somewhere in Texas. The postmark dated this letter eleven years earlier than the one Allison had read first. Kate and Burke would have been in their thirties, Brianna not much more than a toddler.

There were just two pages, pink like the envelope. Allison had come to recognize Kate's neatly rounded handwriting, but this time the script had a slightly forward slant, as if scrawled in haste or even anger.

Bracing herself for whatever she might find, she began to read.

Burke, I am writing this letter because I'm too upset to call you on the phone again. Any conversation we might have at this point would only escalate into an ugly fight.

Yesterday was our anniversary. You forgot, but that's not why I'm writing. Last night, around midnight, I heard Brianna struggling to breathe. I bundled her up and rushed her to the emergency room. The doctor said she had pneumonia. If I hadn't gotten her right in, she could've died. I stayed, scared half to death, while they gave our little girl oxygen and pumped her full of antibiotics. Toward morning her fever broke and she started feeling better, but they kept her for the rest of the day and, of course, I stayed with her. They released her tonight and I brought her home. She's sleeping now, but I'm afraid to close my eyes for fear she'll be sick again.

I don't know how many times I tried calling your room. I phoned the front desk as well, and left messages, but I never heard back. I know your work involves going to clubs and parties at night to check out the talent, but blast it, you have a family. You could have called. Better yet, you should have been here.

Sometimes, like now, I remember how happy we were in that little two-bedroom bungalow in Hollister. I loved waking up with you every morning and snuggling Brianna between us. And I never minded living on a budget. But that wasn't enough for you. You had to buy this big, expensive house—a "surprise," you said. After that, it was the boat and a couple of fancy cars. And to pay for everything, you had to build up the agency with more talent and take on the theater, which meant spending more time on the road than at home.

I never asked for this, Burke—not the house, not the cars, not any of it. All I ever wanted was you and me and Brianna together.

I know you take pride in the fact that your family lives in a showplace with a view of the lake, and that you work hard to provide the best of everything for us. But in all this time, you never once asked me what I wanted. If you had, I would have answered with one word—you.

The letter ended abruptly, without a closing or a signature, as if Kate had exhausted her supply of words. Or maybe she'd heard Brianna stirring and gone to check on her.

Allison folded the pages and slipped them back into the envelope. What had she learned from this letter? That Burke's workaholic nature hadn't changed and probably never would? She already knew that. But Kate's frustration had come as a surprise. The woman hadn't been a paragon of patience and unconditional love after all. She'd struggled against loneliness and anger, and she hadn't been afraid to express herself—not in the letter at least.

The letter had offered some insights into the marriage and how Kate had coped with her work-obsessed husband. But it wasn't enough. Evidently Burke hadn't changed much over the years. But how had Kate made the journey from frustrated young wife to the loving, accepting woman who'd written about her cancer?

Allison slipped the letter back into the manila envelope with the others. By now, she knew that she wouldn't be satisfied until she'd read all the letters in order—not in a single sitting, but one by one, giving herself time to study, ponder, and hopefully learn from each of them.

Upending the envelope, she dumped the letters onto the desk and began sorting them. Going by what she'd seen, Kate hadn't dated her letters. Only the blurred and faded postmarks, some barely readable, told her when they'd been mailed.

Burke hadn't talked much about his road trips. But he must have stayed in the same places long enough for Kate's letters to reach him. The envelopes were addressed to various hotels, motels, and lodges, most of them in neighboring states, where he scouted the local talent and signed up the most promising with his agency—the family acts for Branson and other conservative settings, the adult fare for places like Las Vegas and Atlantic City. In return for a percentage, he would find the talent new gigs all over the country. He was good at his job, making money for himself and his clients, some of whom were still with the agency after more than twenty years.

It took Allison about fifteen minutes to arrange the letters in order, including the one thick envelope that bore only Burke's name and the request to open it after Kate's death. Surprisingly, the letter with the earliest postmark was the one she'd just finished reading.

She ignored the temptation to read the next letter in the stack. She'd done enough for tonight. It was time to put the letters away and go upstairs to bed. Tomorrow was bound to be a trying day. It would be even worse if she was ragged from lack of sleep.

After replacing the letters and closing the drawer, she switched off the desk lamp and made her way back to the stairs, where the light in the hallway lit her way to the second floor. She could feel her fatigue in every step she took. Still, as she passed the door to Brianna's room, an unexpected urge compelled her to step inside and turn on the wall switch.

The family photograph stood on Brianna's bookshelf. Holding it by the edges of the frame, Allison studied the three faces—the proud, handsome man she loved, the young girl just emerging from childhood, and the woman whose mischievous smile hid a world of secrets.

Kate.

A woman who was no longer a stranger.

Burke woke to a raw pain that made him feel as if he were being sawed in two from behind. Straining to reach, he punched the call button on his bed. When the light came on, he fell back on the pillow to wait for the nurse.

He'd been dreaming again—another of the vivid, lifelike dreams that had come to him in the hospital, probably an effect of the pain meds. This time he'd been lying with Allison on a secluded beach, her body molding to his, her sun-bleached hair spread on the sand. Both of them were naked. He could feel the sun on his skin, hear the lapping of the surf and her whispers of love as her long, tanned legs wrapped his hips. It was heaven . . .

And hell was the shock of waking up, understanding where he was and why he was here, and knowing that, whatever happened, his warm, passionate relationship with Allison would never be the same again.

Earlier he'd had a different kind of dream. This time he'd been sitting next to Kate's hospital bed, holding her hand as she slipped from life—swimming in morphine, her hair gone, her weight down to less than a hundred pounds. Her passing had come as a blessed relief, followed by a sense of loss that was like having his heart ripped out. Only the need to be there for Brianna had kept him connected to life.

Until Allison.

"Here you go. Down the hatch." His new nurse had shown up sometime in the night and was still here for morning rounds. Pushing sixty and looking tough enough to wrestle a grizzly bear, she had not once called him "honey."

She handed him a paper cup. By now Burke knew the drill. He took the cup and swallowed the pills inside with a sip from the water bottle she gave him. "How's the pain?" she asked, pointing to a chart on the wall that rated pain levels from one to ten. "Can you give me a number?"

"What number would you give the devil stabbing you in the back with his pitchfork?" He glanced out the window at the pewter sky. "What time is it?"

"Almost seven. Your wife called a few minutes ago. She said she'd be here soon."

"I don't suppose you told her not to come."

"That's not in my job description. How's the pain in your head?"

"Still there. Maybe a little better."

"Any confusion?"

"How the hell would I know?"

"Well, let's get you to the bathroom and into a clean gown before your wife arrives. Then you can rest and have some breakfast."

Burke submitted to the indignity of letting her help him. So far his plumbing was pretty much out of control. The doctor had assured him that would change. But what if it didn't? How could he expect Allison to do the things a nurse would do? And what if the accident and the surgery had left him unable to perform in the bedroom?

All the more reason she needed to call that divorce lawyer.

Back in bed, he could feel the oxycodone working. It dulled the pain in his back and head, but it also made him drowsy, not what he wanted. Sleeping through the pain was tempting, but he had decisions to make and people to deal with. He needed to be sharp.

Burke willed himself to stay awake, but as the minutes passed and the medication took effect, his eyelids began to droop. He was sinking into a fog when, suddenly, it cleared at the sound of Allison's voice. He opened his eyes again.

"Hello, Burke." She was standing next to the bed, holding a tray. She placed it on the over-bed table and moved it within his reach. "The nurses let me bring your breakfast. You must be starved."

"Take it back. I'm not hungry."

"At least have some coffee, and maybe some of those scrambled eggs. You can't get strong by starving yourself."

Grumbling his displeasure, Burke took a sip of the black coffee, which wasn't bad. But the eggs were too bland for his taste. He gave up after a few bites and put down his fork.

Allison had pulled the chair close to the bed. She looked fresh and pretty in a red cashmere sweater and gray slacks, with her honey-gold hair falling over one shoulder. Burke resisted the urge to reach out and skim his finger down her cheek. He'd meant what he'd said about that divorce, even though the thought of her finding someone else—and she would—was almost more than he could stand.

"Brianna left me a voicemail," she said. "I'll be picking her up at the airport this afternoon. I'm guessing she'll want to come straight here."

"And you couldn't talk her out of coming? She doesn't need to see me like this. It'll only upset her."

"Cut her some slack, Burke. She's already lost one parent. She's bound to be worried sick about you."

Burke finished the coffee and sank back onto the pillow. "I've never wanted Brianna to be worried about anything. But if my business goes belly-up, I don't know how I'm going to manage tuition at Northwestern. And that new car I promised her might have to wait."

"She could have my Lexus. I've driven old cars most of my life. And if need be, Brianna could move back home and go to College of the Ozarks. The students there all work for their tuition."

"I know. But she wants to be a journalist, and Northwestern is the big league. She wouldn't be happy if she had to leave."

"Maybe not, but if she's as tough as you are, she'll do fine wherever she is."

Right now Burke didn't feel tough, but he wasn't about to say so. "Somebody needs to take care of the car," he said, changing the subject. "I'm assuming it's totaled."

"I can do that," Allison said.

"Fine. The policy is in my desk—lower left-hand drawer, where the files are. I'm guessing the police had the car hauled away. You'll want to get me my phone if it's still in there, and clean out the glove box and the trunk."

"I'll take care of that this morning. Anything else?"

"The divorce lawyer." As Burke spoke, he saw her cheerful expression freeze. "I mean it, Allison," he said. "At least talk to somebody so you'll know what you're looking at if I go under. It's your only chance of salvaging anything out of this mess."

"I told you, I don't want a divorce. That's the last time I'm going to say it." Her voice was cold. "Is there anything you want me to pass on to Garrett?"

"I'll deal with Garrett myself. I'm sure he'll be coming by. Meanwhile, I know you've got better things to do than babysit me, so you might as well get out of here and get on with your day."

"All right." She rose. "I'll check on the car and see you later, when I bring Brianna by."

"Fine. I'll be right here. It's not like I can get up and leave."

She hesitated, as if about to lean over the bed and kiss him. Burke turned his head away. He knew he'd hurt her, but it was for her own good, he told himself. Allison would be better off without him. Whatever it took, he needed to convince her of that. Losing her would kill him. But even that would be better than having her stay and see him humiliated.

Allison had barely made it into the hall before the tears spilled over. She stumbled blindly ahead, almost bumping into a grim-looking, silver-haired nurse dressed in lavender scrubs.

"Are you all right?" the woman asked.

"I'll be fine." Embarrassed, Allison wiped her eyes. "It's just that . . . oh, I don't know. Seeing him like this, so helpless and so angry . . . it's going to take some getting used to."

"You know he has a good chance of recovery, don't you?" The nurse guided Allison into an unoccupied room, where they could talk in private without disturbing patients. "It's just going to take time and a lot of patience."

"Yes, I know. But he's being so hateful—mostly to me." Allison gave an apologetic shake of her head. "I'm sorry for unloading on you this way. You've got more important things to do than listen to a blubbering fool like me."

"Let me give you some advice," the nurse said. "I've been working this ward a long time, and I've seen a lot of patients come and go. Your husband is a proud man. But underneath that pride, he's scared to death. He's scared of losing his dignity and his manhood. He's even more scared of losing you. And that's the one thing he doesn't want you to know."

"But why is he pushing me away?"

"Because he doesn't want you to know how much he needs you. He doesn't want you to see him as anything but strong and masterful. Think about it." She glanced away at the sound of a call signal. "That's for me. Got to go. All I can do is wish you luck."

"Thanks." Allison left the room and walked down the hall to the exit. Was the nurse right? Was Burke pushing her away because he was afraid of losing her? The logic didn't make sense. But in a crazy sort of way, it did. At least it had given her something to think about.

In the parking lot, she was heading for her car when Garrett drove past. Allison hoped he hadn't noticed her. She was too emotional to talk to him about Burke. But this wasn't her lucky day. Garrett stopped, backed up, and rolled down the window of his black Cadillac Escalade.

"Hey, I was hoping to see you," he said. "How's it going?"

"About the way you'd expect. I was just leaving."

"Well, before you rush off, I've got some big news you'll want to hear. Climb in. We can talk while I drive you to your car."

Did he sense her hesitation? "Come on," he said. "It's warm in here, and private. I won't keep you long."

Acquiescing, she climbed into the big SUV. The

morning was chilly, the heated leather seats pleasantly warm. "I was just on my way to find out about Burke's Porsche and call the insurance company," she said. "Do you happen to know what the police did with the wreck?"

"It's been towed to the impound lot, pending any investigation." Garrett kept driving. "But don't worry about the insurance. I snapped a photo of the car and gave the insurance company a call—the policy information was in the glove box. The claim's already been filed. From the looks of the car, I'm guessing it'll be a total loss. Burke's lucky to be alive."

Allison suppressed a shudder. "So you cleaned out the car?"

"The police did. Everything's in a bag, in my briefcase. I'll give it to you before I let you off."

"Did they find Burke's phone?"

"They did. I can give it to you or take it when I go up to see him."

"Thanks. He seemed anxious to have it." Allison didn't want to owe Garrett, but he'd just taken a load off her mind. Now she could look ahead, to dealing with Brianna. "You said you had some news."

"That's right." He pulled into the empty slot next to her Lexus. "I've nailed down an investor for the American Heartland."

"That's wonderful," Allison said, hoping it really was.

"They're ready to commit the full amount. I've got the contracts with me. All I need is Burke's signature, and it's a done deal."

"Does it have to be today? Burke's on pain medication. He's in no condition to sign anything. I'm not even sure it would be legal."

"I've thought of that," Garrett said. "But if Burke were to give you power of attorney, you could sign it. The investors haven't given me a deadline, but the longer we make them wait, the more likely they might be to lose interest and walk away."

"I can't imagine Burke would give me power of attorney," Allison said. "Things have been . . . tense between us since the night of the party. And I'm not sure I'd even want it. It would be a huge responsibility."

"Not even if it would save the American Heartland?"

Allison's hand went to the door latch. "I can't make that decision now," she said. "Talk to Burke. He's the only one who can answer your questions."

"Wait." Allison had opened the door. He reached out and put a hand on her arm. "You're forgetting something."

He reached behind the seat for his briefcase, opened it, and took out a plastic ziplock bag. "This is everything from Burke's Porsche, including the keys," he said. "The phone's in there, too. Do you want to keep it for him, or should I take it up to him now?"

Allison lifted out the phone and the charger. "Take these to Burke. Maybe being able to call his friends will make him feel less disconnected. Thanks for the ride and the news, Garrett. Brianna is flying in this afternoon. While she's here, I won't have much spare time. But I hope you'll keep me posted about the business."

He caught her shoulder as she moved to step out of the door. "I'm hoping you'll do more than let me keep you posted, Allison. With Burke out of action,

I'm going to need your help making decisions. I know you ran a small business yourself, so you understand what it takes. I'm willing to take you in, show you the ropes, and make you part of the agency."

"Is that an offer?"

"If you want to call it that. Think about it and let me know."

"All right. But no promises. Burke never wanted a working wife."

"But things have changed. You could be a lot of help to him, and to me. Don't worry, I won't say anything to Burke. If it's a yes, I'll leave telling him to you."

"Thanks . . . I think. But I'll let you know."

"That's all I'm asking. Give my best to Brianna."

Allison closed the door, climbed into her car, and pulled out of the visitor lot. Garrett had given her plenty to think about. But with Burke lying helpless and in pain, she wasn't about to rush any decisions.

Morning sunlight had brightened the day. The sky had cleared to a dazzling blue. The hillsides blazed with autumn colors as Allison drove the winding mountain highway toward home. The Ozarks were old mountains. Worn and rounded by time, they were very different from the jutting peaks of the Sierras and Rockies. But they held their own kind of beauty—a beauty that whispered of ancient wisdom and magic when the wind blew through the trees. And never was this country more beautiful than on a sun-sparkled autumn day after a night of rain.

No one had shown Allison the spot where Burke's car had gone off the highway and rolled down the slope, but she knew the dangerous curve where the accident had most likely happened. She slowed the car as she rounded the sharp turn, looking for skid marks, but there were none. The road had been wet, she reminded herself. The Porsche would likely have hydroplaned, jumped the guardrail, and tumbled over the edge. As Garrett had said, Burke was lucky to be alive.

She'd planned to go home, find the policy, and call the insurance company about the car. But now that Garrett had taken care of that, she had time on her hands. Brianna wouldn't be getting in for several hours yet. She could stop at a convenience store for milk and sodas, then go home and do some last-minute tidying of the house, or better yet, put on her sneakers and try to walk off some nervous energy.

Arriving home after her stop at the roadside store, she put the snacks away in the kitchen and went upstairs to change her shoes. Then, with her phone and the house key in her jacket, she went back outside and hit the jogging path that ran along the shore of the lake.

The morning air, smelling of last night's rain, was cool on her face, the calm surface of Table Rock Lake like a smooth blue mirror. A heron, stalking fish in the shallows, flapped skyward at her approach.

She wasn't alone on the path. Approaching from the other direction, a fit young mother in tights was pushing her baby in a jogging stroller. Allison gave them a smile as she stepped aside to let them pass. Just looking at the pair made her feel old.

Before they were married, Burke had made it clear that he'd already raised one child and had no desire for others. Allison, already past thirty, had understood and gone along with his wishes. Sometimes she caught herself wondering what she'd missed, but now that Burke was injured, maybe it was just as well that she didn't have a baby to worry about.

If Kate's letters were any indication, she'd done most of the child raising while Brianna was young. But Allison had to give Burke credit. After Kate's death he'd cut back on traveling and restructured his life to be present for his daughter. It was a shame he couldn't have done it while Kate was alive and still in good health. But it appeared they'd had some wonderful times when he was home, with the boat and their friends. And somehow, through good times and bad, they'd been able to keep their love alive.

Would she be as lucky? Allison wondered. Or was it already too late to save her marriage to this proud, stubborn, driven man?

Her thoughts shifted to Garrett's offer that she come and work for the agency. In some ways it sounded like a good idea. It would keep her busy, and possibly sane, while Burke was recovering. She'd be earning a salary, she supposed—but since it would be Burke's money, there wasn't much financial incentive to take the job. Still, if she could be Burke's eyes and ears, making sure that no employee or client took advantage of his absence to bend the rules, that could be important.

But wasn't that Garrett's job?

And what about being home to aid Burke with his recovery? How much was he going to need her? How much would he allow her to help him?

Her decision would have to wait. Right now there were too many uncertainties involved.

She'd walked more than a mile along the path, to a long, little-used wooden pier that jutted out into the lake. Making her way to the end of it, she stood for a moment, gazing out across the water toward the marina on the far shore, where Burke's boat was stored on its trailer. When was the last time he'd taken it on the water? If he had no plans to use the expensive craft, why hadn't he sold it? Only Burke could answer those questions, and this was no time to ask him.

Turning around, she started back. Where the shoreline curved, she could see the tree-sheltered houses along Peaceful Lane. All of them had been built back in the 1970s with high windows and broad balconies offering magnificent views of the lake. These days, most of the owners were either retirees or wealthy people who used the houses as vacation homes. None of them had much in common with a young bride who didn't fish and had never even been on the water.

Burke had been smart to buy the house when he did. The property was worth more than twice what he'd paid for it. Maybe if they fell on hard times, he could sell it, and they could move to a smaller place. But would he let it go when it held so many memories of Kate? Would Brianna?

Kate had resented the expensive home, which Burke had evidently bought without consulting her. But she'd lived in it for a long time. Had she grown to accept the place, even to love it?

She glanced at her watch. It was early yet. Brianna's flight wouldn't be landing until midafternoon. Once Burke's daughter arrived at the house, reading Kate's letters would be out of the question. But there was time to read one now.

Allison hadn't meant to read the next letter so soon. But with Burke pushing her away, Garrett pursuing his own agenda, and Brianna about to blow in like an unpredictable storm, she needed a steady voice, a voice she could trust.

Right now, that voice was Kate's.

CHAPTER 5

The second letter had been mailed fifteen months after the first. Allison could feel a slight stiffness inside the blue envelope. When she tugged at the pages, a photograph fell out, fluttering facedown onto Burke's desk. She recognized Kate's handwriting on the back.

Brianna, age 4, with Captain

Turning the photo over, Allison found herself looking at the image of a child with challenging eyes and unruly russet curls. She was hugging a furry black puppy with outsized paws. Even given the difference in size and age, Allison recognized the huge black dog from the family picture in Brianna's room. Laying the photo to one side, she slid the pages out of the envelope, braced herself for what she might discover, and began to read.

> *Dearest Burke,*
> *If you've looked at the picture, you'll know that we have a new family member. Captain is a registered*

Newfoundland retriever. He's going to get bigger—a lot bigger. But he's a water dog, so he'll be great in the boat. And Brianna is already head over heels in love with him.

I probably should've asked you first. But after the past wonderful weeks with you at home, Brianna was desolate when you left. You know what a daddy's girl she is. She wouldn't stop moping. I tried taking her out for burgers and movies. I even took her to Silver Dollar City for a day of old-fashioned rides and treats. Nothing could make up for missing you. That was when I thought of getting her a puppy. She brightened right up.

We found a book with pictures of dog breeds, and I asked her to show me the kind of dog she wanted. I expected her to choose something little and cute. But when she saw the photo of an animal that looked like a huge, shaggy bear, there was no changing her mind. When it comes to stubbornness, she's your daughter through and through. I found a good breeder in Spring-field, and we came home with Captain. So far, he's been a good boy. He's very calm, doesn't bark much, and is learning to go potty outside. He and Brianna are inseparable. He even sleeps in her room. So whether you like it or not, my darling husband, I'm afraid the dog is here to stay. Just know that your little girl is happy.

As for your big girl . . . Where should I begin?

It's late here. Brianna and her new friend are asleep. I'm sitting up in bed, using a clipboard from your desk for a writing surface. The doors to the balcony are open to let in the fresh air. I know you've warned me about going to sleep without locking them, but I can see the full moon reflecting on the lake, and it's so beautiful, I can't stand the thought of shutting myself away from it.

After the last three weeks of having you here, this big bed feels cold and empty. I'll never get used to having you gone, but I'm learning to accept it as the price of being your wife. And even though you spent a lot of hours at the office, didn't we have a wonderful time while you were here? I loved taking the boat out on the lake and fishing for bass with Brianna. She was so excited when she caught a fish, and you made such a wonderful fuss over her—taking the fish home and grilling it for her dinner.

And the nights . . . oh, my sainted aunt, even the memory makes me blush! In the bed, in the shower, and even on the bedroom balcony with the moon smiling down on us—if the moon can truly smile. I know I was smiling at the time. Even thinking about it now makes me tingle—your body, the way you held me, the little sound you made when you climaxed . . .

We got pretty wild, which comes to the second reason I'm writing this letter (the dog being first). I was planning to keep the news to myself a little longer, but you know me. I'm no good at keeping secrets. So I'll just end the suspense and tell you.

The test I bought and used was positive.

I'm pregnant.

The letter ended with a few affectionate lines. Allison folded the pages, slipped them back into the envelope, along with the photo, and buried her face in her hands.

What had possessed her to read this letter—or any of the letters? Kate's tender, intimate words were powerful enough to crush her. She would remember them every time she looked at Burke, and whenever they made love—if it ever happened again. Burke had belonged to Kate in a way that he would never belong to Allison. Maybe he was right in asking for a divorce. Maybe she was wrong in refusing.

Forcing herself to move, she put the letter back with the others and shoved the manila envelope into the rear of the file drawer. Burke had never mentioned a second baby. Clearly, something had gone wrong—a miscarriage or an even more tragic loss. Did she want to learn more, or was she better off not knowing?

In the kitchen, Allison found an opened bottle of Chardonnay from the party. Feeling raw inside, she poured three fingers into a glass, walked back through her perfect living room, and stepped out onto the first-floor balcony. The alcohol in the wine burned her throat as she sipped from the glass.

Leave the letters alone, she told herself. *You're already dealing with enough grief.*

The autumn breeze had taken on a chill. Allison shivered beneath the light denim jacket she was still wearing from her walk. She checked her watch again. She still had plenty of time before Brianna's flight was due.

In a way, it was good to have Brianna coming, if only for a few days. With Burke's daughter around, there'd be no temptation to open that Pandora's box and read more of those heartbreaking letters— letters that she should never have touched in the first place.

She was walking back to the kitchen when her cell phone jangled. Startled, she pulled it out of her pocket. The call was from the hospital.

"Mrs. Caldwell." The voice was a woman's. "This is Dr. Moorcroft. Your husband's had a setback. We've got him stabilized now, but you may want to come to the hospital and be here when he wakes up."

Allison's heart slammed. "I'll be right there. What happened?"

"He was having chest pains and shortness of breath. At first we thought it might be a heart attack, but that doesn't seem to be the case. We think it was more likely a bad reaction to the pain medication, or the anesthesia—maybe even some injury we've missed. We've put him on oxygen and given him a sedative while we finish testing."

"Will he be all right?" Allison forced the words out of her tight throat.

"He's stable and sleeping. We're monitoring his vitals." The implications of what the doctor had left unsaid were terrifying.

"I'm leaving now. I'll be there in twenty minutes—half an hour at most."

She grabbed her purse, flew to the car, and backed out of the garage. The traffic was light at this hour. She floored the gas pedal, then forced herself to slow down. A ticket or an accident wasn't going to help her get to Burke.

What if this setback was serious? What if—God forbid—she were to lose him? Allison tried to imagine what the loss would mean, especially with things so troubled between them and no chance to save their marriage. If Burke didn't survive, she would always remember how she'd walked out of his hospital room hurt and angry, missing the last chance to tell him that she loved him.

Then there was Brianna. Burke's daughter didn't know what had just happened. She was bound to be frantic when she found out. And her plane would be landing in less than an hour. Someone would need to be there to meet the flight and prepare her.

If Allison went to the hospital and stayed with Burke, there was no way she could make it to the airport in time to meet Brianna's plane. She would have to call somebody else to pick her up and bring her to the hospital. The most logical person to do that was Garrett.

She used the voice command in her car to make the call. Garrett answered on the second ring. He listened as Allison told him what had happened and what she needed.

"Damn," he muttered. "I saw Burke right after you did. He seemed fine when I left. And the doctor doesn't know what happened?"

"Not yet. They're still trying to find out."

"Sure, I'll be glad to meet Brianna's flight. She knows me, so it won't be like a stranger is picking her up."

"You'll need to tell her what's going on with her dad. Please do it gently. She's bound to be upset."

"Don't worry. I know how to handle her."

Before Allison could ask him what he meant, Garrett ended the call. It would be all right, she told herself as she crossed the Lake Taneycomo Bridge into town. Garrett knew Brianna and would take care of the girl. Right now, for her, the only thing that really mattered was getting to Burke.

She pulled into the parking lot at the rambling, one-story Ortho-Neuro Center, found a space, and dashed for the entrance. Her pulse galloped as she rushed to Burke's room. The doctor had said he was stable. What did that mean? He could be in a coma and be stable.

A woman who looked too young to be a doctor was just coming out of his room. She gave Allison a smile—hopefully a good sign.

"If you're Mrs. Caldwell, you'll be glad to know your husband's awake. We still haven't discovered what happened to him. We're beginning to think it might be stress-related."

"Thank you." Allison began to breathe normally again. "Can I go in and see him?"

"Of course. He asked for you as he was waking up. Remember, we want to keep him as quiet as possible. If he seems agitated, call the nurse." The doctor walked away, then turned back. "You're Brianna, right?"

"Brianna's his daughter. I'm his wife—Allison." At least Burke hadn't asked for Kate this time. "Brianna will be here later this afternoon. She has red hair— like her mother."

"Oh—thanks for straightening me out." The doctor smiled again and hurried off down the hall. Allison opened the door to Burke's room and walked softly inside.

Burke was lying back on the pillow. Beneath the bruises from the accident, his face was fearfully pale. An oxygen clip was fastened to his nose. He looked awful. But the monitors above his head showed that his vitals were good. Thank heaven for that.

Tears welled in Allison's eyes as she leaned over him. What if she'd lost this stubborn, impossible, precious man?

His eyes opened, a surprising alertness flickering in their dark blue depths. He hadn't spoken, but she could tell that he knew her.

"Hello, sleepyhead," she whispered. "You look like hell."

A feeble smile tugged at his lips. "I feel like hell," he muttered. "What happened to me?"

"The doctor isn't sure. They thought you might be having a heart attack, but that didn't check out. What do you remember?"

"Not much. Just some chest pain, and then the monitors went crazy. After that, I must've blacked out, or they gave me something."

Allison reached for his hand and held it, grateful that he wasn't trying to push her away. "After the doctor called me, I couldn't get here fast enough. You scared me half to death."

"No need for that. I'm a tough sonofabitch. You should know that by now."

"I do." Allison blinked back tears. Her fingers tightened around his hand. "Brianna's on her way. Her flight will be landing soon."

"Damn, Brianna didn't need to come. One look at me and she'll probably turn around and run."

"She's your daughter. She loves you. And don't worry about the way you look. Garrett promised to prepare her."

"Garrett?" He scowled.

"I asked him to meet Brianna's flight so I could be here with you."

Burke didn't respond. He was still scowling.

"I spoke with Garrett as I was leaving this morning," Allison said. "He told me he'd already filed a claim with the auto insurance company. And he told me something else. He said he's found an investor for the American Heartland. All he needs is your signature, and it's a done deal." She paused, puzzled by his stormy expression. "Did he tell you?"

"He told me."

"Did you sign? I warned him that your signature might not be valid, since you were on painkillers."

"I didn't sign. And I won't."

Startled, Allison stared at him. "Not even if it would keep your business from going under?"

"Not even then."

Allison shook her head. "I've always trusted your judgment, Burke. Now I'm confused. Is there something you're not telling me?"

"Only that I know who Garrett is talking to, and I don't like them."

"But who—?"

"Don't ask." He cut her off angrily. "I've told you enough. You can't be involved in this mess. Get a lawyer, Allison. You're going to need somebody to fight for your rights before it's over. I can give you a couple of names if you need them."

Fight against whom? Against you?

Allison might have voiced the question, but just then his oxygen monitor began to beep. Heart lurching, she checked the clip. It was on his finger, where it belonged.

Allison sprang to her feet. "Breathe!" she urged him, punching the call button. "Take deep, deep breaths!"

By the time the nurse—a tall brunette this time—came rushing into the room, Burke's oxygen level was rising again. The nurse turned up the oxygen and stayed to coach him until he was stable again. Allison sank back into the chair, her legs quivering. Only now that the brief crisis was over did she realize how scared she'd been.

When he was resting, his vitals stable again, the nurse beckoned Allison out into the hall. "We're still trying to figure out what happened to him earlier," she said. "Did anything change before his oxygen level started dropping?"

"We were just talking. But when the conversation turned to business issues, he started getting upset."

"And probably forgot to relax and breathe," the nurse said. "I'll mention that to the doctor."

"What happened before?" Allison asked. "Was it the same thing?"

"His business partner was here—younger man, dark hair?"

"Yes, I know him."

"He closed the door, but after a few minutes, their conversation got loud. We couldn't make out words but we could hear your husband shouting. Not long after that, the partner left, with his briefcase. I was concerned enough to check on your husband. His oxygen was dropping, and his blood pressure was elevated. When we couldn't calm him down, we gave him a light sedative. He was just coming out of it when you walked in."

So something was going on—something between Burke and Garrett. And until she knew what it was, she would be no more help to her husband than a child groping in the dark.

"Thanks for helping me make sense of this," Allison said. "His daughter will be here a little later. I hope that seeing her will raise his spirits."

"So do I. Meanwhile, do your best to keep him calm and quiet. Stress isn't good for his body."

"I'll be here for as long as he needs me," Allison said.

"Good. Call if you notice anything that doesn't seem right." The nurse turned and headed back toward her station.

Actually, nothing seemed right, Allison thought.

It was as if Garrett and Burke were locked in some kind of power struggle; and Garrett seemed as eager to involve her as Burke was to keep her in the dark.

But whether she liked it or not, she was already involved. If Burke wouldn't tell her what was going on, maybe Garrett would.

When Allison stepped back into Burke's room again, she found that he'd gone back to sleep. His breathing was deep and even, his vitals stable. Relieved, she stood by his bed for a moment, her eyes tracing the chiseled lines of his face. This was the man who'd vowed to cherish and protect her to the end of his life; the man who'd thrilled her with his loving and provided her with every material thing she could possibly have wished for.

But what had she given him in return? Was it enough? Or was he still mourning his beloved Kate? Was she really what his friends called her—his trophy wife, with nothing to offer but youth and looks?

Leaving him, she walked down the hall to the visitors' lounge and chose a popular women's magazine from the rack. Back in his room, she settled in the chair by the bed and leafed through the pages, seeing mostly ads and celebrity photos. Her mind wandered back to the day Burke had walked into her little Capitola gallery to buy a silver charm for his daughter. She'd been attracted to him at once. The man had exuded power and self-confidence. But what had drawn her to him was the glimpsed vulnerability, the loneliness in his deep blue eyes. They'd started talking. He'd invited her on a dinner date that had lasted until the next morning. By then they'd become close. He made her feel treasured and protected, but also needed.

The connection between them had been instantaneous, deep, hot, and strong enough to get them through a long-distance courtship, ending in a proposal.

Their wedding, in the stone and wood chapel at Top of the Rock in Big Cedar, accompanied by the strains of a bagpipe, had been a dream. Even though Brianna had pouted her displeasure through the entire ceremony, Allison had believed herself the luckiest woman in the world. And she had made herself a silent promise that she would be the perfect wife to this wonderful man.

She'd tried—tried to the point of exhaustion. But nothing she did was ever good enough for Burke's daughter or the friends who'd kept Kate's memory alive.

She glanced up at the wall clock. Brianna would be here soon. Hopefully, Garrett would just let her off at the hospital and leave. If he came into the room, Allison knew that it would be up to her to keep him from upsetting Burke again.

Putting the magazine aside, she stepped into the bathroom, finished, and stood to wash her hands. The mirror above the sink reflected a tired face, bare of makeup, the eyes ringed in shadows. A bitter smile tugged at her lips. Nobody would call her a trophy wife now.

Brianna stood in the hospital parking lot, watching Garrett lift her suitcase out of his SUV. At seventeen, she'd had a schoolgirl crush on the man. But now that she'd met Liam, she could see Garrett's flaws. He was showing his age, his hair thinning on top, his teeth slightly yellowed, and his muscles losing their tone. And she'd noticed he had a way of putting other people down to make himself look good. She no longer found him attractive, but she still liked him. He was easy to talk to, and he was one of the few people who'd always treated her like an adult.

Wearing distressed jeans, high-heeled boots, and a black leather jacket, she strode toward the building, with Garrett trailing her. She'd dressed to give herself confidence, but now that she was here, she realized that how she looked didn't matter.

"Are you okay?" he asked as they walked through the main entrance.

"I'll have to be okay, won't I?" The truth was she felt shaky and scared. But she couldn't let it show. She had to be brave for her father.

She pictured him in her mind—tall and strong and energetic, the man who'd always taken care of her and provided for her every need. Maybe his condition wouldn't be as serious as she'd been told. Maybe she would walk in to find him sitting up and smiling, ready to get out of the hospital and get back to work. He was still young—not yet fifty. Surely, whatever had happened to him, he would be strong enough to bounce right back to normal.

Forcing a smile, she walked into the room. The man in the bed was asleep—his face ashen, his head bandaged, his jaw rough with unshaven stubble. An oxygen clip was attached to his nose. IV and monitor tubes were attached to his arms and hands. Brianna blinked back tears. Her father looked even worse than she'd feared he would.

And he was all alone. Where was the nurse? And where was Allison? How could she go off and leave him like this?

She leaned over him, as close as she could. "It's all

right, Daddy," she whispered. "I'm here. I've come home."

His eyelids fluttered. His blue eyes—almost as blue as Liam's—opened. She expected him to smile, but he looked more perturbed than happy. "What are you doing here, Brianna?" he demanded. "Why aren't you in school?"

She drew back a little. "I came to make sure you were all right," she said. "Who's taking care of you? Isn't Allison supposed to be here? Or is she afraid of breaking a fingernail?"

Just then the bathroom door opened and Allison stepped out, drying her hands on a paper towel. She looked exhausted, her hair mussed, her bloodshot eyes sunk in shadows, and her tired face bare of makeup.

"Hello, Brianna," she said. "I'm glad you got here safely."

Garrett had walked into the room, carrying Brianna's suitcase, which he set behind the door. The small room suddenly seemed crowded, as if the people in it were sucking out all the air.

Brianna's expression darkened as she looked at Allison. "How *could* you?" she demanded. "How could you let him go out at night in a storm, on that awful, slick road? He could have died in that wreck!"

"Now, honey, it wasn't Allison's fault," Burke said. "She tried to talk me out of going, but you know your stubborn old dad. I've got nobody to blame but myself."

"He's right, Brianna," Garrett said. "When the problem at the theater came up, I offered to go myself, but he insisted on taking care of it in person. Maybe you should apologize to Allison."

Brianna hated being treated like a child. "I'm

sorry," she mumbled, turning away from Allison and back to her father.

"Apology accepted." Allison looked as if she wanted to make an excuse and leave. But she had clearly staked out her territory in the room. It was clear that she meant to stay and keep the situation under control.

Brianna remembered what Garrett had told her on the way to the hospital. In a way, the accident *had* been Allison's fault. If she hadn't quarreled with Burke before he'd walked out of the party, he might not have been driving so fast. But she knew better than to mention that now. Instead she changed the subject.

"Garrett mentioned something about the theater having money troubles, Daddy," Brianna said. "I guess that means you won't be getting me a new car."

Allison glanced at Burke's blood pressure monitor, then spoke. "Brianna, this is hardly the time for this conversation."

"No, it's all right," Burke said. "I know you've got your heart set on that car, Brianna. So don't you worry about that. I promised you a new car, and you're going to get one. Any car you like."

"And the money for school? If I have to drop out of the program at Northwestern, they might not give me a second chance."

"Don't worry, it'll be taken care of." Burke's voice sounded strained. Allison gave Brianna an anxious glance.

"Brianna, I need you to step out into the hall with me," she said. "Come on, it'll just be a minute."

"Can Garrett come with us?" Brianna felt as if she needed an ally.

"No," Allison said. "Just us girls." She opened the door, closing it after Brianna followed her into the hall.

"What's this about?" Brianna demanded. "Are you going to tell me there's plenty of money for you to turn the house into an art museum, but nothing for school?"

Allison was obviously struggling to hold her temper. "Listen to me. Your father needs to rest. Talking to him about money will only raise his stress level to the danger point. For now, just be kind and loving to him. You can talk about money when he's stronger."

"But . . ." She was confused. "Garrett told me that all Dad has to do is sign a contract with the new investors, and there'll be plenty of money for everything."

"Brianna, your father's in no condition to sign anything. And he has some issues with the contract and the people behind it. That's all I can tell you, except that right now he needs time to rest and heal. Please tell me you understand."

"I'll try. But this is a shock. What'll happen if he doesn't sign?"

"Right now all that matters is that he get his strength back. And for as long as you're here, your job is to help him feel better, not stress him out over financial problems." Allison opened the door and ushered Brianna back into the room. Brianna could sense the tension, as if Allison and Garrett were engaged in a tug-of-war, with her father in the middle. She couldn't take sides until she knew who had her dad's best interests at heart; and she wouldn't know who that was until she knew more about the issues involved.

Much as she disliked her stepmother, Brianna knew Allison was right about one thing. If her dad was to get well, he needed to be protected from stress and worry.

But how could she do that if nobody would tell her what was going on? Between Allison and Garrett, she'd have more luck with her father's business partner. She would see how much she could find out.

Allison had been worried about leaving Burke alone with Garrett, but she found them making awkward small talk. "Thank you for picking up Brianna, Garrett," she told him. "There's no need for you to stay. I can take Brianna home with me when I leave tonight."

"Oh, but I'll be starving by then," Brianna said. "All I've had today is coffee."

"No problem," Allison said. "I'll give you some money and you can go down to the cafeteria. They've got good soup and sandwiches, and their shakes aren't bad either."

"I'm hungrier than that," Brianna said. "Garrett, could you be a sweetheart and take me to the Chateau? I've been craving their chicken marsala all day."

If Garrett hesitated, it was only for an instant. "Sure, I could use a good meal myself. All right with you, Burke?"

Burke didn't look happy, Allison observed. But his daughter was nineteen. He could hardly forbid her to go out to dinner, even with a man he no longer trusted. "Fine," he said with a sigh. "I'm just sorry I can't go with you. Allison, if you want to go along with them, feel free."

Did he want her to go—maybe to keep Garrett from pushing his influence on Brianna? Allison was torn. But she'd already resolved to stay with her husband. And trying to chaperone Brianna would only earn her more resentment.

"Thanks, but I'll stay here," she said. "Go on, you two. Enjoy your meal. Can I assume you'll be back here afterward, Brianna? Maybe in an hour?"

"Sure." Brianna's shrug seemed to show indifference. "Come on, Garrett. I'll owe you one for this." She tugged him out the door and down the hall. Allison already knew that the Chateau, an elegant resort and spa with a tower overlooking the lake, was Brianna's favorite dining place. But she sensed that this escape wasn't just about food. Something was going on, and she didn't like it. Neither would Burke.

Maybe she should have insisted on going with Brianna and Garrett.

Burke's gaze followed Allison as she walked around the bed and sat down in the chair that Garrett had vacated. She looked impossibly tired. Part of him wanted to reach out, pull her down to him, and thank her for staying at his side. But that would only confuse her. For her own good, he needed to keep her at a distance. Still, it wasn't easy when he needed her so much.

"Can I get you anything?" she asked. "Some fresh water, maybe, or a soda?"

He shook his head.

"Are you all right?" she asked.

"Are you?"

"You wanted me to go with them, didn't you?" she said.

"It doesn't matter. Brianna's nineteen, and she's got a mind of her own. She'll do what she wants to."

Burke kept the rest of his concerns to himself. He wondered if Brianna was attracted to Garrett. The man was handsome, witty, and newly single. And the ten-year difference in their ages was less than the age gap between himself and Allison. But Garrett was capable of playing games with the girl's romantic heart, or, worse, gaining her trust and using it to further his own ambitions.

Until this current financial crisis raised its ugly head, he would have trusted Garrett with his life. Now he no longer trusted the man with anything, especially with his strong-willed daughter.

He'd spoiled Brianna after her mother's death, giving her everything she wanted in an effort to make up for Kate's absence. Now she was an adult, and it was payback time. Whatever the issue, come hell or high water, Brianna was used to getting her own way. He could only hope she'd have the common sense to make the right choices.

Damn, he hated being trapped in a hospital bed when he needed to stand up and take charge. He had never felt more helpless in his life.

"Have they told you how much longer you need to be here?" Allison seemed to read his thoughts.

"A couple of days. Then I'll go to the rehab wing for some short-term therapy. After that I'll be going home. But I've arranged for help to come in, so you won't have to worry about taking care of me."

"You know I'd gladly do it—take care of you, I mean."

"I know. But it would kill me to see you tied down to nursing a broken man."

"I'm your wife."

"That can be changed. I'm still hoping you'll make the sensible decision. I wanted to give you the world. I can't do that anymore."

She shook her head. Her face was a stoic mask. Only her lovely violet eyes showed pain. "What about Brianna? You can't divorce her."

"She might have to grow up fast."

"Well, I've already grown up," she said. "And I need to know what's going on with you and Garrett and the real reason you won't sign that contract with the investors. Saying you don't like them isn't enough. Stop treating me like a child, Burke. I need to hear the truth—the whole story."

CHAPTER 6

Allison reached past the monitor cords, found her husband's hand, and clasped it hard. "You're asking me to make the most heartbreaking decision of my life," she said. "You're telling me I'll need a lawyer to fight for my rights. But I don't understand what those rights are, or whom I'd be fighting. This is no time to keep secrets from me, Burke. Not even for my own good."

Burke closed his eyes. He appeared to be resting, but Allison knew he was thinking about what to say and how much to tell her. When he opened his eyes again, he looked tired and in pain. "How much do you know?" he asked.

"Only what Garrett told me—that the American Heartland is in danger of going under and maybe taking the agency with it. He said that in order to survive, you'll need to remodel the theater and hire some big-name acts."

He took a deep breath, bringing his oxygen level up. "Did he tell you there's no money for that, and that the loan we took out to get the building up to code is due at the end of the year? And did he tell you what our options are?"

"As I understand it, you could either try to refinance for enough to pay off the existing loan and make the improvements, or bring an investor on board."

"That's right. I was working after hours on an application for the refinance, taking time to cover all the bases, when this damned accident happened. I figure the loan is a risk, but an honest risk. If we can pull the American Heartland out of this slump, we should be able to make the monthly payments and come out with our ownership intact. If not, it'll be abandon ship, every man for himself."

His eyes narrowed. "That's just one of the reasons you need a lawyer in your corner. You'll need to get out of this marriage and take everything you can get your hands on, before the whole house of cards collapses and me with it—if that's what's going to happen. Take my word for it—you won't want what's left of me by the time this is over."

Allison's stoic expression masked a storm of emotions. Her husband was telling her to divorce him, for the most mercenary reason she could imagine. How could he believe her capable of such a cold-blooded act? She had vowed to take him for better or for worse, and she'd never intended to break that vow.

But right now, her hurt feelings couldn't be allowed to matter. She was here to learn and understand, not to judge.

"You say you were working on the refinance," she said. "If you go ahead with the application, what are its chances of being approved?"

"They were fair, at least before I had this cursed accident. I've got good credit history with the bank, and the theater's free and clear, except for that short-term loan I took out. But now—" Burke shook his head. "The trouble is, I can't do anything from this blasted hospital bed. Hell, I can't even sit up long enough to fill out the paperwork or drive to talk to the loan officer. And Garrett has no interest in working with the bank. He wants to take the easy way out."

"With an investor. I know about that. Garrett says he's got one ready to sign on. So what's the problem? Wouldn't that solve everything? What's holding you back?"

He exhaled with a pain-wracked breath. "You've been talking to Garrett. He's a smart man. But he's not telling you everything."

"So far, neither are you. What am I missing?"

His eyes locked on hers. "Just this. Good, solid investors don't grow on trees. And the American Heartland is an old theater. It would take a major upgrade to turn it into a moneymaker."

"Go on," Allison urged into the stillness.

"To find that investor he's so keen on, Garrett had to scrape the mucky bottom of the barrel. Have you ever heard of the Edgeway Investment Group?"

Allison shook her head.

"I hadn't either, until Garrett brought them by the office," Burke said. "I did a background check on them—even talked to some connections I have in the FBI."

He paused. Allison let her silence ask the next question.

"Edgeway is a front for the Mob, Allison," he said.

"They've been trying to get a foothold in Branson for years."

Allison stifled a gasp. "Does Garrett know?"

"Of course he does. But the Edgeway people have convinced him that this will be a legitimate venture, and that they'll be silent partners, collecting their share of the profits, but otherwise leaving us to run the business."

"I take it you don't believe that."

"Hell, no!" The words exploded out of him. "They'll be running the show by the time the ink's dry on the contract. Garrett's naïve and more than a little greedy. He wants quick cash and a bigger piece of the pie. What he doesn't see is money laundering, drugs, pornography, and worse. I've read the contract. It would give the bastards free rein. I won't sign it. I'll let the American Heartland go under first, or burn it to the ground!"

The monitors above the bed were beeping an alarm. A nurse rushed into the room to give him more oxygen and encourage him to relax. After a few minutes Burke's vitals stabilized. He lay back on the pillow, breathing deeply.

"What happened to him?" the nurse asked Allison.

"My fault, I'm afraid." Allison said. "We were discussing something he felt strongly about, and he got carried away. I'm sorry, I'll see that he gets some rest."

"We mustn't let this happen again," the nurse said. "Call me if he becomes agitated."

Allison leaned over the bed as the nurse left. "You heard the lady," she said. "No more talking. You need to rest. I should be still and let you take a nap before Brianna gets back." She found his hand again. "Thank you for helping me understand the problems. It helps, at least, to know what's going on."

"Then you know why I need you to get away from this mess, legally and physically, before you get sucked into it. These are ugly people. If they won't take no for an answer, they could even threaten you or Brianna to get to me."

"Hush. Close your eyes and rest." She squeezed his hand and released it. "I'm going to the nurses' station to see if I can talk them out of some coffee. When I come back, I want to find you asleep—or at least making a good show of it."

"Call that damned lawyer," he said as she walked out the door.

Allison pretended not to hear him.

She took her time, getting coffee and chatting with the nurse on duty. When she walked back into the room with her cup, Burke was sleeping peacefully, his vitals stable.

She sank onto the chair beside his bed, still taking in what he'd told her and trying to make sense of it all. Was he really in danger? Was she? Should she jump in and try to help him or keep her distance and protect her own interests?

What would Kate have done?

But why even wonder? Something told Allison that Kate had never faced this kind of choice.

Needing a distraction, she finished her coffee, picked up the magazine she'd abandoned earlier, and leafed through the pages. But the slick ads and celebrity faces blurred in her vision. It was as if someone had pulled the plug, draining every drop of energy and emotion from her body.

What if Burke was being overly cautious? What if

Garrett was right, and the Edgeway Group was offering a legitimate bailout of the theater?

That was the last thought that filtered through her weary mind before her head drooped, and she fell into a doze.

"Hi, Daddy!" Brianna's cheerful voice shattered the silence in the room. Allison woke with a jerk that was like being dropped off a twenty-foot ladder. Burke was awake, too, stirring in the bed. A glance at the monitors showed that his vitals were still good.

He gave his daughter a smile. "Hello, sweetheart. How was lunch?"

"Scrumptious. You know how much I love the Chateau."

"Did Garrett come back into the hospital with you, Brianna?" she asked.

"No, he let me off at the main entrance. He said he had a meeting with the investors." She looked as if she'd been about to say more, then thought better of it.

Allison saw Burke frown. She knew he was worried about Garrett's influence on his impressionable daughter.

Brianna danced around the foot of his bed, to the far side. "Garrett suggested a way I might be able to help you. Since I'm your daughter and over eighteen, you could give me power of attorney, to act in your behalf. That way I could help with your business while you rest and get better? Do you think that's a good idea?"

Burke's face was a thundercloud. "If I gave anybody power of attorney, it would be Allison. But I have no intention of doing that. My mind is sound, and I can make my own decisions. If Garrett asks you, you can pass on what I said."

"All right. I told Garrett you'd probably say no, but he wanted me to ask anyway. So I guess that's the answer."

Allison said nothing. She was surprised and flattered that Burke would consider giving her legal power, but he wasn't helping the situation by pitting his daughter against his wife.

The rising tension in the room eased slightly when a nurse bustled in. "I have orders to help you to the bathroom, Mr. Caldwell," she said. "Then the physical therapist is coming to get you walking up and down the hall. After that, it'll be time for a late lunch. Do you want to take it in a chair?"

"Fine." Burke raised the upper part of the bed so the nurse could help him get up. Pausing, he scowled at his wife and daughter. "I don't need an audience for this, or for walking down the hall with my damned gown flapping open behind me," he said. "You two, go get a snack or something. You can come back in about twenty minutes. I should be eating by then."

Allison didn't need to be told twice. "Come on, Brianna," she said. "The cafeteria's down the hall. I know you just had lunch, but you might want some dessert or a Coke."

"Whatever." Brianna shrugged and followed her out of the room. Allison had never felt comfortable with her stepdaughter. In the past, the fact that Brianna was at school most of the time had made things easier. But now that this crisis had thrown them together, they had a common concern—Burke's recovery. Maybe now they could bury the hatchet. At least it was worth a try.

In the cafeteria, they went through the line. Allison, who hadn't had anything but coffee all day, ordered a cranberry chicken salad with a wheat roll. Brianna went for a hot fudge sundae. Like Burke, she seemed able to eat anything without gaining an ounce.

Allison paid for their food, then chose a table near the window. "So how is school going, Brianna?" she asked, making small talk.

Brianna gave her a sour look. "Do we have to have a conversation?" she asked.

"I guess not." Allison poured dressing on her salad and buttered her roll. She'd tried, but if Burke's daughter wanted to shut her out, there wasn't much she could do.

Brianna played with her sundae, stirring the hot fudge into the melting ice cream and taking occasional bites, licking the chocolate off the plastic spoon like a child. At last she spoke. "Do you think my dad is going to die?"

Given the past, it wasn't a surprising question. "Not from this," Allison said. "He's a tough man, and his injuries aren't life-threatening. But it's going to take time and rest for him to heal. And in the meantime, the less stress he has to deal with, the sooner he'll recover. For you, that means not making demands on him or trying to force him where he doesn't want to go. And don't let Garrett use you to push his agenda. There are good reasons your father doesn't want to sign that contract."

Had she said too much? Allison studied her stepdaughter across the table. In Brianna's defiant gaze, which was so like her father's, she could see the girl's defenses springing up.

"I would never let Garrett use me," Brianna said. "I'm smarter than that. He's a good friend, that's all. Anyway, I have a boyfriend back in Evanston—oh!" Her fingers flew to her lips, as if she knew she'd revealed too much. "Please don't tell my dad. He doesn't need to know, and I don't want him to know. Not yet."

"All right, I can keep a secret for now," Allison said. "But don't put too much trust in Garrett. He's a charming, sophisticated man who knows how to manipulate people and get what he wants."

"Like you've manipulated my dad into giving you anything you want?"

"That's not what we were talking about." Allison refused to be baited. "I'm just telling you to be careful. I don't want to see you or your father get hurt."

"You've already hurt us! We were happy, Daddy and I, before he married *you*." Brianna thrust her spoon upright into her ice cream and rose from her chair. "And I won't have you talking about Garrett that way! He's a good person! He's trying to save the theater, which is more than you're doing!"

Turning away, she stalked out of the cafeteria.

Let her go. Allison resolved to stay at the table and finish her meal. Running after the girl would only create more drama. Brianna had no place to go except back to her father, who might be able to talk some sense into her. The information about the Edgeway Group was Burke's to share. Whether he chose to share it with his daughter would be up to him.

* * *

Burke had finished a painful and frustratingly slow trip up and down the hall. Leaning on a walker and trailed by the nurse with his saline drip hanging from a wheeled pole, he'd felt every step like a knife stab in his back. Despite the pain, he'd welcomed the chance to be on his feet, but his slow progress was maddening. Damn it, he wanted his life back!

He was seated in a cushioned armchair, waiting for his lunch, when Brianna burst into the room. Burke could tell from the glint in her eyes and the set of her jaw that she was upset.

"Daddy, you've got to do something about *her*! She's trying to run my life!"

Burke had heard it all before. He'd hoped his bride and his daughter would become close, but Brianna had resented Allison from the first time she'd set foot in the house.

"Give it a rest, honey," he said. "Allison's been under a strain since the accident. We all have, even you. Emotions are pretty raw right now. You have to understand that."

She took a seat on the side of the bed, close to his chair. "Well, I don't care what Allison thinks of me. I've long since gotten past that. But when she starts picking on my friend—"

"What friend?" Burke should've known better than to ask.

"Garrett. She told me I shouldn't trust him. She said that he's trying to manipulate me. That's ridiculous!"

Burke stifled a groan as the nurse brought in his tray and set it in front of him. He remembered the happy little girl his daughter had once been, content to be his best pal and fishing buddy. At times like this, he couldn't help missing that little girl, and wishing he'd been around to spend more time with her.

"I'll tell you what," he said. "Let's stop bickering and enjoy our time together. Where's Allison, by the way?"

"I left her in the cafeteria. She didn't say when she'd be coming back. You need to eat, Daddy."

Burke lifted the cover off his plate and eyed the meatloaf with creamed corn. He hadn't been hungry since the accident, but he knew he needed to eat. With his fork, he cut off a corner of the meatloaf and forced himself to eat it. Not wonderful, but not bad. He took another bite, chewed and swallowed it.

"I know you need to get back to school," he said to his daughter. "When's your return flight?"

"Not till Sunday—if I decide to go."

"No ifs. You need to be on that plane. You're already missing too much school."

"I'll be fine," she said. "While I'm here I can do my assignments on my laptop."

Burke forced a laugh. "Amazing. We didn't have things like that in my school days."

"Your school days were a long time ago, Daddy." Her dimpled smile gave him a glimpse of Kate that swiftly faded as she continued speaking. "Are you really going to go ahead and buy me a new car?"

"Sure, why not?" Burke forced himself to eat a spoonful of creamed corn, bracing himself for what was sure to be a challenge.

"It's a red BMW convertible. I fell in love as soon as I saw it. The dealer's holding it for a few days, but you'll need to call him by the end of the week to arrange payment."

Burke knew better than to ask the price. Even if he could talk the dealer down, it would be more than he could afford right now. Maybe it was time to sell his beloved boat, or apply the insurance payment from the wrecked Porsche to the deposit. A lease, if Brianna would settle for that, would be easier to arrange than a financed purchase, and less consequential if everything went south and he couldn't make the payments.

She'd caught his hesitation. "Is everything all right, Daddy?"

"Don't worry, we'll work it out."

She smiled. "I have the dealer's card in my purse."

"Keep it for now. I'll call him in the next couple of days, when I'm feeling sharp enough to negotiate."

"Oh—and you won't need to worry about my having a car to drive while I'm here. Garrett's offered me the company car for a few days. He'll be bringing it by after work. After I drive him back to his SUV, I can drive the car home."

Garrett again. Burke pushed the tray aside, his meager appetite gone. "He could have asked me."

"Don't frown, Daddy. Your Porsche is trashed, and I could hardly expect Allison to chauffeur me. I need my own wheels."

Burke sighed. "No, it's fine." It wasn't fine, but arguing would be a waste of breath. Maybe Garrett was just being thoughtful. But more than likely, he was using the girl to push his agenda. The hell of it was, Burke couldn't object without sounding petty and overprotective. And he couldn't do much else as long as he was trapped in this damned hospital.

At least Allison was trying to steer the girl away from Garrett. But given the way their marriage was headed, Burke knew better than to burden her with too much responsibility. She was doing her best to deal with his bad luck; but at times like this he missed Kate's Irish spunk and salty, practical wisdom.

Putting the subject aside for now, he turned back to his daughter. "So tell me about your classes," he said. "Which one's your favorite?"

Allison came back from the cafeteria to find Burke and Brianna chatting and laughing together. This was just the medicine Burke needed. Now would be a good time for her to carry out the plan she'd made.

Walking quietly into the room, she lifted her jacket off the back of the chair. "I'm going to run a few errands," she said. "Call my cell if you need me."

With that, she hurried out the door, strode down the hall and out the exit to the parking lot. She'd learned enough from Burke to convince her that she couldn't just sit back and watch him fight a solitary battle to save the American Heartland. Whether he wanted it or not, he was going to need her help.

The agency office was on Atlantic Street, behind Branson Landing. Allison had been there a few times in the past, mostly to pick her husband up for lunch. She'd met the agents who worked for Burke, along with some of the people who managed the theater, and of course she knew Garrett. Still, as she opened the front door and walked in, she couldn't help feeling like an intruder.

"Hello, Mrs. Caldwell." Fran, the middle-aged receptionist, greeted her with a smile. "How's Burke doing? We've all been worried about him."

"He's mending, but still in a lot of pain." Allison

glanced around for Garrett, but she didn't see him, and she hadn't seen his car outside. So much the better. "Burke wanted some things from his files. I hope you won't mind my going into his office and rummaging around for them."

"Not at all." The woman stood. "I can let you into his office, but Burke keeps his file cabinet locked. I hope you have the key."

Allison's heart sank. Then she remembered the ziplock bag Garrett had given her with the things from the wrecked Porsche in it. She'd never taken it out of her car. Dared she hope his key ring was there?

"Silly me, I must've left the key outside. I'll be right back." She rushed out the door to her car. What if the keys weren't in the bag? Maybe the police had kept them—or worse, Garrett could have taken them. Before the accident she would have trusted the man with her husband's life. Now that had changed.

She opened the car door. The bag was nowhere in sight. Panic seized her until she remembered that she'd dropped it into the console between the two front seats. The bag was still there, and she could see the key ring, with five keys on it, through the transparent plastic. She reached in and looped the ring over her finger. She could only hope that one of those keys would open the desk.

"Found it!" She breezed past the receptionist's desk, past the large cubicle room where the agents worked, and into Burke's office, which had been opened for her. The office was enclosed by glass windows, but the venetian blinds were closed, giving her some privacy.

After shutting the door behind her, she examined

the ring of keys. She recognized the key to the wrecked Porsche, as well as the key to the house. She assumed that the other two larger keys opened office doors, which left just one small one. If it didn't open the tall metal file cabinet, she would be out of luck.

Burke had mentioned that he'd spent hours working on the loan application for the theater update. She had to get her hands on that application, keep it safe, and maybe help him finish and submit it to the bank.

Allison already knew the application wasn't in the house. She'd rifled the desk looking for the missing contracts Garrett had wanted. The unfinished application had to be here, in Burke's office, probably in the file cabinet.

Her hand shook slightly as she thrust the small key into the lock.

The lock didn't open.

She stared at the key. The brand logo stamped onto it matched the one on the filing cabinet, and the key slid easily into the lock, but nothing moved. Allison tried again, jiggling and twisting the key. Again, nothing.

After dropping the keys into her pocket, she sank onto the padded leather chair behind the desk, her thoughts racing in circles, always to the same conclusion. Garrett had an identical file cabinet in his office. Before giving her the key ring, could he have switched Burke's key with his own, giving him access to Burke's files?

It didn't make sense that he'd stoop so low. But neither did any other explanation. Could he have been looking for the loan application—maybe to hide or destroy it, so it couldn't be submitted in time to save the theater from foreclosure? If that were to happen, it would leave the Edgeway Group as the only option.

This was crazy, Allison told herself. She was making up stories in her head.

All the same, she was tempted to sneak into Garrett's office and try the key in his file cabinet. But that could turn out to be a bad idea. The receptionist was liable to see her and ask questions. And she had no way of knowing when Garrett might walk in.

If Garrett had taken Burke's key and searched the file cabinet, the loan application would be gone by now. But what if he hadn't found it? What if it was someplace else—like the desk?

Not much chance of that. But as long as she was here, it wouldn't hurt to cover all the bases.

Spurred by a flicker of hope, she began rummaging through the desk drawers, lifting out binders, envelopes, and trade magazines and returning them to their places. If Burke had been working late nights on the application, he might have been too tired to lock the documents in the file cabinet. But the faint hope grew fainter as she searched. It wasn't here, she told herself. She was wasting her time.

One drawer to go. Then she would get up, leave, and try to make new plans on the way back to the hospital.

A large, softcover office-supply catalog took up most of the space in the bottom drawer. Allison picked it up and saw something tucked between the pages. Her pulse galloped as she opened the catalog and found what she was looking for—the ten-page application and supporting financial statements protected by a manila folder.

Most banks might have put their loan applications on line. But Burke's bank was as traditional as he was. Everything had to be filled in and submitted on paper.

She'd planned to take the folder and leave the hefty catalog behind. But just then she heard Garrett's voice outside the door, speaking to the receptionist. Hastily, she thrust the folder between the pages and, with the catalog under her arm, stepped out of Burke's office, and closed the door behind her.

Garrett replaced his startled look with a smile. "Hello, Allison. What are you doing here? Have you decided to accept my offer? And what are you doing with that catalog?"

Her smile was almost as fake as his. "The jury's still out on your offer. As for the catalog, Burke will be working out of the house for a while. I'm hoping some updated furnishings and supplies will make it easier for him."

"You can find all that stuff online," Garrett said.

"I know." The fiction was necessary. "But Burke's hospital room isn't set up for online shopping. With the catalog, I can browse while I keep him company and get his take on what to choose. Don't worry, I'll bring the catalog back in a few days."

Garrett was still eyeing her with suspicion. He was also blocking her way to the exit. Allison tightened her grip on the catalog and took an evasive move to one side. "Thanks, by the way, for offering to lend Brianna the company car. That'll save me from having to play chauffeur."

"Brianna was the one who brought it up," he said.

"She wanted the freedom to come and go as she pleased. I'll say this for the girl—she knows how to get what she wants."

Whatever he'd meant by that last remark, Allison didn't like the sound of it. All she really wanted was to leave, but she knew that if she didn't speak up now, she might regret it later.

"Garrett," she said, "Brianna's going through a difficult time right now. She's very vulnerable. No matter what she says or how she might behave, she needs to be protected. I hope you'll respect that need. If you take advantage of her in any way, you'll answer to me."

Garrett sucked in a breath. He looked as if she'd slapped him. "I know you're concerned. But give me a break, Allison! What kind of predatory jerk do you think I am? Brianna's like my kid sister, and that's the way I treat her—the only way, always." His gaze narrowed. "Do you understand? Are we good?"

Allison sighed. "We're good. I just had to say it. I had to be sure."

"Fine. Then let's forget it. Tell Brianna I'll be bringing the car around a little later."

"I will. Right now I need to be getting back to the hospital."

Before he could ask her any more questions, she dodged around him and hurried outside to her car. Her hand shook as she laid the catalog on the seat, thrust the key into the ignition, shifted into reverse, and backed out of the parking space.

Was Garrett less innocent than his protests proclaimed him to be? Had he really switched the keys to the file cabinet? Had he bought her story about needing the catalog, or had her own nervousness given her away?

Maybe her imagination was working overtime. But Allison had learned to trust her instincts—and unless those instincts were wrong, she had just made a ruthless and unprincipled enemy.

CHAPTER 7

Allison parked in the visitor's lot and hid the catalog under the seat before getting out and locking the car. The sun, setting above the hills, cast long shadows across the asphalt. Overhead, a V of migrating ducks glided low, to settle on the placid waters of Lake Taneycomo.

She returned to her husband's hospital room to find Burke asleep in bed and Brianna in the armchair, playing with her phone and looking bored. She glanced up as Allison walked in.

"It's about time you got back," she said.

Allison glanced at the wall clock. "I was gone less than an hour. Has your father been all right?"

"He's been fine," Brianna said. "After he finished eating, the nurses came in and took the drain out of his incision. They said that he'll be more comfortable now, and that he could be transferred to rehab in the morning."

"Oh, that's wonderful!" Allison blinked back grateful tears. Burke would still be in pain, but at least the frustration of lying helpless in bed would be eased. He could focus on getting his strength back.

"I stopped by the office to pick up some things," she said, keeping her voice low. "Garrett was there. He said to tell you he'll be bringing the car in a little while."

"Awesome. He's on his way now. I just got a text from him." Brianna looked up from her phone. "I mean, I want to be here for Daddy and all that, but it's pretty boring, just sitting around here and watching him sleep. I've texted my friends. We're getting together for a party tonight."

A red flag went up in the back of Allison's mind. But Brianna was an adult, she reminded herself. Grilling her about whom she'd be with and when she'd be home would only trigger a snarky response. "Have a good time," she said, staying on safe ground. "I'll call your cell if there's any change here."

"Will you be here all night?" Brianna asked.

"I'll be here for a while. Later on, if your dad's doing all right, I may go home and get some sleep. You'll be able to reach me anytime. Do I need to give you my cell number?"

"No, I've got it." Brianna lapsed into silence and went back to checking her phone. Allison took a seat on the chair next to Burke's bed, her senses taking him in. His breathing was deep and even, his face less pale than she remembered from earlier that afternoon. He hadn't shaved since the accident. The silver stubble that frosted his cheeks and jaw made him look like a sexy movie star.

A fierce love welled inside her. Her husband was a strong-willed man, a fighter to the end. She would sacrifice anything to fight at his side. But would his cursed pride let her?

Don't push me away, Burke. I'm your wife. Let me be here for you.

Garrett walked in without knocking. His gaze scanned the room. Was he looking for the catalog? Did he suspect what she'd found between its pages?

Allison put a finger to her lips, a signal for him to keep his voice low. But she kept silent. For now, she'd said all she needed to say.

Brianna put her phone in her purse, rose from the chair, and reached for her jacket. "Thanks for getting here so soon, Garrett," she said. "Oh—would you grab my suitcase on the way out? It's behind the door."

"Got it. Keep me posted, Allison." He gave her a sharp glance and followed Brianna out the door.

Through the open blinds, the sunset was fading to twilight. Allison took a moment to use the restroom. She stepped out to find that Burke was awake.

Smiling, she walked toward the bed. "Hello, sleepyhead," she said softly. "I hear you're going to rehab tomorrow."

"That's right. One more step toward getting out of this hellhole." He raised the upper part of the bed a few inches. "Did Brianna leave?"

"A few minutes ago. Garrett brought the company car for her. She said something about a party with her friends."

"Well, I can't fault her for that. She's young, and her old man isn't very exciting company these days." His cobalt eyes narrowed. "I can't be very exciting company for you, either. You look tired, Allison. You don't have to stay here and mother me. Go home and get some rest."

"Maybe later. First I have something to tell you."

She pulled the chair in close to the bed and sat down. "You told me how you'd been working to finish the loan application for the theater. This afternoon I went to your office and found the paperwork in your desk. I smuggled it out to my car. That's where it is now. I thought that maybe, when you're feeling stronger, I could help you finish it and take it to the bank."

Allison waited for him to respond. She'd hoped her husband would be pleased, but his expression revealed nothing. "You didn't have to do that," he said.

"I know. But I wanted to help. The loan won't have a chance if we don't get the application to the bank before the foreclosure deadline." She'd already decided against sharing her suspicions about Garrett and the switched keys. She had no proof, and even if she did, sharing it would only cause Burke more distress.

He shook his head, gazing at her with joyless eyes. "This isn't your fight, Allison. Take the application and put it in my desk. I'll finish it when I get home."

She stared at him. "But—"

"No. As I said, this isn't your fight. I know you mean well, but I can't let you be part of this mess. If things get ugly—and they might—I can't have anybody thinking you're with me on this."

"And Brianna?"

"She needs to be back in school. I'll find a way to pay for it—whatever it takes. Meanwhile, you go home and get some sleep. In the morning, call a lawyer. There's a small firm called Gentry and Smith—not close friends of mine, but good people. You can trust them. I don't want to see you tomorrow until you've got one of them in your corner."

"Burke, what are you trying to do—to me, to us?"

"I'm trying to save you. And there's no more us. You've got to stop thinking that way. Now go home and rest." He paused. "Damn it, just go."

Clasping her purse, Allison stumbled out of the hospital. By now it was almost dark. Her tear-blurred eyes could barely find her car. What was happening to her marriage—and to her husband?

Maybe it was the concussion he'd suffered in the wreck. He'd been all right before the accident—stressed and short-tempered, to be sure. That was nothing new. But the rest—the Mob, Garrett's betrayal, and some perceived danger to her and Brianna—could it all be in his mind? Maybe she should schedule a private talk with his neurologist.

But what about the key—the key that didn't fit the lock on his file cabinet? Was her own imagination working overtime? Had some simple mistake kept her from opening the lock, or had Garrett actually switched the keys?

There was just one way to find out.

Acting on impulse, she turned her car onto the business loop and headed for the agency office. She arrived to find the parking lot empty and the windows dark except for a light above the front door.

After parking across the street, where her car was less apt to be noticed, she took Burke's key ring and a small flashlight out of the glove box. Then, making sure she wasn't being watched, she climbed out of the car and crossed the street.

One of the larger keys opened the front door of the office. There was no alarm system—nothing to steal except some outdated PC desktops. The real value here was in the contracts and other documents contained in the files.

She switched on her flashlight. Keeping the beam
low, she made her way down the hall to the room
with Garrett's nameplate on the door. She turned
the knob, expecting to find the door locked. To her
surprise, it opened. Perhaps Garrett had been in a
hurry to pick up Brianna at the hospital. Or maybe
he'd meant to come back to the office, but changed
his mind.

He could still come back, Allison reminded herself. The sooner she got out of here the better.

She tugged at the top drawer of Garrett's file cabinet. It slid open—no surprise. If Garrett had
switched keys he would've had no way to lock and
unlock it. But now for the final test. If the key on
Burke's ring worked in this lock, she would know that
the two keys had been switched.

Focusing the beam of her flashlight, she closed the
drawer and thrust the small key into the lock. It fit—
again no surprise. But would it turn? Her heart
seemed to stop as she gave the key a gentle twist and
felt it turn, moving the small tumblers that locked
the drawer. This was Garrett's key. And there was
only one way it could've gotten onto Burke's key
ring.

With a shaking hand, she unlocked the drawer
again and withdrew the key from the lock. After taking a moment to make sure everything was as she'd
found it, she left the building and hurried across the
street to her car.

Her thoughts raced as she drove home. The
switched key was irrefutable evidence that Garrett
was up to something. And if that was true, she had
little reason to doubt Burke's other suspicions.

The question now was what could she do to help

her husband—especially since he'd insisted that she mustn't be involved?

Burke was watching a mindless sitcom on TV when the door opened and a familiar voice boomed above the commercial.

"Hot damn, Burke, you look like you got run over by a cow stampede! What did those doctors do to you in this place?" The burly figure of his old friend Hoagie Atkinson lumbered into the room. "I wanted to bring you a beer, but my wife said they'd throw me out of the hospital if I tried."

"Too bad, I could use one." Burke switched off the TV. "Come over here and sit down, Hoagie. I'm glad to see you."

And he *was* glad, Burke reflected. Hoagie was one friend who wouldn't fuss over him and make him feel like a useless invalid.

"So when do we break you out of this place?" Hoagie, a bear of a man with a balding head and a thick mustache, lowered his bulk to the chair.

"I get transferred to rehab tomorrow. When they think I'm ready, I'll go home. I've signed up for some home help until I get back to normal." He shifted in the bed, wincing as the pain shot up his back.

"Hurts like hell, does it?"

"You're damn right it does."

"Have they got you on painkillers? Those things can get you hooked."

"Don't worry, I know better than to let that happen."

Hoagie shifted on the chair. "How's that little wife of yours handling all this?"

"Allison's holding her own."

"Hell, Kate would be runnin' this place by now. She'd have those nurses hopping every time she said jump."

"Maybe." Burke didn't want to talk about Kate. He didn't want to compare her to Allison, who was doing her best to shoulder the load that had been so unfairly dumped on her. And he didn't want to talk about the state of his marriage, not even with Hoagie.

"Allison isn't Kate," he said. "She didn't sign on for any of this crap. But she's tough in her own way. She'd be here now, but she's worn herself out looking after me. I sent her home to rest."

"Well, good for her," Hoagie said. "I was thinking she'd probably packed her car and cleaned out your bank account by now."

Burke didn't reply. He was accustomed to his friend's blunt way of speaking and he'd long since learned not to let it bother him. But this time Hoagie was pretty much on target. He was describing what Burke had told Allison to do—and coming from somebody else, it sounded damned cold.

"I never thought I'd see you with one of those high maintenance types," Hoagie continued. "I always hoped that you'd find another woman like Kate. You know, a woman who liked things simple and never put on airs—a woman who could steer a boat and gut a fish like a pro—a woman who didn't mind getting dirt under her fingernails. Allison's a looker, and I'll bet she's dynamite in bed, but she's about as useful as a wind-up doll—"

"That's enough, Hoagie. You're headed down the wrong road," Burke said, cutting him off. "Allison may not be another Kate, but I fell in love with her for my own reasons. If you don't understand those reasons, that's your problem. I don't want to hear about it."

"Well, all right." Hoagie threw up his hands in a gesture of surrender. "You don't have to bite my head off."

A moment of awkward silence hung between the two friends. Then Burke changed the subject. "I've been thinking of selling my boat," he said. "If you know anyone who might be interested—"

"You'd sell your boat? The *Lady Brianna?*" Hoagie was aghast. "But you love that boat. Kate loved her, too. Think of all the good times we had on her, all the fish we caught—all those great memories."

"That's just it," Burke said. "I put the boat in dry dock after Kate died. Brianna didn't want to go out in it anymore, without her mother. Neither did I. And Allison's never shown any interest in boating or fishing. Why pay storage to the marina for a boat that doesn't get used?"

Hoagie gave him a mournful look. "I'll ask around. Somebody's bound to want her. She's a great boat. But, damn it all, Burke, selling her would be like selling a member of your family!"

"I know. But my daughter's got her heart set on a new BMW convertible. Selling the boat would make it easier for me to buy it."

Hoagie shook his head. "Blast it, Burke, I know you love that girl. And I know you've knocked yourself out trying to make up for her mother being gone, and that you've got some guilt over marrying a woman Brianna doesn't like. But a college student doesn't need a new BMW. A decent used car for ten or fifteen thousand would get her anywhere she needs to go. If she wants fancy new wheels, she can graduate and earn the money herself! She'll appreciate it more that way."

Burke exhaled and took a sip of water. "You're probably right. But I promised her any car she wanted. And I've always taught her that promises were meant to be kept."

Hoagie swore under his breath. "I never thought I'd say this to your face, but I'm saying it as a friend. That girl hasn't heard the word *no* from you since her mother got sick. And it hasn't done her any good."

"You're saying I've spoiled Brianna?"

"Well . . . yes. And even though you haven't talked about it, I know your business is having money problems. Hell, we all know it, the whole gang."

"So what are you saying?"

"I'm saying maybe it's time for Brianna to grow up. And maybe that classy new wife of yours needs to grow up, too. Look at the money she spent fixing up your house, when it was fine the way it was before. Hell, man, Kate would never have—"

"I told you, that's enough, Hoagie," Burke said. "I know you mean well, but when you criticize my wife, that crosses a line. Leave it at that, and I'll forget what you just said. All right?"

Hoagie shrugged. "All right. I was just giving you a little friendly advice, that's all."

"I know. But I've got to ride out this storm in my own way. All the friendly advice in the world won't make any difference."

"You always were a stubborn son-of-a-gun." Hoagie rose to his feet. "Even flat on your back and hooked up to machines, you don't back down. You may be my best friend, but sometimes you can be a mule-headed idiot."

Burke forced a smile. "Thanks, Hoagie. I can always count on you to say what you think. You'll ask around about the boat?"

"Sure. But I still think you'd be crazy to sell it. You get better, okay?"

"Just watch me!" Burke managed to hold his smile until his friend walked out the door. Then, clenching his teeth against the pain, he pressed the call button for the nurse.

By the time Allison pulled the car into the garage, exhaustion had caught up with her. She knew she needed to rest, but it was early yet, not much past nine thirty. And she was too wired to sleep, especially with Brianna out partying and likely to be home late.

In the kitchen she laid the loan application on the counter while she checked the landline for messages. There were none, and none on her cell phone. She didn't have much appetite, but the unfinished bottle of Chardonnay in the fridge had some appeal. She poured a glass half full, crossed the living room, and stopped in front of the fireplace, where the Kathleen Petyarre painting hung above the mantel. It was titled *Mountain Devil Lizard*, a traditional "dreaming" of the Aboriginal artist. Burke and his friends had made fun of it, asking why she didn't just hang up a slab of cement. Allison had forgiven them for not understanding. But she loved the nuances of light and shadow and the deep, hidden meanings in that painting.

How much would it be worth now? Ten thousand?

Fifteen? At least the money should be enough to make a small dent in the short-term loan on the American Heartland, or pay for a few more months of Brianna's education.

It wouldn't be enough to solve any of Burke's problems. But the painting was the one valuable thing she owned outright—the one thing that was hers to sacrifice.

The San Francisco art dealer she'd bought it from was a friend. Tomorrow she would call him to ask how much he could get her for the painting and how soon he could find a buyer. With luck, if she lowered the price, the sale might not take long.

Still holding the glass, she wandered out onto the balcony and stood at the rail, gazing at the lights on the far shore. The night breeze was cool on her face, the wine burning a cold trail down her throat.

A single tear trickled over her cheek. Burke was the love of her life. When they'd married in that dream of a ceremony, she'd promised herself that she would be the perfect wife to him. Now everything was falling apart, and she didn't know how to hold it together.

The glass was empty. Leaving the balcony, she walked back to the kitchen and set it next to the sink. The loan application lay on the counter where she'd left it. For now she would put it away in the desk. But she hadn't given up on finding a way to help her proud, stubborn husband. She could only hope that, with time and healing, he might allow her to be a true partner to him.

What would Kate have done? But she wasn't Kate. She wasn't tough or wise. She didn't know how to bond with her stepdaughter or understand the man she loved—or even throw a proper party. She had never felt more inadequate in her life.

With the documents in hand, she walked down the hall to Burke's study. Even before she opened the door, she knew what would happen. Brianna wouldn't be home for hours, and the contents of the desk were drawing her like a magnet. If she opened the drawer to put the application away, she'd be helpless to turn aside. There would be no way she could leave the room without reading one more heart-crushing letter.

But first she would look at the loan application. If she was to deal intelligently with this crisis, she would need to know how much Burke hoped to borrow and on what terms.

She sank into the chair, switched on the lamp, and spread the papers on the desk.

Allison had taken out a small business loan to upgrade her gallery—a loan that had to be paid off when she sold the gallery to marry Burke. The experience helped her understand the complex document she was looking at now.

Burke had been very thorough. He'd listed all the improvements he wanted to make on the American Heartland. There would be a new, revolving stage with multiple levels, along with sound and lighting to support spectacular productions. Additional seating would accommodate more customers, and luxurious dressing rooms would bring in more demanding talent. A new flashing marquee would be visible even from a distance, and there would also be money set aside for publicity.

Knowing Burke, he would have researched every item and even gotten some bids. Still, the amount of money needed to make the old theater a showplace was staggering. No wonder Garrett was pushing to sell out to the Mob.

The next few pages contained a breakdown of projected revenue, expenses, and proposed loan repayment schedules. The bottom line: the theater would have to run at near capacity to make the monthly payments, which would start in three months, hopefully after the remodeling was done and the American Heartland was open for the spring season.

The final pages of the document listed Burke's assets that could be put up as collateral against the loan. There was the theater itself, and the real estate—mostly condos and apartments. Burke had even listed the house. Only the talent agency—which didn't qualify as property—had been spared. He was risking everything he had to get this loan.

Was that why he'd asked her to divorce him—so she could salvage some of his assets before they became collateral that would be lost in the event of foreclosure or bankruptcy? Or did he simply want to spare her the humiliation of watching him go down if his gamble didn't pay off?

Given what she knew about Burke, his reasons were bound to be complicated. But he was her husband, and she loved him. Any choice she made would be made with her heart. And her heart was telling her to stand by her man and do everything in her power to help him win.

The only question was how.

What would Kate have done? And what would Burke have done if he'd still been married to her?

With the file drawer open, she slipped the loan papers into the front. Then, braced for an emotional battering, she opened the file drawer, lifted the packet of letters out of the back and opened the next envelope.

Dearest Burke,

I'd almost forgotten what pregnancy is like—the morning sickness, the cravings, the mood swings, and the magic of that first little flutter kick, the sudden awareness that there's somebody home down there—a sweet little somebody who is growing into a real live person.

This morning as I was loading the dishwasher, I felt our baby move. Instinctively, I looked around for you to share the news and invite you to feel with your hand on my belly. But of course you were five hundred miles away, Brianna was in preschool, and I was alone in the house. Only Captain was here to gaze up at me and wonder, in his doggy way, why I was bawling like an emotional fool. It was as if all the joy, the worry, and the loneliness had hit me at once, like a doubled-up fist.

It will pass, of course. I'll be fine. I'm always fine. You know that all too well. I just wish I wasn't so blasted easy for you to leave . . .

Kate's schoolgirl script stopped in midsentence, halfway down the page, leaving a blank space at the bottom. But the letter wasn't finished. Two more pages followed, as if she'd left off writing, then continued some time later.

Burke,

I wrote the first part of this letter five days ago. I was going to throw it away, but changed my mind and decided to share it. How else can I help you under-

*stand how swiftly things can change, and how easily a
heart can be torn to pieces?*

*Our baby is gone. While I was writing to you, I felt
the pains start, hard and sharp. I knew what was
happening and that it was far too soon. My only
faint hope was that the labor could be stopped.*

*Brianna was asleep. I called my cousin, Tricia, to
come and take her. Then I called the paramedics, unlocked the front door, and shut myself in the bathroom
with my phone.*

*I won't go into details, but by the time everyone got
to the house, it was over. I had lost the baby alone in
the bathroom. Brianna was still asleep. Tricia stayed
with her while the paramedics cleaned up and took
me to the hospital.*

*Again, I'll spare you the details, which you can
learn when you get home. In the hospital, there were
complications. To save my life, the doctors had to perform an emergency hysterectomy. That's right, my
love, no more babies ever. We will have to settle for
our beautiful, perfect Brianna.*

Allison laid the pages on the desk, her tears blurring the lamplight into rainbows. *Oh, Kate, Kate . . .
How did you survive this terrible loss alone? How could
you be so strong?*

Wiping her eyes, she picked up the pages and
read the rest of Kate's letter.

*I am at home now, recovering as well as could be
expected, so there's no need for you to rush back from
your trip to take care of me. Brianna knows about the
baby, but she doesn't really understand what happened, which is just as well. I am doing my best to be
"normal" for her sake. I don't want you to feel guilty*

*about not being here. There was no way you could
have known, and nothing you could have done.*

*So we will move on, my love. We will enjoy our
daughter and each other and try to focus on the good
things life has given us—and not to wish for what
can no longer be.*

Your Kate

Allison folded the pages, slipped them back into
the envelope, and put the letters away. She couldn't
imagine being as strong as Kate. Yes, she was facing
her own crisis and trying to bear up under stress, but
it was nothing compared to what Kate had gone
through. This heartbreaking letter had been timely,
a lesson in resignation and acceptance.

Still musing over the letter, Allison climbed the
stairs and walked down the hall to Brianna's room.
The family photograph sat in its place on the bookshelf. She picked it up and studied the image of the
young girl, a cherished child, lavished with love and
attention—a child whose world would all too soon
be shattered by the loss of her mother.

Kate's death would have had a deep effect on Brianna. But the girl had survived to grow up strong
and resilient, like her mother. Allison had always
thought of her as Burke's daughter—stubborn, will-
ful, possessive, and quick to defend her territory.
But she was Kate's child, too, loyal and loving, with a
woman's strength.

Maybe if she made an effort to see Brianna as
Kate's daughter, it would be easier to understand
and deal with her, Allison thought. That might be
worth remembering in the difficult days ahead. Maybe
the shared secret of Brianna's boyfriend would grow
into a bond between them. Or maybe not. Maybe, in

Brianna's eyes, Allison would always be the wicked stepmother.

Allison replaced the photograph, closed the door, and made her way down the hall to the master bedroom. A long shower and an old pair of warm flannel pajamas helped relax her for bed, but she still felt restless. Before turning off the bedside lamp, she called the nurses' station outside Burke's room. The nurse who answered told her he was sleeping peacefully. Maybe, knowing that, she could do the same.

She turned off the lamp, punched her pillow into shape, and stretched out in the bed. The house was eerily quiet, every small settling sound making her nerves jump. She would have to get used to sleeping without Burke for the near future. A hospital bed and other equipment for his recovery was to be set up in the downstairs guest room, where he would stay until he was strong enough to climb stairs, which could take weeks, even months.

What would their relationship be by then? Would he even want her? Up until the night of the accident, their sex life had been wonderful. But the man in that hospital bed was a stranger behind a closed door. She no longer knew what to expect from him.

She was beginning to drift. Grateful for sleep, she let it pull her under like a riptide, deeper into the soothing dark.

Sometime later her cell phone rang. Startled awake, she turned on the lamp and grabbed the phone where she'd left it on the nightstand.

"Hello?" she mumbled.

"Allison, this is Garrett."

"What is it?" She sat bolt upright, her heart pounding. "Is Burke—"

"Burke's fine, as far as I know. But I just got a call from Brianna."

"Is she all right?"

"She's fine, except—"

"Except what?" Allison struggled to clear the sleep from her mind.

"Just this," Garrett said. "She was calling from the police station. Evidently she's been arrested."

CHAPTER 8

"Arrested? For what?" Allison blinked her eyes into focus and glanced at the bedside clock. It was 2:25.

"The police stopped her because of a missing tail-light," Garrett said. "She had some alcohol on her breath, and because she was driving the company car, she had no proof that she hadn't stolen it."

"And she called *you*?"

"It wasn't as if she could call her father."

And she wouldn't call me, Allison thought. "I'm assuming one of us needs to go and get her."

"Brianna asked me to come," Garrett said. "But it might not look so good, me showing up at this hour to pick up a girl. I mean, I'm not even family." There was a moment of silence on the line, broken by a female giggle in the background.

Clearly he wasn't alone, but she wasn't about to mention it. "Fine," she said. "I should probably be the one to do it. I'll go and get her. But for now we won't say anything to upset Burke. Agreed?"

"Of course. Thanks, Allison." She could hear the giggle again as Garrett ended the call. The man hadn't wasted any time since his separation from his wife. But that was none of her business. Right now her concern was dealing with Brianna and getting her safely home.

Dressed in jeans, a sweatshirt, and a light jacket, she grabbed her purse and headed for her car. A misting rain was falling outside. She turned on the wipers to clear the windshield as she drove. What was she going to say to her stepdaughter? Nineteen was a typical age for sowing wild oats; but to get into trouble while her father was in the hospital was crossing the line. Brianna needed a crash course in responsibility. But would she listen to the stepmother she viewed as an interloper?

The police station was on Maddux Street, west of the Landing. Allison pulled into an empty parking space, turned off the key, and took a deep breath. There was just one way—if any—that she might be able to reach Brianna. Tell her the truth.

She gave her name and showed her ID to the sergeant at the desk. "I can confirm that the car wasn't stolen," she said. "It belongs to my husband's business, as you'll see on the registration. Brianna borrowed it to drive while she's in town, visiting her father in the hospital." Allison forced herself to stop talking. The sergeant's expression told her she'd said enough.

"The car isn't the issue," he said. "It's the alcohol. The legal drinking age in Missouri is twenty-one. This young lady is nineteen. Her blood alcohol level was .07, under the legal limit for an adult. But for a minor caught driving, anything over .02 qualifies as a DUI, punishable by a fine of up to a thousand dollars and up to a year in jail."

"But she's in college, and her father's recovering from an accident, and . . ." Allison stifled a groan as she realized her words carried no weight with the stone-faced cop.

"Five hundred dollars bail and you can take her home now. You can pick up the car tomorrow. You'll hear when we've set a trial date. Meanwhile you might want to get her a lawyer."

Allison produced her credit card at the window and collected Brianna's purse and suitcase, which had been taken from the car. A few minutes later a policewoman ushered a scared and bedraggled Brianna into the waiting area. She looked so pathetic that Allison wavered between hugging the girl and shaking her till her fool teeth rattled.

"Come on, Brianna. Let's go home." She turned away and headed for the exit. "You can't drive tonight. You'll have to ride with me."

Brianna trailed after her without a word. But her demeanor changed when they reached the parking lot. "Where's Garrett?" she demanded. "He's the one I called, not you."

"Garrett's busy. He asked me to pick you up." Allison opened the passenger door. Brianna plopped into the seat, staring straight ahead as Allison put her suitcase and—after a moment's thought—her purse in the trunk and walked around to the driver's side of the car.

"Where's my phone?" Brianna asked.

"I'm guessing it's in your purse. You can have it after we get home." Allison started the car and drove out of the parking lot. She kept quiet, giving the situation time to sink in.

By the time they'd reached the highway, Brianna was sobbing. "Please don't tell my dad about this!" she pleaded.

"What if Garrett tells him?" Allison asked, playing devil's advocate.

"He won't. He promised me. But you need to promise, too. Please. Dad will be so upset with me. That can't be good for him right now."

"We don't have to tell him right away," Allison said. "But sooner or later, he'll have to know. When the time comes, you need to take responsibility. You should be the one to tell him. Agreed?"

"Oh, all right." Brianna sighed. "I just hope he won't change his mind about buying me that new car."

Allison swung her car onto a side street, pulled up to the curb, and turned in the seat toward her stepdaughter.

"It's time you faced reality and grew up, Brianna," she said. "There's not going to be any new car. Your father's financial troubles are worse than Garrett told you. A lot worse. If things don't go right, he could be in danger of losing everything—the theater, the real estate properties, maybe even the house."

"But . . ." Emotion welled in her voice. "Dad said it wouldn't be a problem."

"Your dad loves you," Allison said. "He'd do anything to make you happy. But the truth is, buying an expensive car like the one you want would be a huge sacrifice for him right now. It would put him that much closer to financial ruin."

"But what about you?" Brianna flung the words at her. "What about all the money you spent fixing up the house, and this car? He's given you everything you ever asked for. And now you're telling me I can't have the one thing I really want."

The accusations hit home. They stung, but this was a time for truth. "You're right, and I understand why you're angry," Allison said. "But so help me, at the time I was redecorating the house, I didn't know about the money problems. Burke told me to spend as much as I wanted. And I didn't ask for the car. He surprised me with it. I had no idea what was happening with his finances until the night of the accident. If I'd been aware that he was strapped for money, I would've made do with the house as it was. As for the car—now that I know, I'll probably sell it and get something cheap. And once your dad's on his feet, I plan to look for a job. I'll do everything I can to help him weather this crisis. As long as you're here, you'll want to help him, too."

"But what about the investors? Garrett says they've got plenty of money, and the contract is drawn up and waiting. It would solve everything. Why won't Dad sign?"

"You'll understand if I tell you." Allison took a deep breath, feeling as if she were about to step off a precipice. Telling Brianna could be a game changer— for better or for worse. "Here's the thing," she said. "It's got to be our secret. You can't tell anybody, not even your boyfriend."

"But why?"

"Because your father wants to protect you. He's keeping you in the dark for your own safety. If he knew I was about to tell you, he wouldn't be happy with me."

"What about Garrett? Does he know?"

"He knows, and he thinks it's all right. But you're not to talk to him about it. You can't be involved in any way. But knowing will help you understand what's going on. So, can I trust you to keep this to yourself?"

She shrugged. "I guess."

"That's not good enough. Can I trust you? Or would you rather not have the secret to keep?"

"All right. You can trust me."

In the simplest terms possible, Allison told Brianna about the Edgeway Group, their Mob connection, and why Burke was refusing to sign with them. She left out her suspicions about Garrett. There was too much risk that Brianna wouldn't believe her, or worse, that she would warn the man she thought of as a friend.

"So how does my dad plan to save the theater?" Brianna asked.

"He's working on a bank loan for enough to repay the short-term loan and remodel the theater. But we're talking a lot of money. If the bank agrees, he'll need to put up collateral—amounting to almost all the property he owns. Do you understand?"

"I'm not stupid. I know what collateral is. If he can't pay the money back, he'll lose everything. That's why you're saying I can't have a new convertible."

"Right. Then there's that bad decision you made tonight. Lawyers don't come cheap, and you're going to need one."

Brianna gazed down at her hands, saying nothing. Allison was about to start her car and pull away when she spoke again.

"What about school? That costs money, too."

"School's important," Allison said. "It's a lot more important than a car. I know your father will do everything he can to keep you at Northwestern—and if the money becomes an issue, you can always get a job or take out a student loan. There's just one problem. The court may not allow you to leave the state until your DUI case is resolved—and not even then if you're on probation."

"No! That's not fair! I wasn't even drunk!"

"I'm sorry, Brianna. But fair or not, I'm not the one who made the laws." Allison felt genuine pity for the girl.

"But Northwestern has one of the best journalism programs in the country!" Brianna argued. "I was lucky to get in. And if I have to drop out, they might not let me come back. I'm talking about my future— my career!"

And her boyfriend, Allison thought as she turned the car around and headed back to the main road. Brianna had made a youthful mistake and been unlucky enough to get caught. The consequences could change the course of her life. But all Allison could do was get the girl a good lawyer and hope for the best. Burke had suggested she contact Gentry and Smith about the divorce—something she had no intention of doing. But maybe they could help Brianna. She would call them in the morning.

Brianna was crying again, weeping quietly in the shadowed passenger seat. With nothing left to say to her, Allison drove on toward Peaceful Lane and home.

Back in her childhood room, Brianna wheeled her suitcase into a corner, fished her phone out of her purse, and collapsed on the bed. She had cried her eyes out in Allison's car. But she was still hurting. How could she have been so careless—and so unlucky?

One of her friends had brought a couple six-packs of beer to the party. Laughing and talking with her old schoolmates, Brianna had lost track of how much beer she'd drunk, but she certainly hadn't been impaired. Certainly she could drive home.

Blast that crappy Crown Victoria. Its broken taillight had turned a simple lapse in judgment into the worst mistake of her life!

Lying back on the bed, she used her phone to call the one person she needed most.

"Brianna?" Liam sounded muzzy from sleep. She pictured his tawny hair tangled on the pillow, his blue eyes barely open beneath thick, golden lashes. What she wouldn't give to lose herself in his arms and drown her senses in his warmth and in the clean, leather aroma of his skin. The longing stabbed her, triggering a fresh surge of tears.

"Brianna, are you all right?"

"I'm . . . fine," she muttered.

"You're not fine. I can tell you're crying," he said. "What's wrong? Is it your dad?"

"My dad's in the hospital, getting better. It's just—" She broke down. "Oh, Liam, I've made such a mess of things!"

Little by little she told him what was going on, leaving out nothing. She and Liam had no secrets from each other.

She finished and waited for his response. For the space of a breath he was silent. Was he going to berate her, or worse, hang up and never speak to her again?

When he spoke, his voice was almost gentle. "Brianna, remember when I told you how I was in a teenage gang? We did some pretty stupid stuff— shoplifting, vandalism, beating up kids we didn't like. I've smoked pot. I've been in court, and I'll probably be going to AA meetings for the rest of my life. Hell, I've served time in jail, more than once. You know that. And you know that I was about your age when I decided to turn my life around."

"Yes, I know all that. Why are you bringing it up now?"

"Because you've just made a mistake. But I've learned that one mistake isn't the end of the road. It might cost you some time and cause you some pain, but you'll survive this. *We'll* survive this and move on."

"Even if my dad loses everything he owns? Even if I have to drop out of Northwestern and they won't let me back in?"

"Even then. And even if you don't get that fancy red convertible your heart's set on. I love you. Nothing's going to change that."

"Stop it! This sucks!"

"Life sucks."

"What if I can't go back to school?"

"You'll find another school."

"What if I can't come back, and we never see each other again?"

"That's enough, Brianna. We can't control everything in our lives, but if we want to see each other again, we'll make it happen."

"I'm scared, Liam. Bad things happen, like my mother dying, and my dad's accident."

"Don't be scared. You're tougher than you think you are. Now get some sleep. I love you." He paused. "While I'm thinking about it, have you told your father about us?"

"I'm just waiting for a good time."

"*This* might be a good time. Goodnight, Brianna."

He ended the call, a bit abruptly, Brianna thought. Maybe she shouldn't have called him expecting sympathy and comfort. Maybe he was tired of her waking him up to whine in the middle of the night.

As for telling her father about their relationship, Brianna knew it was a test. He had too much honor in him to sneak around behind her father's back. If she wanted Liam in her life she needed to show it by involving him in her family.

But what would her father have to say about her dating a long-haired, motorcycle-riding, high school dropout who worked in a garage—even if he was kind, decent, and responsible? And even if she loved him.

She undressed, brushed her teeth in the bathroom, and crawled into bed. The day had been long and miserable, and tomorrow was bound to be worse.

For a time she lay awake, going over their conversation in her mind. Liam was right. It was time for her to stop being a spoiled, entitled baby. Grow up, survive, and move on. And be honest about who she was and whom she loved. That was all she could do. But sometimes being a grownup sucked.

What if she couldn't measure up to Liam's expectations? What if he was already falling out of love with her?

Why did she have to be so blasted insecure?

Closing her eyes, she sank into exhausted sleep.

After bringing Brianna home, Allison had been too keyed up to sleep. Now, in the darkness before dawn, she sat before the computer on Burke's desk, studying the photos on the web page she'd brought up. Gentry and Smith, the lawyers Burke had recommended, were mother and daughter. Rae Ann Smith, the daughter, appeared to be in her midforties, thin and blond. With a beauty shop hairstyle and a friendly smile, she looked like somebody's soccer mom. Her mother, Roberta, square-jawed with short, iron-gray hair, looked so much like the nurse who'd taken Allison aside in the hospital that they could have been sisters. Maybe they were. Either way, Allison liked what she saw. Both women were experienced and well qualified. And she sensed that Brianna might be more at ease with a woman lawyer than with a man.

Leaning back in her chair, she shut down the computer and massaged the back of her neck. She would call the law office as soon as they opened. She would also call her art dealer friend in San Francisco and ask him to find a buyer for her painting. Then it would be time to visit Burke in rehab. Meanwhile, as long as Brianna was asleep, a predawn walk might ease her strained nerves.

She was standing up to stretch when she remembered Kate's letters in the desk. It was too soon to read another one—especially since the last letter had left her emotionally bruised. But if she planned to read more later, it might be wise to take them upstairs now. The guest room where Burke's bed and exercise equipment would be set up was right across the hall. And Brianna would likely be around, too. Once he was home, reading the letters at the desk would become impossible.

Decision made, she opened the drawer and lifted the crumpled manila envelope out of the back. When she was finished with the letters, she would put them back where she'd found them.

Hearing no sound from Brianna's room, she carried the envelope upstairs, slid it between the mattress and box spring, and went to the closet to get her running shoes.

Brianna climbed out of Allison's car in the hospital parking lot. Two days had passed since her early morning arrest and her visit with the lawyer. Now it was time for the task she'd dreaded most—breaking the news to her father.

Burke was in rehab now, pushing himself hard and making good progress. In a few days he'd be going home. Brianna and Allison had agreed that now would be the best time to tell him.

"Do you want me to go in with you, Brianna, or would you rather talk to him alone?" Allison had been pretty cool, Brianna conceded. She hadn't lectured or scolded, just helped her through the steps of what needed to be done. And the older woman lawyer had been all right, too, even though much of what she'd delivered had been bad news. There would be no easy way out of this mess.

"I'm a big girl," Brianna said. "If it gets ugly, you won't want to be there. I'll tell him alone."

"Fine," Allison said. "I've got a couple of errands to run. Will half an hour be enough time before I come back?"

"I'll text you," Brianna said, and closed the car door.

As Allison drove off, she walked through the front entrance of the rehab wing. She loved her father, and they'd always been close. But she had never disappointed him as cruelly as she was about to this morning. It was all she could do to keep from turning around and running out of the building.

Last night she'd resisted the urge to call Liam and cry on his shoulder again. She knew what he would tell her—take responsibility and face up to it like an adult. She didn't want to call him again until she'd proven she could do just that.

She found her father in the gym, using a cane to walk with the help of a therapist. He was dressed in sweats, his color good, his face freshly shaven, but he still winced with every step. He was in obvious pain.

He glanced up and saw her. "Hello, honey. Did Allison come with you?"

"She'll be here a little later." Brianna took a deep breath. "Daddy, we need to talk."

He gave her a puzzled frown. "If it's about your car—"

"No. It isn't about the car."

He glanced at the therapist. "Can we go back to my room? I think I've walked enough for now."

The husky young man walked him back down the hall to his room and settled him in a cushioned armchair. Brianna followed, closing the door after the therapist left.

"So it's that kind of talk, is it?" Burke's voice had taken on an edge.

"I'm afraid so." Brianna sat on the side of the bed.

"You look like you just lost your best friend. What's the matter?"

"I'm in trouble. Just listen, all right?"

In a voice that shook sometimes, she told him about the party and the beers she'd drunk, about being stopped by the police and arrested because she was under the legal drinking age.

"Allison posted bail and picked me up," she said, deciding not to mention that she'd called Garrett first. "She read me the riot act on the way home. She even told me I wasn't going to get the new car you promised me."

"She was right. You're not."

"Oh, I know that. I don't deserve a new car. And with the theater in trouble, I know you can't afford one."

"Go on." He was stone-faced. She could sense his displeasure building.

"Allison took me to a lawyer the next day. She— the lawyer—said that the best I could hope for would be to get the DUI charge dropped and plead guilty to underage drinking, but only if I'm very lucky. Either way, I'd at least get a fine and probation with community service, maybe even jail time. And I wouldn't be able to leave the state until I served it."

"What about school?" He spoke in a flat, measured tone as if controlling himself by force of will.

"That's the worst part. I'll probably have to drop out of Northwestern, and they might not readmit me. The lawyer called the court and got permission for Allison to drive me back to Evanston so I can clean out my dorm room and talk to the dean. I'll be able to tell you more after that."

"So when are you and Allison going?"

"Tomorrow. We want to do it while you're still in rehab so we can be with you when you come home."

"You make it sound like I'm going to need babysitters."

"Dad—"

"Why didn't you tell me right away when you got arrested? At least I could've given you some sensible advice. Damn it, I'm your father. And I'm tired of being treated like a helpless invalid who doesn't know what day it is!"

"Daddy—"

"I've arranged for a home care service to come in when I'm home. And I'll be doing plenty for myself. You and Allison won't have to lift a finger to help me!"

"Daddy, listen to me. I have something else to tell you." Brianna summoned her courage. "I have a boyfriend in Evanston. His name is Liam, and I love him."

Brianna watched him deflate as if he'd been punctured. She'd dated boys in high school, but only as friends. She'd never given her father reason to believe she loved any of them. This was new. This was serious.

He sighed. "Well, I guess it was bound to happen sooner or later. What's he studying? Journalism, like you?"

"No." Brianna braced herself for his reaction. "Liam isn't a student. He works full time. He has a good job, repairing foreign automobiles."

"He's a *mechanic*?"

"Yes." Brianna stood her ground. "He's a very good mechanic. And you might as well know the rest. He's twenty-three, and he drives a vintage Harley-Davidson. When we go out, he makes me wear his helmet, so you don't have to worry about that."

"Believe me, that's the least of my worries," Burke muttered. "Brianna, you're nineteen! You've got your whole life ahead of you! I won't allow you to throw it away on some greasy biker! Is he the one who started you drinking? Is this mess his fault?"

"No. Liam's a recovering alcoholic. He doesn't drink at all, and he wasn't happy when he found out what I'd done. He's a good man. He's mature and responsible and kind. He even insisted that I tell you about him because he didn't want to date me behind your back. You'd like him if you gave yourself half a chance."

"How about no chance?" Burke's fist tightened on the arm of the chair. "Your boyfriend sounds to me like a recipe for trouble. I can't forbid you to see him, but if your legal problems keep you from going back to Evanston, that might be a blessing in disguise."

"That's not true!" Brianna battled mounting tears of frustration. "How can you judge Liam when you don't even know him?"

"I know the type, sweetheart," Burke said. "One day, when you're happy, with the right kind of man, you'll look back on this time and wonder what you were thinking. Trust me. I know."

"Do you?" Brianna could have said more about her father's own choice. But it didn't seem right to criticize Allison, who'd done her best to be helpful these past two days. Instead, she said, "I love you, Dad," and walked out of the room.

After leaving Brianna at the hospital, Allison drove to the talent agency. She hadn't made a final decision to take Garrett up on his job offer, but she was leaning in that direction. With Burke still a long way from recovery, somebody needed to look out for his interests and keep an eye on Garrett.

The office-supply catalog, which had concealed the loan application, was still in her car. Returning it would give her an excuse for today's visit.

With the catalog in hand and Burke's keys in her purse, she walked in the front door, which was unlocked today. The receptionist, platinum blond with movie star makeup, was new. Allison introduced herself and asked for Garrett.

"Hang on, I'll buzz him." She pressed a button on the phone. "Garrett, Mrs. Caldwell is here to see you," she said, then turned back to Allison. "Have a seat. He won't be long."

Allison sat down on a brown imitation leather loveseat. She leafed through a theater trade magazine, but her mind was on other things. Accepting a job here would be a waste of time unless she could find a way to help Burke.

She knew that Garrett had offered her the job for a reason—most likely to win her to his side and use her to influence Burke, or even work around him. But what if she pretended to go along with Garrett's plans, or at least to be open to them? Gaining his trust could give her access to vital secrets, and maybe even a measure of control over what was happening.

A few minutes later, Garrett came striding out of the hallway. "Allison! Does this visit mean you've decided to accept my offer?"

She managed a smile. "I'm still thinking about it, but I'd like to know more, if you've got time to talk. Oh—and I wanted to return this." She thrust the catalog toward him.

"Oh, thanks. Would you put this away please, Monica?" He laid it on the receptionist's desk, then turned back to Allison. "Did Burke find anything he liked?"

"Actually I gave up on the whole idea," she said. "You know Burke. He prefers things just the way they are."

"Yes, I know. That's part of the problem." He glanced down the hall. "Do you mind if we talk in Burke's office? I've got things going on in mine."

"You're sure this is a good time?" Allison asked.

"For you, anytime is good."

His hand brushed the small of her back as he ushered her down the hall. A chill passed through Allison's body. This was her last chance to say no, she reminded herself. Otherwise, if she followed the plan she had in mind, she would be playing a dangerous game, with dangerous people.

CHAPTER 9

Burke's office appeared untouched since the last time she'd seen it. Garrett motioned her to a seat at one end of the worn leather couch, then took his place at the other end.

"I can't stay long," Allison said. "I left Brianna with Burke. I promised I'd pick her up when she texted me."

"So how's Brianna taking this new chapter of her life?"

"As well as you could expect. She's got a lawyer, and she's waiting for a court date. She's not happy about it, but at least she seems to be accepting responsibility."

"And Burke? How's he doing?"

"Better. He's in rehab now. Haven't you been to see him?"

"Things have become testy between us. I'm giving him a break for now, hoping he'll come around—or that you can talk him into seeing things my way."

Allison knew what he wanted to hear—something

she wasn't going to say—but she needed to dangle the bait a little longer. "Suppose I take you up on the job offer," she said. "What would I be expected to do?"

He shrugged. "Whatever you like. Act as liaison with Burke until he's ready to come back. Talk to clients and charm them into signing with us. Brainstorm new publicity ideas and carry them out. You'll find plenty of work to keep you busy. But what about Burke? Won't he need you at home?"

"Burke has made it clear that he doesn't want me taking care of him. He'll have help coming in, and Brianna will be around at least part of the time. So my working shouldn't be a problem—in fact, it might even help keep me sane."

"So it's a yes?"

She forced herself to smile. "Yes, I suppose it is. But it'll have to be part-time for now. And don't expect me for a few more days, at least. Tomorrow I'll be driving Brianna to Evanston to meet with the dean and pick up her things from the dorm. The court wouldn't let her make the trip alone. We'll be getting home on Friday, in time for the weekend. And we don't know how soon Burke will be coming home. I'll have to let you know when I'm coming in." She glanced at her phone and stood. "I just got Brianna's text. She's waiting for me now."

Garrett rose with her. "So welcome aboard. Let us know when you'll be starting." He caught her arm as she turned to leave. "If you'll wait just one more minute, there's somebody in my office I'd like you to meet. Come on. It won't take long." He tugged her out of the room, toward his own office down the hall.

Inside, a stocky, silver-haired man wearing tailored khakis and a black golf shirt rose from a chair.

"Allison," Garrett said, "I'd like you to meet Joe Kaplan, one of the attorneys for the Edgeway Group. He'll be here a lot. You'll get to know him. Joe, this is Allison Caldwell, who needs no introduction."

"Mrs. Caldwell." Kaplan shook her hand. Up close, he smelled of expensive cigars. "I was very sorry to hear about your husband's accident. I hope he's doing all right."

"He's getting better, thank you." Allison accepted the man's smooth handshake. Everything about the man was smooth, from the palm of his hand to his thick, flawlessly coiffed hair.

"Allison's just agreed to work with us," Garrett said.

"Excellent. I hope we'll become friends, Allison—if I may."

"Of course," Allison said. "Now if you'll excuse me, I have someone waiting for a ride. It's been nice meeting you."

Turning, she headed for the door and down the hall toward the front office. Was Garrett going ahead with the Edgeway partnership on his own? Why else would their lawyer be here? And what were they doing to get around Burke? This was a frightening development—a dangerous development. But she couldn't tell Burke while his health was at risk. Somehow, she would have to handle this on her own.

In the front office, Monica, the receptionist, was on the phone, chatting in an animated way that suggested the call wasn't business related. As Allison passed the desk, the person on the other end of the call must've said something funny, because Monica chuckled, then broke into a distinctive, high-pitched giggle that matched Allison's memory of Garrett's late-night phone call.

Allison stifled a groan. This was like a scene from a badly written movie.

Eyes straight ahead, she strode out the front door and fled to her car. Her hand shook as she thrust the key into the ignition.

She had never been one to believe in coincidences. The switched key, the presence of the Edgeway lawyer, the new receptionist who was sleeping with Garrett—somehow they all had to be connected. It made sense that Monica was working for Edgeway, and that she was being paid to watch Garrett and find her way into his bed. But what about Garrett? Was he a naïve puppet, being manipulated by the Mob, or was he pulling some of the strings?

Her instincts told her to run from this situation before she found herself trapped in a web of lies and deceit. But that would mean leaving Burke unprotected at his most vulnerable time. Right now, whether he liked it or not, she was the only help he had. She needed to be here for him.

Heaven save her, what had she gotten herself into?

Early the next morning, Allison and Brianna left home for the day-long drive to Evanston. Barely awake, Brianna curled up in the back seat with a pillow and a blanket, closed her eyes, and went back to sleep. Not that Allison minded. Conversing with her stepdaughter still wasn't easy. She much preferred the peace and quiet of solitary driving, which calmed her nerves and gave her time to think.

Last night, torn by doubts and fears, Allison had felt the need to read another of Kate's letters. Burke's first wife had faced the loss of her baby with so much strength. Allison needed to borrow from that strength. She'd come to depend on Kate's words to help her face what she was facing now.

After making sure that Brianna was asleep, she'd opened another letter and read it sitting up in bed. Written about six weeks after the previous one, the letter, a single page—had hit so hard that the words still burned in Allison's memory.

> *My dearest Burke,*
>
> *Thank you for coming home, even though you couldn't stay long. I told you I was fine. I told you I'd recovered from the loss of our baby—that I was moving on. I wanted it to be the truth. But I lied.*
>
> *Two days ago I walked out onto the end of the long pier and stood there for half an hour trying to make myself jump off into the deep water. Brianna was at Tricia's—I knew she'd be safe. And I felt that no one else would miss me, not even you. But then Captain found me. I knew that if I jumped, he would go after me, and maybe drown himself trying to save me. In the end, I couldn't do it. But I wanted to. I still want to. I feel utterly joyless. I cry myself to sleep every night.*
>
> *Today I called the pastor at our church. He has referred me to a weekly support group. I'll be going for the first time tonight. I can only hope that sharing with others will help me grieve.*
>
> *No need to come home again. You don't need to see*

*me like this. Just know that you and Brianna are my
life, and I am doing my best to find my way back to
you.*
   K.

The memory of that letter raised a lump in Allison's throat. Kate hadn't been made of steel. She
was flesh and blood, and she had suffered terribly.
But somehow she'd made it through the darkness,
to face the end of her short life with serenity and
spirit. She was strong in a deeply human way that Allison could only admire and envy.

And Burke? Surely he'd loved her. But had he
known how to show it? Had he even tried to understand her? Had he wanted to be there for her, or had
he taken the easy way out, leaving her to depend on
her own strength and find her own wisdom?

By lunchtime, Brianna was awake and hungry.
They pulled onto an off-ramp, filled up on drive-in
food, and continued on their way, this time with Brianna in the passenger seat.

"Are you going to let me see Liam?" she asked.

"Something tells me I wouldn't be able to stop
you. So I might as well say yes," Allison said. "Have
you told your father about him?"

"Yes—not that it did any good. When Dad heard
that Liam dropped out of school and works as a mechanic, he threw a fit."

"Your dad wants the best for you, that's all."

"Liam *is* the best. He's kind and smart and honest,
and he works hard. He wants to have his own garage
someday."

"I'll tell you what," Allison said. "Why don't I take
the two of you out to a nice dinner tonight? I'd like

to meet Liam and get to know him for myself. Would that be all right?"

"Sure," Brianna said. "There's a good Italian place close to where we'll be staying. I'll text Liam and make sure he can make it."

Her fingers flew over the surface of her phone. "Yes!" she exclaimed. "He'll meet us there at seven. You'll like him, I guarantee it!"

She fell into silence. When Allison glanced her way a few minutes later, she was plugged into her phone, absorbed in texting.

By six fifteen they'd reached Evanston, a northern extension of Chicago that sprawled along the shore of Lake Michigan. They checked into their motel in time to change and clean up for dinner.

As they headed for the door, Brianna glanced at her phone. "Liam's already there. He's saving a booth for us."

Score one for Liam, Allison thought. She found herself wanting to like Brianna's boyfriend. But the responsibility to protect Burke's daughter lay heavy on her. She hadn't come here to make friends.

A few minutes later they walked into the restaurant. Rustic booths and tables, a college-age crowd, and the aroma of good Italian food—the place took Allison back to the years when she was married to Kevin and waiting tables to keep a roof over their heads while he pursued his movie career. It hadn't been an easy time, but being young and in love had had its moments.

The man who rose from a nearby booth to greet them was beautiful in a wild, masculine way that would stir any girl's heart. He reminded Allison of Kevin—not that they looked alike, but he had the same grace, the same air of charm. But if he turned out to be like Kevin in other ways, Brianna was headed for heartbreak.

Proceed with caution, she warned herself as Brianna made the introductions.

"Brianna tells me you're a mechanic," Allison said after they'd given the server their orders.

"Not just a mechanic," Brianna said. "Tell her, Liam."

"I specialize in vintage and foreign cars," Liam said after a modest pause. "Like today, I replaced the clutch on a '53 Aston Martin. The hardest thing about it was finding authentic parts—that goes along with the job. It's a privilege to work on a beautiful old car like that. I could almost do it for nothing." His smile showed a dimple. "But of course, I don't."

"Liam's work brings the shop lots of clients," Brianna said. "But he's saving up to start his own business. He lives over the garage where he works, and he doesn't even own a car. He rides his Harley everywhere. That's because most of what he makes goes into the bank."

"And I buy used books to read." Liam gave Brianna a wink. "That was how we met."

No, Allison thought, this young man was nothing like Kevin. He had skill, ambition, and common sense. So far, so good.

"But that's enough about me," Liam said. "It's Brianna I'm concerned about. Will she have to drop out of Northwestern?"

"For the semester at least," Allison said. "Her father's accident would be enough reason to take time off. But the rest—the DUI charge and the sentencing—will be up to the judge."

"I'll have to tell the dean the truth," Brianna said. "I can't lie my way back into school. My arrest will be on the public record. It would be too easy for them to check." Her voice broke, but she managed not to cry. Liam's arm went around her shoulders in a reassuring hug.

"I've learned my share of lessons the hard way," he said. "But seeing Brianna pay such a high price for one mistake . . ." He shook his head. "It just kills me. I love this girl. I want what's best for her."

Looking at the two of them, Allison had no doubt he spoke the truth. But Liam was a mature man. Brianna still had a lot of growing up to do—just as Allison had had to grow up when she'd married Kevin at the same age.

The server brought their meals and they settled into eating and small talk. "Is there a college in Branson?" Liam asked.

"College of the Ozarks," Allison said. "It's a good school. The students earn their tuition by working, which gives kids who can't afford to pay a chance for an education."

"But it isn't Northwestern," Brianna added. "They offer a minor in journalism but not a major. I suppose I could take a few classes and hope to transfer later. But it's not my plan. It's not my dream."

"I know," Allison said. "I could tell you that you'll get back what you've lost or find another dream. But right now I know better than to say that."

"Would you mind if I took Brianna for a ride after dinner?" Liam asked. "We've got a lot to talk about. I promise to have her back at the motel by ten."

"Fine." It would be bending the rules set by the court, but Allison sensed that if she said no, Brianna would slip out anyway. Why create bad feelings over a fight she was bound to lose? "Just be careful," she said.

"We don't go fast, and Liam always makes me wear his helmet," Brianna said.

"Then he should take some of that money in the bank and buy an extra helmet for himself," Allison said, feeling old and wondering if he'd take her advice.

They finished their meals. Allison had planned to pay, but Liam snatched the check from the server and had the cash out before she could argue. Another point scored.

"Ready?" He stood and held Brianna's leather coat while she slid her arms into the sleeves. Turning, she looked up at him, her eyes brimming with love. They were so beautiful together, Allison thought. But only time would tell whether the magic would—or even should—last.

They walked Allison to her car, and she watched them climb onto Liam's motorcycle, Brianna holding tightly to his back as they roared away. Had she done the right thing, letting Burke's daughter go off with a man her father had already judged to be unsuitable? What if they had an accident, or what if they just kept going and never came back?

But they were responsible young people, Allison reminded herself. Liam treated Brianna like a treasure and would die before he let her come to harm. He would have her safely back, as he'd promised, by ten o'clock that night.

She watched them until the motorcycle vanished from sight, then climbed into her car and drove back to the motel.

*   *   *

They followed the road to Brianna's favorite place, the deserted beach on the shore of Lake Michigan. The night was unseasonably warm, the west wind blowing clouds across a murky sky, heralding the cold front that was forecast for morning.

They secured the bike, kicked off their boots and socks, and walked hand in hand along the beach. The sand was like cool silk under their bare feet. White-caps on the dark water crashed against the shoreline.

"Will I see you tomorrow?" Brianna asked him.

"I have to work tomorrow. And Allison mentioned that you'll be leaving right after your meeting with the dean. She's a nice woman, by the way. After listening to you, I wasn't sure what to expect. You made her sound like the Wicked Witch of the West."

"I did not!" She swung a playful punch at his chest. "I only said that she was the wrong woman for my father. But I have to say, she's been pretty decent since my arrest."

There was a moment of silence. She let him pull her closer, nestling into the curve of his arm. "So I won't see you tomorrow, will I?"

He shook his head. "It'll only make saying good-bye that much harder, Brianna. But I want you to call me after your meeting and let me know what the dean says. All right?"

"All right. But what if I can't stay in the journalism program? What if I can't come back at all? They've got applicants beating down the doors to get in. A journalism degree from Northwestern—that's like the Holy Grail! Why should they keep me—especially if my dad loses his business and can't pay my fees?" She looked up at him. "What if I can't be with you?"

"Hush." He grazed a trail of kisses along her hairline. "You're intelligent and capable, and I love you. Whatever happens, we'll deal with it. You and me together. I'm not going anywhere."

The wind had taken on a chill, whipping the waves to frothy peaks as the storm front moved in. Brianna shivered through her thin leather coat. "Hold me, Liam," she whispered. "Just hold me."

He opened his jacket and wrapped the front around her, holding her against his shirt. She was shivering, more with emotion than with cold. His arms tightened, pressing her into his warmth.

When she tilted her face up toward him, he kissed her—not gently but hungrily, his mouth devouring hers, his tongue thrusting in a desperate pantomime of what couldn't happen—not here, not now, with no place to go and the cold swirling around them. His arousal was a solid ridge, jutting against her belly through his jeans. Desire was an ache in the pulsing core of her body. As she moved against him, his breath deepened to a rasp.

"Liam . . ." she whispered. "I want you . . . I want you so much . . ."

With a muttered oath, he pushed her firmly away from him. His hands gripped her shoulders at arm's length. His eyes blazed into hers. "Damn it, Brianna, haven't you made enough mistakes in the past week?" he growled. "I won't let myself do this to you. Not now, while your life's in a mess on so many fronts—school, your father, your legal problems. Even if we had the right place for it, you don't need me adding to the load by making love to you."

Brianna's chin came up. At some deep, practical level she knew Liam was right. But he was treating her like a foolish child. Worse, he had rebuffed her, and it hurt.

"The wind is getting cold," she said. "We need to go."

"Good idea."

Sand swirled around them as they crossed the beach and returned to where they'd left the bike. Brianna didn't look up at him as she sat on the curb and pulled her socks over her chilled feet. Liam didn't speak as he laced up his boots and handed her his helmet to wear.

Was this the end? Were they breaking up?

She clung to his back, fighting tears as the Harley wove through nighttime traffic. She loved him so much. But that was no guarantee of a happy ending. Life being what it was, when he let her off at the motel tonight, there was a chance she might never see him again.

By the time they reached the motel, a sleety rain was falling, blown almost sideways by the wind. Liam pulled up under the lip of the roof, the bike stopped at an idle. Before he could dismount and help her, Brianna climbed off the back seat and handed him his helmet.

"Put this on. You'll need it tonight." It was the closest she could come to saying goodbye.

He buckled on the helmet. "Call me after your appointment. I'll be wanting to know how it went," he said. Then, he swung the bike away from the building and headed out of the parking lot.

Brianna had pocketed a key to the room. Opening the door with caution, she stepped inside. On a table next to the empty bed, a small lamp lit the warm darkness. In the other bed, Allison was sleeping, or at least pretending to.

Trying not to disturb her, Brianna stripped off her damp boots and clothes, pulled on her pajamas, and turned off the light. Only then did she allow the tears to come, her heaving sobs muffled by the pillow she pressed to her face.

The next morning, Brianna kept her eight fifteen appointment with the dean of students. Half an hour later, feeling numb and shaken, she emerged from the administration building and sank onto a sheltered bench to wait for Allison, who'd gone to the dorm to pick up her boxed possessions. Right now, it was time to phone Liam.

Last night's storm had stripped the leaves from the maples and sycamores, leaving bare branches etched against the chilly blue sky. Brianna shivered as she pulled her phone out of her purse. The color and warmth of autumn was coming to an end. Would the love relationship of her life be coming to an end, as well? She and Liam hadn't exactly quarreled, but things had been cold between them when they'd parted last night.

The phone rang once on the other end. No answer, but Liam had said he'd be working. Brianna waited as the phone rang again, then again. Worry tightened an icy band around her heart. What if he'd gotten in an accident last night? Nobody would have called her. She'd have no way of knowing whether he was all right.

"Brianna?" She heard his voice, and her world slipped back into its orbit. "How did it go with the dean? Are you all right?"

Brianna sighed. "It could've been worse. I've been released on probation. If I make it back to school next semester, I'll be all right. Any later and I'll have to reapply. But I don't know what's going to happen, Liam. This isn't just about my arrest. It's about my father. Northwestern is expensive. What if he can't afford to pay for me to go there? And what if he needs me at home to help him get better? I can't ask Allison to do everything."

Liam was silent for a moment, as if weighing what he'd heard. "You'll be all right," he said. "*We'll* be all right. As long as we love each other, we'll find a way to make this work."

Her heart soared. As long as Liam believed in her and loved her she could make it through this crisis. But it wouldn't be easy. She'd be making some hard decisions over the next few weeks. It was time to become an adult.

She glanced up to see a white Lexus pulling over to the curb.

"Got to go," she said. "Allison's here. We're heading home now."

"Be safe," he said. "Call me."

"I will. I love you," she said. But he was gone by then. She didn't even know if he'd heard her final words.

Brianna tucked her phone in her purse and hurried toward the white car. A world of challenges awaited her at home—her trial, her father's health and financial issues, and her own dreams of an education and a career, and keeping in touch with the man she loved. But Liam was right. Somehow they would work things out.

If only I can keep believing that.

"How did it go with the dean?" Allison asked as Brianna climbed into the front seat.

"I'll tell you on the way," she said. "For now, let's just drive."

Allison wasn't surprised by Brianna's news. The dean had made a reasonable decision. Brianna had been a promising student, but with so many applicants for Northwestern's journalism program, they couldn't hold her place beyond next semester.

"There are good colleges in Missouri," Allison said. "I did some checking. Missouri State in Springfield offers a degree in journalism. You wouldn't be paying out-of-state tuition, and since it's only thirty-five miles from Branson, you could even live at home and commute."

"Yeah, in my shiny red BMW convertible." Brianna sighed. "Sorry, that just came out. I'm trying to look on the positive side, but this whole thing sucks. I can't be Little Miss Perky-face all the time."

"Of course you can't," Allison said. "If you feel like venting, go ahead."

"It won't help," Brianna said. "And it won't help my dad. Right now, what happens to him is more important than a new car, or college, or—"

"Or Liam?"

"Don't. You'll make me cry. Liam said he'd be there for me, but I'm a big girl. I know things can happen."

"I got married when I was about your age," Allison said. "His name was Kevin, and he wanted to be an actor. He was almost as handsome as Liam."

"What happened?" Brianna asked.

"He got in with some bad friends and died of a drug overdose. But we were happy for a while."

"Liam would never do that. He's got plans. He's working hard and saving to get his own business."

"I know."

"And we haven't even talked about getting married. Liam says he doesn't want a wife or kids until he can afford to give them a good life."

Allison gave her a smile. "That sounds a lot like your dad."

"It does, doesn't it?" Brianna sounded mildly surprised. "But my dad doesn't like the idea of my dating Liam. He says I should find someone more suitable."

Allison didn't reply. She liked Liam and could see that he cared for Brianna, but she didn't want to go head-to-head with Burke over his daughter's future. Give it time, she told herself.

"People think I love Liam because he's so good-looking," Brianna said. "But that isn't the reason. I love him because he's honest and kind and smart, and because of the way he treats me. He could be as ugly as a troll, and it wouldn't make any difference."

"I know." Allison eased the Lexus into the right-hand lane and watched the signs for the connection to the southbound freeway. "People think I married your father for his money, but he could lose everything and I'd still love him."

Brianna was quiet for a moment, thinking. "What will we do if Dad loses all his money?" she asked.

"If it were to happen, we'd find ways to manage," Allison said. "But for now, the best we can do is help him get strong so he can manage the situation himself."

It would be wise to keep her own plan for helping Burke a secret, Allison reasoned. Knowing Burke, he'd forbid her to get involved in his business. And telling Brianna would only raise the odds of his finding out.

Sooner or later she would have to tell him. But the next few weeks would be a balancing act with Burke recovering at home, Brianna dealing with her legal issues and long-distance love, and Garrett plotting to turn Burke's business over to the Mob.

She would have to be prepared for the battle of her life.

CHAPTER 10

Brianna sat at the end of the long wooden pier that broke the shoreline of Table Rock Lake. Bundled in her warm coat, she gazed at the reflection of the full moon in the calm, dark water. An eventful week had passed since Allison had driven her home from Evanston with the clothes and other things from her dorm room loaded in the Lexus. In that short time, it was as if her whole life had turned upside down.

After finding her phone in her pocket, she scrolled to Liam's number. Except for a couple of texts, she'd put off calling him. He worked long hours most days, and at night he could be sleeping or out with friends. Maybe she'd really put off calling because she didn't want to discover he was dating somebody else. After all, they'd never promised to be exclusive, and women practically followed him down the street.

But why did she have to be so insecure? Liam loved her. She had to keep believing that.

She made the call. Liam picked up on the second

ring. He sounded sleepy. "Hey," he said. "What are you up to? It's after midnight."

"I know. Did I wake you?"

"Yes. But that's all right. I was getting worried. Are you okay?"

"More or less. But I had my trial today."

She could hear him turning over and sitting up in the bed. "How did it go? Tell me."

"The judge gave me a break because I had a clean record, but the news was still hard to take. A five-hundred-dollar fine and six months' probation, with community service."

"But no jail time?"

"No jail time. But *six months*, Liam! I can't leave the state while I'm on probation. I can't go back to Northwestern—or to . . . you." Brianna had resolved to sound brave, but her voice broke.

She could hear him breathing. "Have you thought about what you're going to do?" he asked.

"Look for a job, I guess. I can't ask Dad to pay my fine or the lawyer's fee. Tomorrow Allison's going to trade in her Lexus for two good used cars, so we'll both have something to drive. She's been pretty cool about all this."

"What about your dad? Is he getting any better?"

"He came home a couple of days ago. He can walk a little but he's still in pain and pretty hard to live with. He wasn't happy about school or the trial, but at least he won't have to visit me behind bars." Brianna muffled a sob. "I miss you, Liam."

"I miss you, too. But six months isn't forever."

"So why does it seem that way? I know you need your work. I can't ask you to take time off and visit me."

"Something tells me I wouldn't be welcome if I came. But the time will pass, and we'll get through it. Call me, okay? I worry about you and I need to hear your voice."

"I will. I love you, Liam." She ended the call, dropped her phone back into her pocket, and pushed to her feet. Life was a bitch sometimes. But she'd already learned that whining was a waste of breath. Deal with it—that was all she could do.

Six months—yes, the time would pass. But where would she and Liam be at the end of it?

Allison paused outside the closed door of the downstairs bedroom, wondering whether to knock or just turn the knob and walk in. Burke had only been home four days, but the little-used guest room already seemed like alien territory. Prior to his homecoming, the room had been rearranged to allow for more floor space. The double bed had been moved against the wall, with a cushioned armchair close by. A tray table, a walker, and some exercise equipment had been moved in, and some attachments added to make the adjoining bathroom more usable.

Samuel, a husky young aide from the home care service, was another addition. For four hours a day, he helped Burke in and out of the bath, helped change his clothes and bedding, checked his healing incision, doled out his pain meds, put him through his daily physical therapy, and fixed his lunch. At the end of the week, when the insurance coverage ran out, he would be gone, and Burke would be on his own.

And that would be fine, Allison told herself. Burke was improving daily and determined to do things by himself. Allison's efforts to help him had been coldly rebuffed. She'd hoped that their talks in the hospital would bring them closer. But the gulf between them was widening with each day she remained at home. He was a proud man, accustomed to being in charge of his business and his home life. Now that control was slipping away, leaving a helpless rage in its place.

Allison could sense what was happening. But how could she just stand back and wring her hands while her husband's world was falling apart?

Yesterday she'd traded in the Lexus for two used Honda Civics and given Brianna first choice of the cars. Now that they both had transportation, it was time to go to work. She had already let Garrett know that she'd be starting at the agency tomorrow. Now, just one step remained—telling Burke.

Allison had been tempted to fabricate a story about the job. But sooner or later Burke would have to know the truth. Confronting him would be painful, but it would be better than keeping a lie between them.

She was raising her hand to knock when the door opened partway. Samuel stepped out into the hall, closing the door behind him. He wore his jacket and carried the leather satchel that held his medical equipment.

"Leaving so soon, Samuel?" Allison asked, surprised.

"Leaving for good, I'm afraid," the young man said. "Your husband just dismissed me and told me not to come back."

"But . . . you've been doing a fine job. What happened?"

"Nothing, really. I was helping him walk, trying to

work on his posture and his gait, and suddenly he just stopped, saying he'd had enough and that he could manage by himself from here on out, and I wasn't to come back. He didn't sound angry, just frustrated and very firm."

"That would be Burke, all right," Allison said. "I'm sorry Samuel. This is no reflection on you."

"I know. And I think he'll be okay. It's just a little startling, that's all."

Allison walked him to the front door and watched him drive away in a compact car that seemed too small for his bulky frame. Burke, she suspected, would not be in an amiable mood. But she'd resolved to tell him about the job, and putting it off would only make the confrontation harder.

Feeling like Daniel about to step into the lions' den, she walked back to the closed door, rapped lightly, then opened it without waiting for an answer.

Burke, dressed in navy blue sweats and gray sneakers, was sitting in the armchair reading the newspaper, with a mug of black coffee on the tray table. The pillows, arranged to support his back and sides, were the only sign that he was still in pain.

He laid the newspaper aside as Allison walked in. "I suppose you've spoken with Samuel," he said.

"Yes. He's gone. He said you'd be fine." Allison moved a straight-backed chair to face him. His eyes narrowed as she sat down. He'd lost weight since the accident. His body was leaner, his features sharper. And he'd grown a short, well-trimmed beard, which was darker than his silver hair. Pain had etched new furrows at the corners of his eyes. He looked good, she conceded. But the husband she remembered was gone, his place taken by an edgy stranger she barely knew. Only his deep blue eyes were the same.

"Do we need to talk?" he asked.

"We do. For one thing, are you sure you'll be all right without Samuel coming in?"

"Positive. I can walk fine. I can manage the shower, get snacks, and use the microwave in the kitchen. The woman who comes in to clean can change the bed and do my laundry. I'm cutting back on my meds. I'll get along fine. But what I really need is to get back to work. For now, I can work in my study. Between the computer and my phone, I should be able to stay in touch with my employees and the clients."

Allison faked a smile. "So you won't be needing me for anything either, right?"

Don't you know how much I want to help you, Burke? Don't you know what I'd give if we could be close again?

She shoved the unspoken words to the back of her mind.

"I'm trying not to need you, Allison. You never signed on to take care of me. If you had any sense, you'd walk out today."

His words cut deep. She willed herself to ignore them.

"You're going to need a car," she said. "But you won't be allowed to drive until you're off the opioid pain meds."

"That won't be much longer. I've already got my dealer on the lookout for a car I can buy with the insurance money from the Porsche. Until I get it, you might have to chauffeur me once in a while. Or maybe Brianna can do it—although I'm still not happy about you trading in the Lexus. That car was my gift to you."

"Brianna needed a car, and that was the easiest way to get her one. She's looking for a job now, and she'll be busy with her community service. She may not have much spare time."

"We'll work it out." He picked up the newspaper again, then glanced at her as if surprised to see that she hadn't gotten up and left. "Anything else?" he asked.

"Yes." Allison braced herself. "There is something else. I've accepted a part-time job, starting tomorrow. I'll be working for the agency, with Garrett."

The newspaper fell to the floor, scattering pages. "Are you out of your mind?" He stared at her. "I don't want you anywhere near the agency. Not with Garrett in charge. I don't trust the man anymore, and I trust his new friends even less."

"Listen to me, Burke." Allison leaned toward him, her eyes holding his. "I don't trust Garrett either. Until you're strong enough to go back to work full-time, you'll need somebody at the agency to be your eyes and ears."

She paused, wondering how much more to tell him. For now, the less said the better, she decided. If she mentioned the key, the new receptionist, and the Mob lawyer who'd shown up, Burke would find a way to interfere with her plan. Or worse, he might go rushing headlong into a dangerous situation.

"But why you?" he demanded. "There must be somebody else I can count on to look out for my interests until I'm back on the job."

"Think about it," she said. "The paid employees can be bought or fired. The agents on commission are pretty much working for themselves. As long as they get paid, they don't care who's in charge. The one person who's loyal to you is your wife."

His jaw tightened as the words sank in. "But

wouldn't Garrett realize that, too? The man isn't stu-pid."

"Neither am I. So far I've got him believing that my only interest is saving the theater, and that I can influence you to change your mind about signing the contract. As long as he trusts me—"

"No!" Burke's fist came down on the table, splat-tering coffee. "It's too risky, Allison. I won't stand for your doing this!"

Allison took a moment to sponge up the spilled coffee with a tissue. "You can't forbid me, Burke. And the only way you could stop me would be to tell Garrett the truth, which would put me in even more danger. We've got to find out what he's up to with the Mob and stop him. Right now I'm the only one who's in a position to do that."

He shook his head. "I have a bad feeling about this. It's my job to take the risks, not yours. If any-thing were to go wrong, I'd never forgive myself."

"No, listen," she said. "All I'll really be doing is stalling for time. When you go to your desk in the other room, you'll find your unfinished loan appli-cation in the front of the file drawer. As soon as you've finished and signed it, I'll take it to the bank, or even drive you there to deliver it in person, if you want. Once it's approved—"

"*If* it's approved."

"Once it's approved, you'll have the cash you need. The Edgeway people will have no reason to be involved."

"True," Burke said. "But even with the loan, we won't be out of the woods. It's a lot of money. If we can't pay it back, we could still lose everything."

"What are you saying? That we should just sit back

and let Garrett hand the American Heartland over to
the Mob?"

"Lord, no! I'm betting everything I own on this
project. I just want you to be aware of the risk."

Allison shook her head. "I'm aware of the risk,
and I'm with you a hundred percent. But somebody
needs to keep an eye on Garrett. If I'm working with
him, I can do that."

He still looked skeptical, but Allison sensed that
she'd gotten through to him. "Maybe," he said. "But
what about Brianna? She thinks Garrett's her friend.
We'd have to keep her out of this."

"You're right. She has to be protected." Allison
had almost forgotten about Brianna's liking for Garrett. "I'll talk to her. I think I can warn her away."

"You'll have to. I won't accept any plan that puts
her at risk."

"I know. Neither will I." She rose, meaning to
leave before he began to have second thoughts. But
as she turned away, his hand caught her wrist. With
surprising strength, he whipped her back around to
face him, pulling her down until their faces were
inches apart. His eyes blazed with an angry despera-
tion. For the space of a breath, she imagined he
might kiss her. But then he spoke.

"Don't do this, Allison. Garrett's fallen in with
some dangerous people. They could be capable of
anything. I'm asking you for the last time."

Allison knew a calm answer would be best; but the
hurt of the past days and weeks rose inside her. Words
emerged like barbs, aimed to wound. "Why should
you care whether it's dangerous? You've been wanting to get rid of me ever since the accident. Maybe
you'll succeed this time. Now let me go."

He released her, his expression rigid, as if she'd

slapped his face. She backed away a step. Then, without giving him time to speak, she turned and stalked out the door, closing it behind her with a click.

As her footsteps crossed the hall and mounted the stairs, her words echoed in Burke's ears. Was that what she really thought, that he was out to get rid of her? How could she believe that? All he wanted—all he'd ever wanted—was to protect her from harm when he couldn't keep her safe, and from need when he could no longer keep her in comfort. Why couldn't she understand that?

Pushing through the pain, he used the chair arms to lever himself to his feet. Without the walker or cane, each step was a study in balance, but he made it to the door, out into the hall, and to the foot of the stairs. Here he stopped, one hand resting on the banister.

Overhead, he could hear Allison's quick, sharp footsteps heading down the hall to the bedroom— *their* bedroom where, night after night, they'd made soul-searing love until they fell asleep in each other's arms.

Last night, too restless to sleep, he'd gotten out of bed and stood in this very spot, thinking of Allison alone in the bed that was no longer his. He imagined her lying with her long legs tangled in her silk nightgown, her honey-gold hair spread on the pillow, her mouth soft in sleep.

The yearning to stride up those stairs and take her where she lay had roused an ache so deep that he'd groaned out loud with it. But the stairs were beyond his limits, and would be for weeks to come.

With a muttered curse, he turned away from the

stairs and walked down the hall to his study. Given what their relationship had become, odds were he might never make love to his wife again—even though he now knew it was physically possible.

The thought of not having her was like dying.

Squaring his jaw, he forced himself to think of other things. Allison had said the loan application was in his desk. If he could finish it today, they could take it to the bank tomorrow—after her work, whenever the hell that would be.

Why had he given in and let her take that damned job? But he knew why. If he hadn't, there would've been all-out war between them. Now he was worried about her—worried sick. Garrett was nothing but a fool. But if she ran afoul of the Mob, her life could be in danger.

His back was throbbing, but he'd vowed to get off the painkillers today. At least he could control that. Clenching his jaw against the pain, he walked into his study, closed the door, and prepared to bury himself in his work.

Allison had left her cell phone on the nightstand. It was ringing as she walked in the door. She rushed to answer it, stumbling on the rug in her haste. Maybe it was Brianna. Maybe she'd gotten the newspaper job she was interviewing for.

But the caller wasn't Brianna. It was Garrett. The sound of his voice tightened her frayed nerves.

"Hi, Allison. Just wondering if you were planning to come in tomorrow."

"Yes, I was. Did we decide on a time?"

"That's up to you. Mornings or afternoons?"

"Afternoons would be better," she said after a moment's thought. "That way I can make sure Burke is up and around before I leave."

"That's fine. How's Burke coming along these days?"

"Still in pain, but he's determined to get back to normal. He'll be working from his study for a while—you'll no doubt be hearing from him." Allison sank onto the edge of the bed. The encounter with Burke had left her shaken, and Garrett's phone call wasn't helping.

"I don't suppose you've talked to him about the contract, have you? We've been hoping you could change his mind."

The *we* was not lost on Allison. "Not yet," she said. "But I did tell him I was taking the job. He wasn't happy about it. Don't worry, he'll come around." That part was a lie. But if she was going to work with Garrett and his mobster friends, lying was something she'd have to get used to.

"We can talk more tomorrow," she said. "Shall we say one o'clock?"

"Sure. I'll tell Monica to get everything ready for you. Again, glad to have you aboard, Allison."

After ending the call, Allison sank backward onto the bed. She wasn't ready for this. But somebody had to keep those slime balls from taking over the American Heartland and Burke's other holdings. She'd volunteered, and now it was time for her to deliver.

She could only hope that Burke would forgive her once he heard the whole story. But she had never known Burke to be a forgiving man.

As she turned over, thinking maybe she should get

up and go for a walk to calm her nerves, she heard a faint crackle from beneath the mattress, where she'd hidden the packet of letters.

Maybe reading Kate's words would lend her the courage she needed.

Standing for a moment, she worked the manila envelope out from between the mattress and box spring, then sat down and drew out the next letter, this one in a peach-colored envelope.

Her own life had been so hectic over the past few days that it took a moment's thought to remember the details of Kate's last letter. Then the memory came into focus. Kate had sunk into depression after losing her baby and learning that there could be no more children. Her pastor had recommended a support group, and she'd planned to go.

The support group must have been helpful. The first letter Allison had read, the one telling Burke that she had cancer, had been written by a loving wife at peace with herself and her marriage. Kate had come a long way from the despairing woman who'd described her life as joyless. Maybe this letter would lend some insight into her journey.

As she slid the letter out of its envelope, Allison glanced at the postmark. This letter had been mailed six weeks after the last one she'd read.

Dear Burke,

Thank you for coming home and trying to make things better for me. I appreciate your efforts—taking Brianna and me out in the boat and to dinner at the Chateau, inviting our friends over for a cookout, and treating me far better than I deserved.

I sensed your frustration when you left again. I'm aware that I was distant and withdrawn when we

*were alone, and that even when we were making love,
I seemed to be somewhere else. You asked me to explain—I couldn't. Not to your face. That's why I'm
writing you this letter. And if my penmanship's a bit
shaky, it's because I know that I'm about to hurt you
terribly.*

   *Burke, I had an affair. You don't know the man
and never will. He was in my support group, both of
us grieving for our lost children, both of us needing
comfort, and it just happened. By the time you came
home, it was over. He was married and felt just as
guilty as I did. We agreed that we would never contact each other again.*

Allison laid the pages on the bed. Her eyes blurred
with tears. *Oh, Kate . . . Kate . . .*
Taking a deep breath, she picked up the letter
again.

   *So there it is. You've done nothing to deserve this
pain. And there's nothing I can do to make it go
away. I am here, prepared to move on with whatever
comes next. You can choose to forgive me or not. You
can stay and hate me forever, or you can walk away.
All I ask is that we do everything we can to protect
Brianna. She's so innocent, and she knows nothing
about what her mother did. Please don't let my terrible mistake destroy her.*

   *I love you with all my heart, Burke. I realize those
words won't mean much right now. You'll be hurt.
You'll be angry. Take your time. Work out your feelings. What happens next is up to you. I promise that
whatever you decide, I will understand.*

   K.

Allison folded the pages and slipped them back into the envelope. With a ragged sigh, she fell back on the bed, one hand still holding the letter.

How much pain would it have taken to drive Kate into another man's arms? And how much love would it have taken for Burke to forgive her?

Burke *had* forgiven her, Allison surmised. Somehow they'd stayed together and made their marriage work. The letter Kate had written after her cancer diagnosis had made that much clear.

But Allison would never know the details of their journey toward forgiveness and healing. After the letter about her affair, Kate had written no more—or if she had, the letters hadn't been saved.

The next letter, postmarked almost seven years later, was the one Kate had written to tell Burke about her cancer. Allison could only imagine that the years between had been good ones, filled with love and happy family times, and that Kate had fought her illness bravely to the end.

There was no way for Allison to know for sure because, for whatever reason, there were no more letters. Maybe the cancer treatments had left Kate too exhausted to write. Or maybe Burke had come home to take care of his wife and daughter.

Now only the thick white envelope, with Burke's name and instructions to open it after Kate's death, remained unopened. It had been sealed for a reason, Allison told herself. Whatever was inside—another letter, a will, a family secret, even money, it wasn't meant to be seen. It appeared that Burke had been given the envelope by Kate while she was still alive, and that after putting it away with the other letters, he'd either forgotten about it or been in too much emotional pain to look at its contents. Or maybe he'd opened it carefully and glued the flap shut again. The only thing Allison knew for sure was that nothing inside was any business of hers.

Standing, she dropped the last of Kate's letters into the large manila envelope and slid it back under the mattress. She had finished reading the letters, but with Burke working downstairs, she would have to keep them hidden until the coast was clear to return the packet to his desk.

She had no sooner turned away from the bed than the door swung open without a knock and Brianna burst into the bedroom. "I got it, Allison! I got the job!" She was literally dancing with excitement.

"The one at the newspaper?" Allison knew that Brianna had interviewed for a part-time position with the *Branson Tri-Lake News*, a biweekly paper that covered local personalities and events.

"Yes!" She flung herself onto the bed, bouncing like a five-year-old. "It isn't exactly the *New York Times*, I know, but I'll be a real live journalist, even doing interviews! And I'll still have time to do my community service."

"Congratulations. That's wonderful," Allison said. "Have you told your dad?"

"I told him just now. It's the first time I've seen a real smile on his face since the accident."

"And have you told Liam?"

"He'll be working today. I'll call him tonight."

"We should celebrate," Allison said, remembering her promise to alert Brianna about Garrett. "Have you had lunch?"

"Not yet. Are you offering to take me?"

"Anywhere you want to go. My treat. And we can bring home a meal in a box for your dad to warm up later."

"That sounds great. I'll tell him we're going and see what he'd like."

Allison grabbed her purse and followed her step-daughter downstairs. She could only hope that the serious conversation she had in mind wouldn't spoil Brianna's happy mood.

CHAPTER 11

On the downstairs balcony, Brianna settled in a lounge chair with her phone and made a call to Liam. It was after eleven. The house was dark and quiet, Burke asleep in his downstairs room and Allison alone upstairs in the king-size bed. Brianna could tell things were strained between her father and stepmother. Not so long ago, she had hoped the marriage wouldn't last. Now that she was getting to know Allison, she found herself wishing it would—and fearing that it might not.

"Hullo." Liam had picked up on the third ring.

"Hi, sleepyhead," Brianna purred into the phone.

"Hi. You sound mighty cheerful for this late hour."

"I am. I got a job today—just part-time, but it's with a local newspaper. I'll be a real reporter!"

"Hey, that's great. I'm happy for you."

"You don't sound too happy."

"Sorry. I've been trying hard not to miss you, but

it's like there's this big hole in my life. I'm counting the days till you can come back here."

"So am I. But I'm scared, Liam. My six-month probation won't be up in time for next semester. I'll have to reapply to go back to Northwestern in the summer or fall. What if they don't accept me? I mean, I was a decent student, but not one of the superstars, and now I've got this blotch on my record. Why should they take me back when they could fill my place with somebody better? And with my dad having money troubles . . ." Brianna's voice trailed off. She'd tried not to worry about her father's business, but today's lunch with Allison had brought the issue front and center.

"Can you reapply now? At least you'll know whether it's even an option."

"That's a good idea. The sooner I find out, the better."

"What if you don't get back in? Do you have a plan B?"

"Sort of. Allison suggested I check out Missouri State in Springfield. They have a good journalism program. It would be a lot cheaper, and I'd be close to home—but I wouldn't be close to you."

Liam took a long, deep breath. "I love you, Brianna," he said. "I've got a good job here but there are other jobs. And I'd never forgive myself if I didn't give you the chance to follow your dream. Figure out where you need to be. If you still want me, I'll find a way to be there for you."

His willingness to accommodate her brought tears to her eyes. "You have a dream, too, Liam," she said. "Yours is just as important as mine."

"If you and I are meant to be together, we'll work

something out," he said. "But not much can happen until you've settled the question of school."

A pause passed between them. "How's your father?" he asked.

"Well enough to be up and around. He's working a little from home, but I can tell he's in a lot of pain. That doesn't make him any easier to live with. We haven't talked about you since the first time. But I get the impression he hasn't changed his mind."

"Well, give it time. Until I can show up and convince him how much I love his daughter, all we can do is be patient."

"For what it's worth, his daughter loves you, too. Now get some sleep."

After ending the call, Brianna settled back in the chair and watched the clouds drift across the moon. The day had been full of surprises—the job with the paper, the sight of her father, up and working, and the unexpected conversation she'd had with Allison over lunch.

They'd driven down to the Landing for Mexican food, in an outdoor restaurant with a view of Lake Taneycomo. They'd talked about Brianna's new job, and Allison had shared the news that she'd be working part-time for the theatrical agency. "It was my choice," she'd said. "Your father wasn't happy about it, but with so much at stake, he needs someone to look out for his interests there."

"Isn't that Garrett's job?" Brianna had asked.

"I don't trust Garrett, and neither should you," Allison replied. "I told you about the Edgeway Group's connection to the Mob. I have every reason to believe Garrett's working with them to get control of your father's business."

"Every reason? What do you mean? What do you know that I don't?"

"I'd rather not say—in fact I haven't told your father what I've learned because he needs to focus on his recovery. But I've been in that office. I've seen what's going on. And I need to warn you. Garrett may pretend to be your friend—just like he's pretending to be mine. But don't believe anything he tells you. In fact, you're better off having nothing to do with him."

"Are you saying he's dangerous?"

"I hope not—although I can't say that for some of his new friends. But Garrett's certainly capable of lying. And he's capable of using you to influence your father. If he can get Burke's signature on that partnership agreement with Edgeway, the Mob will step in and take everything—and I'm pretty sure Garrett's hoping to be the front man."

"I don't know what to say."

"You don't have to say anything," Allison had replied. "Just be aware that Garrett's gone over to the dark side, as they say in the movies."

"For now, I'll take your word for it," Brianna had said. "But I'm not a baby. You don't need to protect me from knowing what's happening."

"I understand. But your father doesn't want you involved. Neither do I. Right now, until we have solid evidence, it's better that you stay away from Garrett and from the agency," Allison had said. "Now let's talk about something else."

Recalling the conversation now, Brianna struggled to make sense of it. Garrett had been her friend for as long as she'd known him. She'd always trusted him. And now, suddenly, he was supposed to be the villain.

Allison had already told her about the Edgeway Mob connection. At the time, she'd found herself wondering if it would be so bad, having plenty of money to remodel the theater and not having to pay it back, versus having her father go into heavy debt to borrow money from the bank. She still didn't fully understand what was going on, except that the Mob was evil. If they financed the theater, they would probably demand control over everything. If he signed that contract, her father would be pushed aside, with no power. If he refused to sign . . .

A chill crept over her as she weighed the implications. The danger was real. But had Garrett joined forces with the Mob, or was he simply guilty of trusting the wrong people?

Allison had warned her to stay away from Garrett. Should she take the warning at face value? Maybe. Or maybe she should talk to the man she'd always believed to be her friend.

Too weary to make a decision, Brianna rose from the chair and wandered back into the house. Tomorrow morning she would start her new job at the newspaper office. To be at her best she would need a good night's sleep.

Upstairs in her old room, she turned on a lamp to get ready for bed. The soft light fell on the framed photo that stood on the bookshelf. Taking it down, she gazed at the happy image of her family. She'd been twelve when the snapshot was taken by one of her father's friends. Her father—barely forty here— looked young and happy. Her mother was the picture of radiant health, even though the cancer that

took her life must have already begun growing inside her.

Wise, funny, loving Mom. How Brianna missed her.
Allison was all right, but she was more like an older
sister than a mother. Mom had been the real deal.

Brianna imagined telling her about Liam, and
about the problems with her father's business. Her
mom always had an answer for her, even if it was just
to be patient and trust her heart.

What advice would she give her troubled daughter
now?

With a sigh, Brianna replaced the photo on the
shelf and got into her pajamas. She was exhausted,
but even after slipping into bed, she lay awake for a
long time, gazing up into the darkness.

Allison had offered to make Burke breakfast that
morning, hoping that, with Brianna already on the
way to her new job, they could sit at the table and
talk awhile. But he'd insisted that all he wanted was
coffee and that he would make it himself. She
shouldn't have been surprised. He was still angry
about her decision to take the part-time job at the
agency. Angry or worried—most likely both.

By the time she'd dressed in leggings and a warm
sweatshirt for her morning walk, he was talking on
the phone in his study, the paperwork on his desk
organized into neat piles. She gave him a wave from
the open doorway. He would know where she was
going—if he even cared.

But she mustn't think that way. Burke did care.
Maybe he cared too much. As a man, he took re-

sponsibility for everything that happened in his world and shouldered the blame for anything that went wrong.

Allison left the house by the back door and made her way down the slope to the jogging path that followed the lakeshore. The morning was cool and cloudy, with a steady breeze from the west. At her approach, a flock of mallards lifted off the water's surface, rising and circling as their beating wings caught the wind.

The words of Kate's letter came back to her as she followed the path. Kate could have kept her secret— the affair was over, the man no longer in her life. But she'd chosen to face the consequences with honesty and courage. And Burke had chosen to come back and save their marriage.

Was there a lesson to be learned here?

The breeze had taken on a chill. Allison thrust her hands into the front pocket of her sweatshirt. Today at one o'clock she would report to the agency for her so-called job. She would lie to Garrett about her intent, just as she'd already lied to Burke about the danger involved. She was tired of lying. But she was doing this for Burke and also for Brianna.

She could only wonder whether Kate would have made the same choice.

Dressed for work in gray slacks and a black silk blouse, Allison stood in the doorway of Burke's study. Burke was still at his desk. "I've got time to make us some lunch before I leave," she said. "Would you like something?"

"Don't bother. Samuel left plenty of frozen dinners in the fridge. I can warm something up later, when I'm hungry."

"You never seem to be hungry these days." *Not even for me.* The thought crossed her mind as she walked into the room, stopping close enough to look over his shoulder.

Swiveling the chair, he looked up at her. His gaze was sharp and hard, traveling from her upswept hair to her black pumps. "So you're really going."

"I told you I was, and I told you why." Maybe she ought to tell him everything she'd seen and heard. But Allison knew where that would lead.

"Have you spoken with Garrett lately?" she asked.

"I left a message, but he hasn't returned my call. There's a new receptionist. I had to tell her who I was. Did something happen to Fran?"

"I don't know. I can ask."

"Never mind. I should finish the loan application today. Can you drive me to the bank in the morning?"

"I can deliver it if you want," Allison said.

"No, the folks at the bank will have heard about the accident. I need to show up on my feet, to let them know I'm fit to do business."

"Fine. I'll be glad to drive you." Allison was about to leave, but something in his expression caused her to hesitate. "Are you sure I can't get you some lunch?" she asked.

"Don't bother, I'm fine." He caught her hand as she turned to go, drawing her back toward him. "You don't have to do this, Allison," he said. "Call Garrett. Tell him you changed your mind."

"It's a little late for that."

But as she spoke, Allison wondered, what if it wasn't? What if she were to give in, abandon the idea of going to work, and do what he wanted her to? Would that close the rift between them? Would he draw her onto his lap and bury his face between her breasts while she wrapped him in her arms, opening to his touch, as she'd yearned to do?

No, that would be taking the easy way. Burke was in danger of losing everything. She had to see this through.

"Listen to me," he said, still gripping her hand. "I'm not a fool, Allison. I know Garrett's doing everything he can to close the deal with Edgeway and get their people in place while I'm out of action. The new receptionist was just one of the clues. The fact that he hasn't returned my calls is another. You might be able to handle Garrett. But he's surrounding himself with some dangerous people. Letting you go to work there would be like watching you walk into a rattlesnake den."

Letting you? She could have challenged him, but she'd be wise to choose her battles. "Don't worry," she said. "I know what I'm getting into."

He shook his head. "I'm not sure you do. Wait a week. By then I'll be strong enough to go back and take care of things myself. With luck, we'll have approval on the bank loan. Then we can move on to a whole new set of challenges."

"We may not have a week. And you'll still be in a lot of pain. The doctor said it would take three months, at least, for your spine to heal."

"I know. I'll just have to take that chance." His strong fingers tightened around her hand. His gaze drilled into hers. "Don't do it, Allison. If anything were to happen to you, I'd never forgive myself."

"Thanks. I'll try to remember that." Acting on a

sudden impulse, she bent and kissed him on the mouth. It was meant to be a quick goodbye peck, but, perhaps because they both wanted it, their lips lingered and warmed. His free hand caught the back of her upswept hair, pulling it loose as the kiss deepened. Something in the depths of Allison's body went molten, pulsing and shimmering, wanting him.

But no, she mustn't do this. Not now, with so much at stake. Summoning all that remained of her will, she pulled free and backed away from him.

"Stay, Allison." His voice was rough with need.

"I can't. I've got to do this. Forgive me."

Before he could change her mind, she turned and hurried out of the room.

"At least promise you'll tell me what the hell's going on there," he called after.

"I will." Allison paused to answer. "I promise."

Then, after grabbing her jacket and purse, she was out the door.

When Allison walked into the agency at one o'clock, she was greeted by Monica, who let her into Burke's office. The blond receptionist was courteous, but not exactly warm, which was all right with Allison. She had no wish to become friends with the woman.

Monica left her and returned a few minutes later with coffee in a Styrofoam cup and a packet of creamer.

"Thanks," Allison said. "Is Garrett around? I didn't see him when I came in."

"Oh." Monica had been about to leave. Then she turned in the doorway. "Mr. Miles and Mr. Kaplan are at the theater, meeting with the designers and contractors. Mr. Miles asked me to get you started on the client contracts."

"The client contracts? Oh, these?" Only then did Allison notice the large file box on the corner of the desk.

"For now you're supposed to read through them. Get familiar with each one—the terms of agreement, the signing and expiration dates, and anything personal about the clients, like addresses and phone numbers. I've set up a file on the computer where you'll enter the information. You know, like a database."

"Thanks, I know what a database is," Allison said. "As long as I'm doing the work, could I ask what the database is for?"

"I guess so. Once the partnership's drawn up, the contracts will be transferred to Edgeway. The clients will be given new contracts to sign. The database will be used for tracking."

"I see. Will I have any trouble accessing the digital file?"

"Your login and password are your first initial and last name. Let me know if you need anything."

"Thanks, I will." Allison finished her coffee and logged into the computer. From the front office, she could hear Monica on the phone, punctuating her conversation with that inane, high-pitched giggle. She was tempted to close the door of her office, but on second thought decided to leave it open. She was here to learn, and she was already learning plenty.

Kaplan, the Mob lawyer, had become a regular at the agency. He and Garrett were already taking bids on the remodeling of the American Heartland. And

Edgeway would be taking over the agency as well. Clients who accepted the new contracts would be unknowingly signing their souls over to the Mob.

The days when she could protect Burke from the truth were over. She'd promised to tell him everything she found out. When he learned what Garrett and his cohorts were up to, her husband would be livid.

Setting her resolve, she started on the database. She'd expected the work to be drudgery, but she soon discovered that each contract had a story behind it. These clients were show business people—singers, dancers, musicians, and actors; stand-up comics, acrobats, and magicians. The paperwork gave her intriguing glimpses into their lives.

What would happen to these people if the Mob were to take over their contracts?

It was almost four o'clock when she looked up to see Garrett standing in the doorway. He was leaning against the frame, an amused grin on his face.

Startled, Allison stifled a gasp. "How long have you been here?" she asked.

He chuckled. "Long enough to see that you're really into this job. How about we break for an early dinner—or a late lunch, if you want to call it that? We can relax and talk over a good steak and a glass of wine."

"That sounds wonderful." Allison was faking her enthusiasm. She didn't relish the thought of an intimate dinner with Garrett, but she needed to hear what he had to say.

She'd promised to tell Burke everything she learned. Her husband was bound to be upset, but it was high time she stopped treating him like an invalid. He deserved to know the truth.

"You can shut down the computer," Garrett said. "After we've had dinner, I'll just let you off at your car."

"Fine. I'll be needing to get home by then." Allison logged off, picked up her purse and jacket, and let him usher her out to his black Escalade. While Garrett steered through late-day traffic, Allison struggled to pull her lines together, like a would-be actress about to walk on stage for the first time. She would have to be open to his ideas, but not too open; curious, but not too curious.

He parked at a nearby steak house, escorted Allison inside, and followed the hostess to a quiet corner booth. She waited until the server brought their wine and took their order before she made her move. Gazing at him over the rim of her wineglass, she said, "I missed you today."

He smiled. "Sorry. I meant to be there to welcome you and show you the ropes myself. But we were meeting with contractors in the theater. Big plans ahead. The place is going to be unbelievable when it's finished. Remind me tomorrow, and I'll show you the blueprints."

"Blueprints?" Allison raised her eyebrows. "So this is really happening."

"It has to happen—and happen now. If Burke keeps dragging his feet, the remodeling won't be done in time for the spring season. That would be a disaster. Everything is planned and ready to go, just waiting for him to get on board." Garrett emptied his wineglass and motioned to the server for more.

"How is Burke, by the way?"

"Getting better, but he still needs rest and therapy. As you might imagine, he's not a happy patient."

"Any luck getting him to sign off on the partnership?"

"I'm working on it. At least he's listening to me, but he's a stubborn man. Maybe if you were to come to the house and show him the blueprints and bids—"

Garrett shook his head. "Burke and I are barely on speaking terms. He'd never listen to me. That's where you come in. If he'd agree to give you power of attorney—"

"He'd never do that. Burke isn't an invalid, and he's not mentally incompetent." She leaned toward him. "Give me a little more time, say, a week to persuade him. I know he's worried about finding the money, especially if the bank doesn't come through. If he doesn't pay off that short-term loan by the end of the year, the American Heartland will go into foreclosure. Come to think of it, why doesn't the Edgeway Group just wait until that happens and buy the place from the bank?"

"I'm sure they've talked about it. But that old theater is in a prime location. The land alone is worth more than they're offering to invest, even at foreclosure prices. Besides, the Edgeway Group likes to work behind the scenes, with the original owners out front."

"And what about the agency?" Allison asked. "Monica mentioned that if the partnership goes through, Edgeway would be taking over the contracts."

"Oh, she did?" Garrett looked startled, as if Monica might have revealed too much. "Well, that's still open to negotiation," he said.

"Of course." Allison paused as the server set down platters of juicy grilled steaks with baked potatoes and asparagus spears, along with a basket of warm buns. She didn't feel much like eating, but she'd have to make a show of it, at least.

"What if you can't change his mind?" he asked.

"Then we'll have to think of something else, won't we? Something like a plan B."

Her use of *we* was not lost on him. He smiled. "Then we might have to think fast. The Edgeway folks are good to go on this project, but they won't wait forever."

"Just a few days," she said. "Understand, I don't want to harm Burke in any way. All I want is to save his business from going under, any way I can."

"Of course you do. I want the same thing. Burke gave me a break and made me partner. We've been friends for years." He sliced off a chunk of rare steak and speared it with his fork. "So are we on the same team?"

"It appears we are." The lie made Allison feel nauseous.

"Then will I see you tomorrow afternoon?"

"If you need me."

Garrett didn't answer right away. Instead, his hand slid across the table and covered hers with its warm, damp weight. A shudder passed through her body. Heaven help her, this could only mean one thing. And it was the last thing she'd expected—especially since she knew he was sleeping with Monica.

"I need you in more ways than you can imagine,

Allison," he said, releasing her hand. "Now what do you say we finish our dinner so I can get you back to your car?"

Allison made an effort to eat, but she could barely swallow her food. If she wanted to learn Garrett's plans, she'd be smart to encourage him. But how far was too far? She was playing a dangerous game, and her husband's conniving partner had just raised the stakes.

By dusk, the rain had moved in, sweeping across the lake in a bank of black clouds, then fading to a sulky drizzle as the night wore on.

Brianna lay on her bed, curled under the pink and blue afghan her mother had crocheted more than a decade ago. She held her phone, cradling it against her cheek as she talked with Liam.

"When I ride the bike, it's like something's missing," he said. "It's you, holding on behind me."

"I miss you, too," she said.

"How was your first day as a reporter?"

She laughed. "Not bad. I got to interview people at the fish hatchery for a feature in the next edition. Not exactly Pulitzer Prize material, but at least it'll help my résumé."

"And the application to Northwestern?"

"I emailed it off tonight. But I don't have a good feeling about it. I'm applying to Missouri State as well, just in case."

"Smart move." He hesitated. "I have some news, too. My boss here at the garage has offered me a buy-in partnership. I pay him what I've saved up, then a percentage of what I make every month.

When he retires in five years, I can refinance the balance and have my own business."

"Oh," Brianna said. Should she be happy or devastated? Owning the garage was Liam's dream. But it would tie him to Evanston for years, if not for life. What if she couldn't go back to Northwestern? Did she love Liam enough to give up her own dream to be with him?

"I don't have to make a decision right away," Liam said. "But it would help to know what you and I would be looking at. You're an important part of all this, Brianna."

After telling him goodnight and ending the call, Brianna lay back on the pillow, tears flooding her eyes. What if Northwestern didn't let her back in? She had a B-plus average—not bad but not outstanding. And the fact that she'd dropped out of fall semester because of an arrest wouldn't help her case.

She couldn't afford to wait for months, or even weeks, for an answer, especially when that answer would likely be no. She would give it a couple of days, then call the dean, she decided. At least, after that, she'd have a better idea of what to expect.

She could only hope that she wouldn't have to choose between getting her education and being with Liam.

So many decisions to make. What if she were to be reaccepted by Northwestern, only to learn that her father couldn't spare the money to pay her tuition? She would have to get a job or a student loan, maybe both—not the end of the world, but these things would take planning.

She'd thought about talking to her father. But

lately, he'd seemed so preoccupied that she could barely get through to him. Garrett had always been willing to lend her an ear. Allison had warned her to avoid him, but surely he was still her friend. Surely he'd be able to give her a clear picture of what was happening with the business, and perhaps offer some practical advice.

Maybe in the next few days she would give him a call, or drop by the office as she'd often done in past years. After all, what harm could it possibly do?

CHAPTER 12

The next morning, Allison drove Burke to the bank to deliver the loan application. Burke had insisted that he could drive himself, but since he was still on pain meds, and not allowed behind the wheel, Allison had talked him out of it.

Even with the low-dose opioids the doctor had limited him to, she could tell he was in pain. Showered, shaved, and dressed in wool slacks, a cashmere polo shirt, and a tweed sport jacket, he looked strong and healthy. But he sat gingerly in the car, bracing his body against the bumps and turns, and grimacing when the small car hit a rough patch of road.

Last night she'd told him everything that she'd seen and heard at the agency, including the presence of the Edgeway lawyer, the plans for the client contracts, and the fact that Garrett was sleeping with the new receptionist.

She'd left out just one thing—Garrett's move on

her at the restaurant. Telling Burke about that small incident would have triggered a blowup.

This morning Burke appeared calm on the surface. But Allison knew he was seething with anxiety. His partner had betrayed him, and the business he'd worked half a lifetime to build was being stolen from him by a gang of criminals.

Only the bank loan could save him.

Allison pulled into a parking spot outside the bank. "Do you want me to go inside with you?" she asked.

"No, wait here." He climbed out of the car with the application in his hand. Allison watched as he walked to the bank entrance, making a painful effort to balance his stride. He was doing his best to appear fully recovered, but he was far from it. She couldn't help being proud of him. He was her warrior, returning to battle in spite of his wounds.

How she loved him, this proud, stubborn, gallant man of hers.

She waited, the minutes crawling past. They'd arrived at the bank at 9:30. It was 9:50 when he came out again and walked toward the car, limping slightly now. He looked pale and shaken. Allison's heart dropped.

"What is it?" she asked as he climbed into the car. "Did they take your application?"

"Yes." He sank into the seat with visible pain. "They said everything looked good, but it's a lot of money. They promised to get back to me in the next couple of days."

"But something's wrong. What is it?"

"Start the car. I'll tell you on the way home," he said.

Allison drove out of the parking lot. "Tell me."

He took a long breath. "When I walked in, the loan officer, Phil Gunderson, was surprised to see me. He said that a few days ago, somebody from the agency—it must've been Garrett—had called and told him to cancel the loan application. He said I'd signed the partnership agreement with Edgeway and wouldn't be needing the money. He even offered to fax the bank a notarized copy of the contract."

Allison gasped. "But you hadn't even submitted the application."

"I know. That's the strangest thing of all. Whoever called the bank assumed I'd already applied for the loan. He sounded almost embarrassed when Phil told him he didn't have the application."

"But they've got it now, and they know that you really do need the loan."

"Yes. But somebody else may have forged my signature on that contract, and notarized it, too. We need to go to the police."

"But first we need evidence that a crime's been committed," Allison said. "You say Garrett, or whoever it was, offered to fax a copy of the contract?"

"Yes, but Phil told him not to bother. Too bad. Otherwise, we could've gotten a copy from the bank."

"I'll be back at work this afternoon," Allison said. "Maybe I can find that forged agreement and make a copy."

"I still don't like your being there, Allison. Those people know how to play rough. Anything could go wrong."

"Don't worry. I'll just play the dumb blonde. I'll be fine." Allison spoke to reassure him, but she knew that finding and making a copy of the contract would be difficult and dangerous. Burke was right, anything could go wrong. But she couldn't let the danger stop her.

"I'm asking you one last time, Allison. Don't go back to that place. Let the police handle this." Dressed in sweats and sneakers again, Burke sat in his armchair, finishing the ham, cheese, and mushroom omelet Allison had cooked for him. The trip to the bank had worn him out and left him in more pain than usual. He was doing his best to hide it, but Allison wasn't fooled.

"You know that getting the police involved would just set off alarms," she said. "Any evidence would vanish as if it had never existed. The same thing would happen if you tried to intervene. I'm the only one Garrett trusts."

"Don't be too sure of that. Garrett isn't stupid. And I met a couple of those Edgeway goons before the accident. They're straight out of central casting for *The Godfather*. Only they're the real thing. They could literally make you disappear. I've even wondered whether the brakes on my Porsche were tampered with."

"Your Porsche was in the garage. And nobody could have known you would leave that night, or that it would rain."

"That's what I keep reminding myself. But when something like this happens, you start questioning your own judgment."

"You don't remember the accident?"

"Not a damned thing worth remembering."

Allison picked up the tray she'd brought into his

room. "Get some rest," she said. "And don't worry. I'll be careful."

"I'd stop you if I could. But I know better," he said. "I'll just ask for one thing. If you feel you're in the slightest danger, promise me you'll walk out of that door, get in your car and leave."

She stood in the doorway, his gaze riveting her in place. "I promise," she said. "Now get some sleep. I'll see you when I get home."

She carried the tray into the kitchen, tidied up, and found her jacket, keys, and purse. When she tiptoed down the hall and opened the door to Burke's room, she saw that he was lying on the bed, his eyes closed in sleep. She had made him a promise to flee from any threat of danger. But what if breaking that promise meant finding the evidence they needed so desperately?

"I love you, Burke," she whispered. Then she turned away and went out to her car.

As she arrived at the agency, she saw Garrett's black Escalade parked out front. Next to it was a high-end model white Lincoln with rental plates. Best guess— someone from Edgeway had flown in for a meeting. This might not be a good day to look for the contract. But maybe she'd get lucky. All she could do was keep her head down and her eyes open.

"Good afternoon, Mrs. Caldwell." Monica greeted Allison from behind the front desk. Her mouth was smiling, but her eyes were not. Did the voluptuous blonde suspect her of being a rival for Garrett's attentions? The thought made Allison shudder, but if it was true, she'd be foolish not to use Monica's jealousy to her advantage.

"Hello, Monica," Allison said. "Is something special going on today?"

One carefully penciled eyebrow twitched upward. "I wouldn't call it special. Just Mr. Kaplan and Mr. Zacharias here to look over the bids for the theater. They're meeting in Mr. Miles's office, so they won't disturb you. You'll be able to review those contracts in peace."

"Thanks." Allison nodded. So much for sneaking into Garrett's office to look for the contract. She still had Burke's keys in her purse. Maybe she'd be better off staying after closing time or coming back at night.

"Oh, just so you'll be aware," Monica said. "We had a security alarm with a motion sensor installed this morning. The Edgeway people ordered and paid for it. It's to be turned on whenever the office is closed. Not that you'd have any reason to come in after hours."

"No, of course not." Scratch that idea, Allison thought. She was about to walk away when another thought occurred to her.

"Does anyone in the office happen to be a notary?" she asked. "A friend of mine needs her will notarized, and I thought maybe . . ." Allison let the words trail off.

"I'm a notary," Monica said. "It'll be useful, with all the contract work we'll be doing here. But I'm not in the habit of doing favors for people's friends. Tell her to go to her bank. Somebody there should be able to help her."

"Thank you, I will." Allison turned and walked away, past the cubicles and down the hall. Burke's office—temporarily hers—was open, the desk piled with more contracts to review and add to the database. The next door, the one to Garrett's office, was closed. She could hear male voices through the wall but couldn't make out anything that was being said.

So much for her daring, dangerous spy mission.

At least she'd learned that Monica could have notarized the fake signature on the document. That, in itself, proved nothing. Copying Burke's scrawling signature would have been easy. He had signed most of these contracts. And Edgeway probably had access to a skilled forger. But what about the date? If the signature had been dated during the time Burke was in the hospital, on painkillers, that would be a red flag.

As Allison worked, she tried to imagine what would happen if Burke were to get the bank loan. Would Edgeway fold their cards and leave, or would they take the fake agreement and dig in, forcing Burke to take them to court in a case that could delay the remodeling for months, causing the theater to miss the profitable spring season and the loan payments to fall into default?

It appeared that Edgeway's original intent had been to block the bank loan, leaving Burke with no choice except to take on his new partners. The forged agreement would enable them to get bids and start the remodeling while they waited for Burke to give in and accept the inevitable.

Now, if Burke were to get the loan, the complications could be just as bad, or even worse.

There was only one sure way to save the situation—prove criminal intent on the part of Garrett and Edgeway. And that, Allison knew, would be up to her.

She worked uninterrupted until about three thirty. She was thinking about a break when she heard the door to Garrett's office open, followed by the sound of approaching footsteps and the murmur of male voices. An instant later, Garrett stepped into her office, followed by two men. Allison recognized Kaplan, the lawyer. The bigger, older man in the tailored Italian suit would be Zacharias.

As Allison rose to take their handshakes, Garrett made the introductions. "Gentlemen, this is Allison Caldwell, the newest member of our team. She'll be bringing her husband on board as soon as he's recovered. Allison, you've already met Joe. Theo Zacharias here is the big boss, so be nice to him."

"I'm sure you're always nice, Allison." Zacharias's voice was startlingly deep, his hand huge. "Welcome aboard."

"We're breaking to go and eat," Garrett said. "Monica will be here in case you need anything."

"I'll be fine, thanks. Enjoy your meal." Allison took her seat again as the men left.

From down the hall she heard Zacharias's booming voice. "Are you crazy, Garrett, bringing Burke Caldwell's wife in here?"

"Relax," Garrett said. "Allison's on our side. If anybody can talk Burke into becoming a team player, she can."

"And if she can't?" The stentorian voice was fading. Garrett's reply was too faint to hear. But the thought of how he might have answered sent a chill through her body.

Once she was sure the men were gone, Allison rose and walked down the hall to the restroom. Coming out, she could hear Monica talking to her friend on the phone. That giggle was as annoying as fingernails scratching a blackboard, but at least it told her that the receptionist was occupied.

Stepping softly, she paused outside the closed door to Garrett's office. If the three men had left without putting important papers away, she might be lucky enough to find what she needed.

Allison had worn a loose-fitting jacket with pockets that would hold her phone. Now she took the phone out of her pocket. Her pulse skipped as her free hand tried the doorknob.

The knob didn't budge. The door was locked. And she already knew that she didn't have the key. The two large keys on Burke's key ring opened the front door and his office. Unless Garrett had switched the office keys, too . . .

Racing back into her office, she found Burke's keys in her purse and tried again. But neither of the large keys on the ring would open Garrett's door. She was out of luck. And Monica was no longer talking on the phone.

Spirits sagging, she slunk back into Burke's office, sat down at the desk and picked up the next contract in the stack. She was still working when the three men returned at four fifteen. They went into Garrett's office and closed the door behind them. They were still inside at five, when Allison logged off the computer and left for home. Her efforts to find the forged contract had come to nothing. But at least Burke would be relieved that she was safe.

On the way home, Allison picked up a big order of Chinese takeout. She was hungry, and hopefully

Burke and Brianna would be, too. Maybe tonight they could even eat together at the table like a real family.

Kate had been a legendary cook, or so Allison had been told by Burke's friends. Allison's own cooking skills were limited to the basics, and when she was working, as she'd done most of her life, she didn't have the time or energy for fancy meals. For tonight, takeout would have to do.

Coming into the house, carrying the large sack, she passed the open door to Burke's study and noticed that the light was on. He was at his desk, working on his computer. He looked up and gave her a smile. "Hey, that smells good," he said.

"Chinese. It'll be on the table in a few minutes. Is Brianna home?"

"I think she's in her room," he said. "I can call her phone if she isn't on it, talking to that long-haired boyfriend of hers. First, how did your afternoon go?"

"So-so. Nothing big to report. I'll tell you later."

"Fine. I'll call Brianna and tell her there's food down here."

He sounded good, Allison thought as she unloaded the sack on the kitchen table and set three places. Maybe he'd gotten some rest, or maybe he was feeling better about getting the loan application to the bank.

"Chinese! Yum! I'm starved!" Brianna burst into the kitchen. As Allison filled glasses with ice water, she rummaged in the cupboard and found napkins and soy sauce. "I hope Dad is going to eat with us."

"He is. Why don't you go tell him everything's ready."

She darted off and came back moments later with Burke. They took their seats and began passing around the paper cartons filled with steamed rice, noodles, dumplings, meat, and vegetables. *This is how it should be*, Allison thought. The three of them together, everybody eating, nobody sulking or fighting. Why couldn't this happen more often?

"How was your job today, Brianna?" Allison asked, hoping to start a conversation.

Brianna wrinkled her pretty nose. "I've had better days. In the morning, I interviewed the supervisor of the sewage disposal plant for the paper. Then in the afternoon I put in three hours of community service helping clean at the county animal shelter. Those poor dogs. It was all I could do to walk out of there without taking three or four of them with me." She turned to her father. "I really miss Captain, Dad. Can't we get another dog?"

"Dogs need a lot of time and attention," Burke said. "You can't take a dog when you go back to school—unless you plan to keep living here."

"But couldn't you and Allison take care of the dog for me?"

"Don't even think about it," Burke said. "Things are going to be crazy enough around here without a dog to worry about."

Brianna added some soy sauce to her cashew chicken. "Liam loves dogs," she said. "Maybe he could . . ." She trailed off, as if realizing she'd said the wrong thing.

"Liam again." Burke's face had become a thundercloud. "How many times do I have to tell you, Brianna? You can do better than a long-haired biker bum who works on cars and lives over a garage."

Tears glistened in Brianna's eyes. "Don't say that! Liam works hard. He's saving money for his own business, and he loves me."

"I love you, too, Brianna. That's why I worry about your throwing your life away for a man who's not worthy of you. What would your mother say?"

Brianna rose from her chair. "My mother would say that you can't judge a book by its cover, and you can't judge a man without getting to know him. Please, Dad, don't jump to conclusions until you've seen Liam and talked with him face-to-face." She turned to Allison, her eyes pleading for support. "You met Liam. What did you think of him, Allison?"

"He seemed very nice," Allison said. "He was polite and responsible, and he even insisted on paying for our dinner. Brianna's right, Burke. You should at least meet him before passing judgment. Liam might have a few rough edges, but not every long-haired biker is, as you say, a bum."

Burke's dark look was enough to let Allison know that she'd come down on the wrong side. But Brianna was right. Liam deserved a chance to prove that he was a worthy man.

"I'll think about meeting him," Burke said. "But don't rush me, you two. I've got more urgent things on my mind right now."

"Thank you, Dad." Brianna sat down again and speared another egg roll from the box. Silence hung over the table.

"I have a question." Allison broke the silence. "Your boat. I've heard your friends mention it, Burke, and I've seen it in photographs. I know you have it in storage at the marina. Why don't we take it out on the water sometime?"

Burke and Brianna glanced at each other. In bringing up the boat, Allison had feared she might be touching on an emotional subject. Evidently she'd been right.

"We haven't taken the boat out since Kate passed," Burke said. "It wasn't that we planned it that way. But without Kate, there just didn't seem much reason to go on the water. As time went by, I had the boat put in dry dock because it was cheaper and easier on the hull. Lately I've thought about selling it. If we run short of cash, I might have to."

"Oh, no, Dad!" Brianna cried. "You can't sell the *Lady Brianna*! Mom loved that boat. I love it, too. And I'd love to go out on the water again! We could take Allison. We could even take Liam if he'll come. You could teach him to fish."

Burke shook his head. "Why do I have the feeling I'm being railroaded here?" he muttered. "All right, I'll think about it. But not until my back's stronger. I can't go climbing around in a boat and risk another injury."

"Thank you, Dad!" Brianna jumped up and ran around the table to give her father a hug and a kiss on the cheek.

"Don't thank me too soon," Burke said. "By the time I'm fit enough to take the boat out, it'll be winter. That means nothing's going to happen until next spring."

"But you won't sell her. Surely you won't!" Brianna's expression could have melted a heart of granite.

"Honey, with all that's going on in the next few months, I can't promise anything," Burke said. "But with winter coming, it's not likely I'll get an offer anytime soon. That's the best I can do for now."

Brianna looked downcast, then brightened. "But we can still invite Liam to come this fall, can't we? We'll want to do it soon, before it gets too cold, in case he wants to ride his motorcycle."

"That strikes me as a very long motorcycle ride," Burke said.

"Not for Liam. A few years ago, he and some friends biked all the way to California and back. He has a book by Jack Kerouac, who used to be his hero. But Liam says he's got more sense than to take off on that kind of road trip now."

Burke scowled. "If I'm supposed to be impressed . . ."

"You'll like him, Dad. I know you will," Brianna said.

"A long-haired king of the road." Burke shook his head. "I'll reserve judgment on that. But all right, go ahead and invite him. Let's see how he behaves around civilized people."

"That's not fair, Dad!" Brianna said. "If you're expecting Liam to act like he's not housebroken, you're going to be pleasantly disappointed!"

They finished the meal under a truce. Brianna offered to clean up the kitchen. Burke mumbled something about paperwork and disappeared into his study. Allison went upstairs to change out of her work clothes. She hung up her jacket and wool slacks, and tossed her blouse and bra in the laundry basket. Finding a stretchy sports bra in the drawer, she pulled it over her head, then put on her warm sweats and slippers. She still needed to tell Burke about her day. After butting heads with his strong-willed daughter, he might be in a sour mood. But Allison couldn't allow that to matter.

Coming out into the hall, she could hear Brianna's shower running. Downstairs, Burke's study was dark and empty. So was the room where he slept these days. Standing in the open doorway, Allison gazed into the shadows, wondering how long this arrangement would go on—her husband sleeping downstairs, while she spent every night alone in their king-size bed on the second floor.

True, Burke wasn't yet able to climb a long flight of stairs. But that didn't mean she couldn't come down and join him in the double bed. Even if they didn't make love—although, with care, that might be possible—just snuggling could go a long way to easing the tension that had sprung up between them since the accident.

But this was Burke's room, not hers. If he wanted her in his bed, he would have to let her know. Joining him without an invitation could prove to be awkward—or even humiliating.

From the den, off the far side of the kitchen, she could hear the faint sound of the big-screen TV. Good. At least Burke had decided to relax instead of laboring in his study.

She followed the sound to find him leaning into the corner of the sofa with cushions supporting his back on both sides. Flames glowed in the gas fireplace. Mounted above the mantel, the TV was showing a nature program about coral reefs. Burke used the remote to switch it off as Allison walked into the room. "Come join me," he said.

She crossed the room and sank down beside him, letting the warmth from the fireplace creep around her. His arm lay lightly behind her shoulders. She settled back against it. "This was a good idea," she said.

"It was, wasn't it? So how did your afternoon go?"

Trust Burke to get right to the point. "Well, I didn't get a chance to look for the contract," she said. "But I did find out that the new receptionist is a notary.

Without the document, there's no proof that she notarized the signature, but she certainly could have
done it."

"It's a start. Was Garrett there?"

"He was. But he spent most of the time shut in his
office with the lawyer and the big boss from Edgeway."

"Theo Zacharias. I met him a few days before my
accident," Burke said.

"Garrett introduced us briefly when they broke to
go out and eat. Just as you said—straight out of central casting for *The Godfather*. While they were gone, I
tried to get into Garrett's office, but it was locked.
Aside from the busywork I was doing, that about
sums up my day."

Burke's arm curved around her shoulders, drawing her into his warmth. "I still don't like your being
there, Allison. Zacharias is a dangerous man. Be
careful."

"You, too." She hesitated, then decided she should
tell him. "As they were walking away down the hall, I
heard Garrett say that I'd been hired to convince
you to join the team. Zacharias asked him what
would happen if you refused."

"And what did Garrett say?"

"I don't know. By then they'd gone too far for me
to hear. But it scared me, Burke. It made me afraid
for you."

His arm tightened in a protective hug. "You don't
have to go back there," he said. "We'll find another
way. I told the people at the bank that we need an
answer on the loan as soon as possible. If we get the
money—"

"I thought about that. The Edgeway Group could

still fight us. We might even have to take them to court, which could hold up the renovations on the theater for months. And what if we don't get the loan?"

"I don't even want to think about that right now."

"I've got to go back there, Burke. We need a copy of that contract with the forged signature—or some other evidence we can take to the authorities. It's the only way we'll beat them."

Burke took a deep breath. "I told you to get out while you could. It's still not too late."

"I know," Allison said. "But I'm not going anywhere, so deal with it, mister." She tilted her face upward and gave his cheek a playful kiss.

A small, broken sound rose from his throat. His arms went around her, pulling her to his chest. When his mouth found hers, his kiss was fierce and hungry, devouring her with his need. Her arms went around his neck, fingers raking his hair. Her mouth opened, her tongue meeting his. The contact triggered a spark that became a bonfire of desire.

Where her hip pressed his sweatpants, she could feel the hard bulge of his erection. It could happen now, she thought. Except it wouldn't because Brianna was still awake and might decide to join them in the den. But it could happen later tonight, if she could find the courage to tiptoe down the stairs and slip into the double bed beside him.

She moved against him. He groaned. His hand found the hem of her shirt and slid up her back to her sports bra, feeling for the clasp that wasn't there. His fingers fumbled in mounting frustration.

"Damn it, Kate," he muttered. "Where's—" He broke off, realizing what he'd just said.

Kate.

Allison went rigid in his arms. Her hands pushed him away. "Not another word," she said. "I have to go."

Half tripping over the ottoman, she stumbled blindly out of the room and headed for the stairs.

CHAPTER 13

Allison closed the bedroom door behind her and sank onto the bed. I'm a big girl. I'm not going to cry, she told herself. Burke had made an honest mistake, something that happened from time to time, especially when he was tired or stressed. Maybe this time, it was talking about the boat that had triggered the name.

She couldn't blame him. After all, how many parents mixed up their children's names, even though they knew better? Burke's calling her by his first wife's name was no more than an innocent slip of the tongue.

But his timing couldn't have been worse!

She didn't want to go back and face him, but it was too early to go to bed. Anyway, she was too upset to sleep. Going to the closet, she switched her slippers for her running shoes. After throwing on a warm jacket, she stole downstairs to the back door. She needed to work off a serious case of angst.

She hit the path running—not a good idea in

near darkness. Her sneaker caught a broken spot in the asphalt pavement. She twisted her ankle and went down hard.

For a moment she lay still, her breath coming in gasps, the tears springing to her eyes. You're all right, she told herself. It just hurts, that's all.

That pretty much summed up her life tonight.

Recovering, she sat up and moved her limbs cautiously. Nothing appeared broken. But her hands were skinned, her knees bruised, and her twisted ankle felt tender when she stood and put weight on it.

Idiot, she chastised herself. Why hadn't she brought a flashlight, or at least had the sense to slow down? She took a few careful steps. The ankle felt all right, and she didn't want to go back to the house yet. It wouldn't hurt to walk a little farther.

She hadn't told Burke or Brianna where she was going, but they both knew she liked to walk along the lakeshore. They probably wouldn't even miss her.

She moved along the path, favoring her ankle. A great horned owl, huge in the darkness, swooped low over her head, then glided away, as if the creature had seen her limping, thought she might be prey, then decided she'd be too heavy to carry off. The thought—ludicrous as it was—brought an ironic smile to Allison's lips.

By now the moon had come up, reflecting like a gold coin in the black water. By its light, she could see the old wooden pier, stretching its length out into the lake. Balancing carefully, she walked out to the end of it and stood there, feeling the night chill on her face, hearing the cry of a loon and watching the ripples spread where a fish jumped.

The time-weathered pier had been here many years. Had Kate walked out here on nights like this, taking a moment to be alone and think? Had she stood in this very spot after her affair had ended, wondering how to tell Burke—or whether to tell him at all? Had she come here to face her cancer diagnosis and to contemplate the end of her life?

Tonight Allison could almost feel Kate's presence. But she didn't believe in ghosts—not her mother's, not Kevin's, or any of the other people she'd known and lost. Kate was gone, leaving only her husband, her daughter, and those blessed, cursed letters as a challenge to the woman who would take her place.

She shivered under her jacket. It was time to go back. Would Burke be waiting by the back door to scold her for going off and worrying him? But no, tonight he would avoid any confrontation that could arise from his having called her by the wrong name.

She entered by the back door to discover that she'd been right. The den was empty, the TV silent. At the foot of the stairs, she saw that Burke's door was closed, with no light showing through the crack underneath.

Limping on her twisted ankle, she climbed the stairs to her room and the solitary king-size bed. There would be no letter from Kate to read tonight. Except for the one that was sealed, she had read them all. Now she was on her own.

Brianna was driving to work the next morning when she got the phone call from the dean at Northwestern. Pulse racing, she pulled off the road and switched off the engine to take the call.

"Thanks for getting back to me so soon," she said. "As I told you, I need to know about my readmission as soon as possible."

"I understand." The dean, a middle-aged woman, was pleasant but not warm. "I got to work this morning with a little time to spare, so I read through your application. Unfortunately . . ." The woman paused. Brianna's heart sank.

"Unfortunately," the dean continued, "your grades aren't high enough to compete with the new students who are applying every day. A B-plus average would be good enough to keep you in school if you were already here. But it's not good enough to get you readmitted—especially since you were barely passing most of your classes before you dropped out this fall. I'm sorry. I know it's a disappointment. But there are other colleges."

"Yes, I know. Thank you for your time." Brianna ended the call, put her forehead on the steering wheel, and cried. She'd known this might happen, and she'd done her best to prepare herself for bad news. But when it came, it was like being punched in the face. Until now she hadn't realized how much she'd wanted to go back to Northwestern—and to Liam.

After wiping her eyes and blowing her nose, she started the car and pulled back onto the road. Last year she'd earned decent grades. But then, this fall, she'd done the unthinkable—she'd fallen head over heels in love.

It hadn't been Liam's fault. He'd encouraged her to study for exams and get her assignments in on time. But all she'd wanted to do was be with him. And when she wasn't with him, all she'd wanted to do was think about him.

And then her father had wrecked the Porsche and almost died. She'd had no choice except to come home, where she'd gotten herself arrested. Now she was trying to grow up, repair the damage, and take charge of her life. But it wasn't going to be easy.

She would wait until tonight to give Liam the bad news. It didn't make sense to call him now and ruin his day. Her father could wait, too. Meanwhile she would need to start looking at other options. She had to work this morning, but later today it might not hurt to get some advice from an old friend.

Allison woke to the aromas of fresh coffee and bacon drifting up the stairs. Sunlight was streaming into the room. It had taken her hours to fall asleep last night. When slumber finally came, it had pulled her under like anesthesia.

She wondered who could be cooking in the kitchen?

Swinging her legs off the bed, she stood. Her ankle was still sore, her hands scraped from falling on the rough asphalt. Wincing with each step, she found her robe, slipped it on, and limped out into the hall.

Brianna had already left for work. Her door was partway open, her bed neatly made. The photo of her family sat in its usual place, on the bookshelf. Kate's sunlit, freckled face smiled at Allison from the frame.

Let him go, Kate! Stop coming between us!

Allison projected the thought, as if it could penetrate the glass and somehow reach its target. But Kate's smile was unchanging, as if she knew that she'd always be first.

Allison closed Brianna's door and went on downstairs. She found Burke standing by the stove, tend-
ing bacon in a cast-iron skillet. Freshly shaved,
dressed in chinos and a long-sleeved polo, he looked
fit and healthy. But fixing breakfast? That was something new.

Was this his way of making up for last night?

Allison blinked herself fully awake. "What are you
doing?" she asked.

"I'm declaring myself recovered," he said. "I've
been off the pain pills for twenty-four hours. I was
hoping you'd let me take you for a drive this morning after breakfast."

"A drive where?"

"To see an old friend. Come on, sit down."

Neither of them mentioned his calling her by
Kate's name last night. It had happened before and
would no doubt happen again. Aggravating as Allison
found it, there was no point in making it an issue.

Allison crossed the kitchen to the table. Only then
did he notice that she was limping. He frowned.
"What on earth—?"

"I went for a walk last night and twisted my ankle.
It's nothing."

"Nothing? I don't think so." He pulled a chair away
from the table. "Sit down. Let's have a look." He motioned her to the chair. Allison sat down and raised
her pajama-clad leg for him to see. He dropped partway to a crouch, wincing with sudden pain. "It seems
I'm not as recovered as I'd hoped," he said, moving
another chair to face hers and sitting down. "Now
let's see that ankle."

His hand cradled her bare foot, strong, gentle fingers testing the pain. "It doesn't seem swollen. Does

it hurt here?" He probed just above the ankle bone. She whimpered.

"Bad?"

"Just a little. Not too much."

"Here?" His hand moved higher, pushing back the loose-fitting leg of her pajamas. His touch sent electric tingles up her thighs. She stifled a moan that had nothing to do with pain. He had to know what was happening—and what might happen if he continued.

Was it too soon? Should she stop him? Could she?

She sensed the slight quickening of his breath as he moved again, higher up the inside of her calf. "What about here?"

Her lips parted. "I think . . ."

"You think what?" His voice was husky.

At that instant, a bitter smell penetrated her nostrils. "I think the bacon's burning!" she exclaimed.

With a muttered oath, Burke lunged toward the stove and moved the smoking skillet off the burner. He gazed down at the charred remains of the bacon. "Would you settle for coffee and toast?" he asked.

At least they could still laugh together.

Half an hour later, they were in Allison's Honda Civic with Burke driving. She could tell he was in some pain, but she knew better than to mention it. Burke's pride wouldn't let him admit he was hurting.

"Where are we going?" she asked.

"You'll see. It isn't far. It feels good to be driving again. I was beginning to feel like a prisoner."

"Now you need to get a car."

"I'm working on it. I didn't get a great settlement for the Porsche—the word *vintage* translates as *old* to an insurance company. I might be driving around in some clunker—or better yet, maybe I can get a motorcycle, grow my hair long, and pal around with Brianna's new boyfriend, what's-his-name."

"It's Liam, and he seems like a decent guy. He deserves a chance to show you who he is before you judge him."

Burke sighed. "Yes, I remember what I promised Brianna. But she's too young to know her own mind. And I didn't raise my daughter to be a damned biker chick. Look what's happening with her. She never got arrested till she met him!"

"For your information, Liam doesn't drink at all. And he wasn't even around when she had those beers with her friends and tried to drive home. All your daughter is asking is that you meet him before you jump to conclusions."

"I said I would, didn't I?" Burke turned off the main road at a sign with an arrow that said MARINA.

"We're going to see your boat?"

"That's right. Brianna got me thinking last night. We could still have a few weeks of good weather left. The *Lady Brianna* deserves better than to end her days with us in dry dock. If there's a chance I'll have to sell her later, why not take her out on the water and enjoy her—even if it's only one last time?"

"Oh! Brianna would love that!" Allison said. "So would I. I've never been out on a boat! Could we fish? I don't know if I could catch one, but I'd love to watch."

Burke pulled into the marina parking lot and turned to look at her. "You'd really like to go out in the boat? You never said a thing. I always assumed you wouldn't want to."

"And I always assumed you didn't want to take me," Allison said. "All the time I've lived here, I've heard how much Kate loved that boat. Now, all those memories . . . Won't it be hard for you?"

"Maybe. But not so much if it makes Brianna happy—and you. Come on. Today I need to inspect the hull and make sure she's shipshape. If nothing needs fixing, we can talk to Brianna and make some plans. I know she'll want to take her boyfriend if he can come for a visit. But we can work that out."

He got out of the car and came around to let Allison out. She handed him the cane she'd brought along. He'd refused to take it into the bank. But on the uneven ground here, he was going to need it. Allison had wrapped her ankle before leaving the house and had no trouble walking.

He took the cane without comment and led her to a long, open-sided shelter where the dry-docked boats were kept. There were about fifteen in storage here, most of them mounted on small trailers.

Allison recognized the *Lady Brianna* from the name painted on the hull. Sleek and white as a gull, it was a beautiful boat. Burke stood back looking at it for a long moment. Allison kept still, thinking of the memories that must be going through his mind—Kate and Brianna with their friends and the dog, the fish they'd caught and the fun they'd had.

"What do you think of her?" he said at last.

"She's breathtaking," Allison said. "And I agree with you. She deserves better than to sit here alone, out of the water."

Burke circled the boat slowly, inspecting every inch of the hull for any cracks or chips. "She looks sound," he said. "Tonight when Brianna's home, we'll make some plans."

"Will you be all right climbing in and out of the boat?" Allison remembered his telling Brianna that his back needed time to heal. But maybe he'd just been making excuses.

"I'll be fine. I'm getting stronger every day." He glanced at the Rolex watch Allison had given him last Christmas. "I guess it's time we were getting you home to change, unless you've come to your senses and changed your mind about going to the agency today."

"You know I have to go," she said. "Maybe today I'll find that contract, or overhear some secret that will make a difference."

"Just be careful," he said. "And remember what you promised me—that you'll get out of there at the first sign of danger."

"I'll remember." Allison wasn't looking forward to going back to the agency and pretending to cooperate with people who were out to steal her husband's business. But she would do whatever it took to get to the truth—and that included breaking her promise to run if things got dangerous.

They were walking toward the car when a thought struck her. She hesitated, then decided to speak her mind. "Where is Kate buried? I'd like to visit her grave sometime, just to leave flowers and pay tribute. Does that sound strange to you?"

He gave her a slightly puzzled look. "Actually, it sounds very nice," he said. "But—" He paused.

"But what?"

"Kate wasn't buried. She was cremated. That was what she wanted. She asked to have her ashes scattered in this lake because she loved it so much. She was never happier than when she was on the water. So, in a way, you've already visited her grave. And now you know."

She walked beside him in silence for a moment. "And the boat? Is that why—?"

Burke nodded. "The last time Brianna and I took the boat out on the water was the day we scattered her mother's ashes."

Burke swung the small Honda back onto the main road and gunned the engine. It felt good to be in the driver's seat, even though the car wasn't exactly a thrill ride. And it felt invigorating to be out doing something, even if it was only inspecting the boat, and even though, by now, his back hurt like hell. Maybe he'd stopped the opioids too soon. But he wasn't about to go back on them. With luck, he could find some ibuprofen in the medicine cabinet to take the edge off.

He glanced at Allison, his eyes tracing her fine-drawn profile against the side window of the car. She was everything a woman should be—beautiful, brave, tender, and passionate. He remembered last night, holding her in his arms, feeling her move against him as he'd kissed her. He'd begun to feel like a whole man again when that damn fool slip of the tongue had ruined the moment. He couldn't blame her for walking out. What he feared was that one of these times, he might push her too far, and she wouldn't come back.

He had loved Kate. Despite the rough patches over the years, they had fit each other like a pair of comfortable old shoes. But his love for Allison was something almost akin to worship. She was so elegant, so perfect, that sometimes he found it hard to believe she was his.

She hadn't signed on for this present mess. But even when he'd told her to leave, she'd stuck by him like a champ. And now she was playing a dangerous game to help him win. The need to pull her back and charge into the fight was driving him crazy. But much as he hated to admit it, she was right. As long as Garrett trusted her, she was the only one who could do what needed to be done.

Still, the thought of her in that place, with those people, was like a waking nightmare. He would rather lose everything he owned than cause harm to come to the woman he loved.

Keeping his eyes on the road, he reached across the console, found her hand, and clasped it. *Don't go*, he wanted to tell her again. But he knew that Allison wouldn't listen.

That afternoon, dressed for work in tailored slacks and a black blazer with an inside pocket, Allison drove to the agency and pulled into an empty parking spot. Garrett's Escalade was parked between her Honda and the front entrance, but the big white rented Lincoln, which would have been parked right in front, was nowhere in sight. Were Kaplan and Zacharias at lunch, or had the creepy pair left town? She could only hope they were gone. They reminded her of a lion and a jackal—powerful, alert, and deadly. And she was certain that they didn't trust her.

In the car, she took a moment to transfer her phone from her purse to the inner pocket of her blazer. If the chance came to photograph the fake contract, or any other document, she might have only seconds to take a picture and get the phone out of sight.

Fixing her face in an impersonal smile, she opened the front door and walked into the front office. Monica, wearing a low-cut pink angora sweater, was checking her makeup in a small compact mirror. She snapped it shut as Allison approached the desk.

"Hello, Monica," she said. "Do you know if Mr. Miles left me more work?"

Monica shook her head. "He said there were still plenty of files left from yesterday. He and the Edgeway people should be back from lunch soon. You can let him know if you run out of things to do."

"Thanks. I will." Allison walked past the cubicle area and down the hall. Garrett's door was closed. A tug at the knob confirmed that it was locked. Burke's office was open. Nothing to hide in here, Allison surmised as she walked into the room and sat down at the desk, which was stacked with files.

Burke's key ring was still in her purse. Yesterday she'd removed the keys to the wrecked Porsche, lessening the bulk. The remaining keys—to the house, to the office, and to what she'd discovered was Garrett's file cabinet—would fit in the pocket of her slacks without a telltale bulge.

She was about to sit down and start work when a distressing thought struck her. Hoping she was wrong, she walked over to the file cabinet, took the key ring out of her pocket and inserted the small key in the lock.

It turned easily.

This wasn't Burke's cabinet. This was Garrett's. The two cabinets had been switched.

She opened the drawers. The two top ones were filled with office supplies—reams of paper, notepads, pens, markers, clipboards, and computer manuals. The bottom two were empty, but the vacant file hangers suggested that the filed contracts on her desk had been stored here. Everything vital to the running of the business had been moved out.

Trembling slightly, she sank into the chair behind the desk. All this time, she'd let herself believe that Garrett trusted her, and that she could play him. Now she wasn't so sure.

Allison turned on her computer, brought up the database, and opened the next client file. She tried to work, but focusing was impossible. She was getting a headache. Questions tortured her mind.

What if there was no forged partnership document for her to find?

But there had to be. Garrett had offered to fax it to the bank. Somewhere, that document existed. She had to find it.

Allison couldn't stay in the chair. She pushed away from the desk and walked to the window, which faced an ugly brick wall. Staring through the glass, she tormented her mind with more possible scenarios.

What if Burke, with no bank loan and no other recourse, were forced to sign the agreement?

It made sense that they'd have an unsigned copy, ready for his signature. Once it was signed, the fake document would be destroyed.

But what if Burke refused to sign, leaving them with a forged document that he could, and would, dispute, perhaps in court?

The men he was up against were capable of getting him out of the way, then claiming that the forged contract was real, signed by Burke sometime before his untimely . . .

Dear God!

She was shaking. She had to sit down.

What if Burke's idea that the Porsche's brakes had been tampered with was right? Allison could almost picture it happening.

Garrett had been at the party. He'd arrived early to mingle with the arriving guests. He'd known where the Porsche was, and he'd known that Burke was the only person who drove it. He could have easily left the party long enough to slip downstairs to the garage, cut the brake lines, and return without being missed.

No one could have predicted the rainstorm or the problem at the theater. But that didn't matter. Sooner or later, Burke would have driven the car, and he always drove it fast on that steep, winding highway. The darkness and rain had only helped things along.

Only one thing had gone wrong. Burke hadn't died.

But no—her theory was ridiculous. Garrett might be a snake in the grass, but he wasn't a murderer. And this wasn't the 1920s. The Mob wouldn't kill somebody over a piece of property that they could just as easily walk away from.

Pulling herself together, she sat down again and went back to work. Somehow she had to find that forged contract. But jumping to wild conclusions wasn't going to help. Stay calm, focused, and alert. Wait for her chance. That was the only way to find what she needed.

A few minutes later, she heard men's voices up front. Garrett, Kaplan, and Zacharias had returned from lunch and were headed back in her direction. With her door partway open, Allison couldn't hear everything they were saying, but Zacharias's booming voice came through loud and clear.

"We've got time for a pit stop, and then we'll be on our way to the airport. We'll be back next month—we'll let you know when. But meanwhile, Garrett, we need this partnership mess straightened out. We can't start spending money based on a fake contract that won't hold up in court. You've got your marching orders. I want Burke Caldwell's signature on a bona fide contract, or I want him out of the picture. Understand?"

"Out of the picture?" The tremor in Garrett's voice was enough to convince Allison that Burke's accident had been just that—an accident.

"Out of the picture, whatever it takes," Zacharias growled. "I hope you're not as stupid as you sound."

"No, don't worry. I'll take care of everything," Garrett said.

"Fine. Call me if you need any help." Zacharias's heavy fist pounded on the door of the men's room. "Get the hell out of there, Kaplan. I've gotta take a leak!"

Allison kept her head down, pretending to work as the two men got ready to leave. Fear gnawed at her stomach. Had Zacharias really meant what he'd said? Was Burke really in danger of being killed if he didn't sign the contract? And did Zacharias really hold Garrett responsible for doing the job? Having met the big man, and knowing who he was, she had no doubt that the sickening answer to every question was yes.

She heard the sound of a toilet flushing, followed by the men's heavy footsteps fading toward the front desk. There were faint, gruff goodbyes, then the closing of a door. After a brief exchange with Monica, Garrett came back down the hall, walked into his office, and closed the door behind him.

Now Allison had a decision to make. She could sit here, play dumb, and wait for a chance to sneak into Garrett's office and look for the contract, or she could be bold enough to play the hand she'd been dealt. If she was going to act, it would have to be now. She was running out of time.

CHAPTER 14

Summoning her courage, she stood, walked out into the hall, and rapped lightly on Garrett's closed door.

"Garrett?"

There was no answer.

"Is it all right for me to come in?" she asked. "I think we need to talk."

"Come on in." His voice sounded muffled. When she opened the door and walked into the room, Garrett was at his desk, pouring himself a shot of Jack Daniel's.

"Have a seat," he said. "Would you like a drink?"

"No thanks," she said, taking the chair opposite the desk. "But go ahead. Something tells me you might need one."

"You heard Zacharias?"

"Without earplugs, it would've been impossible not to."

Garrett downed the shot of whiskey and poured himself another. "So what now?" he asked.

"I know you might not trust me. But for Burke's sake, I want to help you if I can. First I need some honest answers." The necessary lie made her wince. "Zacharias said something about a fake contract. What was he talking about?"

"Oh, hell," said Garrett. "In order for us to get bids on the theater update, we needed something to show the contractors, so they'd know the partnership was real and there'd be money coming in. While Burke was still in rehab, we got signatures on a copy of the partnership agreement and forged Burke's name. Kaplan did the copying, and Monica notarized it, so it looks legit. But it wouldn't fool an expert. And, of course, Burke would know that he didn't sign it. Things could get ugly if he were to see it and decide to sue."

"Which is why Zacharias gave you an ultimatum."

"Yup. The real contract is signed by the Edgeway folks, notarized, and waiting for Burke's John Hancock. No money changes hands until it's done."

Garrett poured himself another shot of whiskey. His face had the look of a man who'd just realized he might have gotten in over his head. Allison had already decided not to mention that she knew about his attempt to block the bank loan. Some surprises were better saved for later.

"Do you have the fake document here?" she asked. "Could I see it?"

He hesitated, then shrugged. "Oh, why the hell not?"

Getting up, he walked to the file cabinet and opened the top drawer. Near the front was a manila folder.

"Here it is." He laid the folder in front of Allison. She opened it and studied the document. Her heart was pounding, but she couldn't let her excitement show. "It looks pretty convincing," she said. "If I didn't know better, I'd have a hard time believing that wasn't Burke's signature. The only thing suspicious would be the date. When it was signed and notarized, Burke was still in the hospital, on opioids for pain."

"Well, it was good enough for the contractors." Garrett closed the folder and put it back in the file drawer. "Once we get Burke's real signature on the real partnership agreement, we can put this one through the shredder. That's where you come in."

He sat down again. His brown eyes studied her face, as if looking for some clue in her expression. "You heard what Zacharias told me. Burke's got to sign that contract."

"And I told you I wouldn't stand for Burke's being harmed," Allison said. "I know you've gotten yourself in pretty deep with Edgeway, Garrett. But I can't believe you'd hurt Burke, let alone have him killed."

"Maybe not. But I know people who would. He's got to sign, Allison. With that short-term note due in a couple of months and the American Heartland bleeding money, Edgeway's our only option. Can't you get that through his stubborn head? Otherwise—"

The ringing desk phone interrupted him. Garrett snatched it up. "What is it, Monica? . . . What? . . . Oh, hell! Tell him I'm on my way."

He gave the receiver an impatient slam. "That was Max at the theater. The matinee's about to start, and the power's gone out. The idiots can't figure out how to turn it on. Probably just the breaker box, but right now, they've got an audience sitting in the pitch-dark, and some of the kids are starting to cry."

Without another word, he dashed out to his car, leaving Allison alone in his office, with the file cabinet unlocked.

Stunned by the incredible stroke of luck, Allison sprang into action. After closing the office door and locking it from the inside, she hurried to the file cabinet and found the forged contract in the drawer where Garrett had put it.

With the pages spread on the desk, she took the phone out of her pocket and started taking pictures. Willing her hands not to shake, she snapped a variety of close-ups and longer-range shots, making sure to miss nothing. She even took shots of the desk and the office, to show where the document had been found. At last, satisfied that she'd done her best, she returned her phone to her pocket, gathered the pages in order, and put them in the folder. Mission accomplished. All she had to do now was put the contract away and leave.

She was opening the file drawer when she heard the faint rattle of someone tugging on the locked door, followed by the click of a key in the lock. The door swung open. Garrett stepped into the room, closing the door behind him. "The idiots didn't need me after all," he said. "I'd only gone a few blocks when I got the call—"

He stared at Allison, who stood frozen with one hand on the open drawer and the other holding the telltale folder. "What in hell's name are you doing, Allison?"

There could be no talking her way out of this. "I wanted another look at the contract," she said.

"You could have asked me."

Allison dropped the folder into the drawer and closed it. "Sorry. I would've asked if you'd been here. But no harm done. Now, if we're finished, I'll get back to work."

Heart pounding, she rounded the desk, intent on leaving. He stepped in front of her, blocking the path between the desk and the door.

"We'll be finished when I say we are," he said.

He moved closer, trapping her against the desk. His face was so close that she could see the pores in his skin and smell the liquor on his breath.

"I've been wondering whose side you're really on, mine or his," he said. "Maybe it's time you showed me."

Resisting would give her away, Allison knew. She had to keep up this masquerade until she got safely out of the room. "This isn't a good time, Garrett," she said. "Not with your girlfriend out there at the front desk."

"Monica?" He laughed, but he didn't let her go. "She's a lot of fun, but we're not exclusive. Believe me, she won't mind."

His arms went around her, hands sliding under her blazer. When he kissed her, thrusting with his tongue, his mouth tasted of onions and whiskey. Allison remembered the phone, tucked into her inside pocket. What if his groping hands were to find it? She had to keep it safe until she could get free of him and get out of here.

From down the hall came the sound of approaching footsteps—a woman's footsteps, probably Monica's. She might get a shock if she opened the door, but right now that was just what Allison wanted— anything that would let her escape. *Please, Monica. Please open that door . . .*

The door opened. Allison heard a gasp as Garrett's arms released her. She stumbled to one side, wiping her mouth. When she looked past Garrett, her heart dropped.

It wasn't Monica who stood in the open doorway. It was Brianna.

Stifling a cry, Brianna wheeled and bolted back down the hall, toward the front desk. From somewhere behind her, she could hear Allison's voice. "Wait, Brianna! Let me explain!"

But Brianna didn't want to hear her stepmother's explanation. She didn't want to look at Allison or hear her voice. All she wanted was to be somewhere else.

One hand fumbled for her car keys as she raced out the front of the building. As she unlocked her car and flung herself into the driver's seat, she could see Allison coming outside, waving and shouting something. Ignoring her, Brianna gunned the engine and roared out of the parking lot.

Half blinded by tears, she drove randomly, scarcely aware of stop signs and traffic lights. Her cell phone had begun ringing and ringing. After glancing at the caller ID and seeing that it was Allison, she turned the phone off and kept driving.

Finally, reminding herself that another traffic violation could land her in jail or cause her to lose her license, she pulled onto a quiet side street and stopped at the curb.

Shaking, she buried her face in her palms. She felt sick to her stomach. She had just begun to like Allison, to see her as a trusted friend. And now this.

Brianna's fist pounded the dashboard. For Allison to betray *her* was bad enough. But to betray her own husband—Brianna's generous, loving father who'd given the woman everything her greedy little heart desired—that was truly unforgivable.

And Garrett—he was a single man now. But that didn't make it all right to carry on with his partner's pretty young wife. For years, Brianna had considered him her friend. But he would never be her friend again. She remembered how Allison had warned her away from him. Never in a million years would she have guessed that Allison wanted Garrett for herself.

The lying, conniving, faithless bitch!

What now? Brianna knew she wasn't ready to go home and face her father. She needed to cool down. And she needed to talk to Liam.

Looking around, she realized that she wasn't far from the Lakeside Forest Wilderness Area, a natural hiking park in the heart of Branson, with miles of winding trails. A peaceful walk might be just the thing to calm her nerves before she decided what to do next.

After parking at the trailhead, she tightened the laces on her sneakers, took her phone, and locked her purse in the trunk. She chose one of the easier trails that wound through thickets of oak, redbud, hickory, and the tall, cedar-like trees called ash junipers. As a little girl, Brianna had hiked this trail many times with her mother, who had known all the trees, flowers, and animals along the way. How she wished her mother could be with her now.

Allison had tried to call Burke twice. There was no answer on his cell or on the house landline. Only after the third try did she remember overhearing a phone conversation yesterday between Burke and his friend Hoagie—something about going out for burgers and beer today.

It would be like Burke to turn off his cell phone, or even leave it at home, when he was with friends. He hated having a good conversation interrupted by a ringing phone. If he was out with Hoagie, she'd have no way of letting him know about finding the fake contract until he got home. Worse, she couldn't tell him about the fiasco in Garrett's office.

All she could do was keep looking for Brianna.

When she'd run outside to stop the girl, Allison had left her purse, with her car keys, in her desk. By the time she'd run back to get it—without encountering Garrett, thank heaven—Brianna's car was nowhere in sight.

Calling her had been useless, although Allison had tried. All she could do was drive, trying to remember Brianna's favorite places where she might go to be alone, think, and maybe phone Liam.

Now, after half an hour of frantic driving, Allison was running out of options. Maybe it was time to go home and wait for Brianna to show up. But something told her that right now, home was the last place Brianna would want to be. All she could do was keep calling and keep looking.

She was headed down a side street when her car engine sputtered and stalled. Using the forward momentum that remained, she steered to the right and made a rolling stop at the curb. Cranking the ignition, she tried to start the car again. Nothing. Then she noticed the fuel gauge.

Not only was she out of options—she was out of gas.

* * *

Brianna walked along the trail, fallen leaves crunching beneath her feet. She could feel her heart pumping adrenaline through her body. Tears stung her eyes. She was so hurt, so angry. How could Allison betray her family like this?

A half mile down the trail she came to a sheltered bench. By now she was ready to sit down and phone Liam. She didn't usually call him when he was working, but this was an emergency. She needed to hear his voice and know that, even at a distance, he was there for her. It wouldn't make everything all right. At this moment it seemed as if nothing would ever be all right again.

When she turned on her phone, she saw several voice mails from Allison. She deleted them without listening. Then she called Liam.

Liam answered on the third ring. In the background she could hear the clatter of metal tools and the sound of an engine starting up.

"Brianna, are you okay?" he asked anxiously.

"More or less," she said. "I know I'm interrupting your work. But, oh, Liam, I'm having the most awful day! I just had to hear your voice."

"It's okay that you called," he said. "Hang on, let me get someplace quiet where I can hear you."

She could hear the garage sounds fading, then the closing of a door. "That's better," he said. "Now, what's wrong?"

She began with the news from Northwestern. "They're not letting me come back. My grades are okay but not good enough. Liam, I miss you so much. Maybe I could just come back to Evanston and get some kind of job, as a waitress or a receptionist. At least we'd be together."

"Don't even think about that, Brianna. We can work things out, but you've got to get back into school."

"I did apply to Missouri State in Springfield. It's cheaper and closer than Northwestern. But I'm still waiting to hear. Oh—and here's some good news. My dad is willing to meet you. He wants you to let us know when you can come."

"That's great—I hope. I'll see when I can get time off. Is that all? Your bad news doesn't sound like the end of the world."

"That's because I haven't told you the worst."

She told him then, about walking into Garrett's office and catching Allison in his arms.

"You're talking about your stepmother? The woman who came here with you? She seemed pretty cool. That's hard to believe. Are you sure that's what you saw? Could she have been trying to fight him off?"

"They were all over each other—and no, she wasn't trying to fight him off. Oh, Liam! I don't know what to do! I don't want her in our house. I don't want to talk to her, or even look at her. And my poor dad—this is going to kill him!"

"Have you talked to your dad?" Liam asked.

"I don't know if I can. It would devastate him."

"Listen," Liam said. "I know what can happen when secrets fester. Put yourself in his place. Would you rather hear the truth from someone who loves you, or have it come out—as it will come out—some other way?" His voice gentled. "I'm not telling you what to do. I'm only asking you to think about it. Ask yourself how long you can hide a lie?"

Tears welled in Brianna's eyes. Liam was right. Much as it would hurt her father to tell him what she'd seen, it would hurt more for him to find out she'd known the truth and kept it from him.

"I'll think about it—and try to be brave," she said. "Thank you, Liam. Just hearing your voice helps. Let us know when you can come."

"I will—and you'll get through this all right, Brianna. You're a strong person and I love you."

"I love you, too." Wiping her eyes, Brianna ended the call and headed back toward the trailhead. She thought about calling her father, but that would only make him worry about her. It would be better to just show up.

What if Allison had already called him? She could have fed him a string of lies—lies that he would believe because he loved her. Whatever the story turned out to be, Brianna knew she could no longer stay in the house with that woman. Her father had a choice to make. Either Allison would have to go, or she would.

Half an hour later she pulled into the empty garage and went upstairs to the main floor of the house. Nobody appeared to be home, but as she looked out the window toward Peaceful Lane, she saw Hoagie's Jeep Wagoneer pull up in front of the house. Her father eased himself out of the passenger side. As the Jeep pulled away, he came up the walk to the front door, moving slowly as if in pain.

Brianna ran to open the door for him. He gave her a smile as she closed the door behind him. "Home so early? Didn't you have community service today?"

"I decided to skip. I need to talk to you, Dad."

His eyes narrowed. "This sounds serious. Is Allison home yet?"

"I guess not. Her car isn't in the garage. Sit down. You look tired. Can I get you anything to drink?"

He settled onto the living room sofa with a cushion behind his back. "A glass of water would be nice. And could you get me a couple of ibuprofen tablets from that bottle on the nightstand? I'm afraid I overdid it a little this afternoon."

Brianna scurried off and came back with water and pills. While he swallowed them, she moved a black leather footstool in front of his chair and sat down to face him.

"Now what is it?" he asked her. "And how bad could it be? We're both here, aren't we?"

"You're always such an optimist." She took one of his hands and held it in hers. He'd lost weight since the accident. His fingers felt thinner than she remembered—or maybe it was because she wasn't a little girl anymore. "Here's the first thing. I heard from the dean at Northwestern about my reapplication. I won't be going back there."

"I'm sorry, honey. I know you had your heart set on it. But it's not the end of the world. There are plenty of good colleges, some of them close by. You'll be fine."

"I know. But here's the other thing I have to tell you."

"Lord, you're not pregnant, are you?" His face had gone slightly pale.

"No, Dad! Heavens no! Nothing like that. But in its own way, it's even worse." She took a deep breath. "It's about Allison."

He listened then, his sad but gentle expression

never changing as she told him how she'd wanted to talk with Garrett about her college rejection and how she'd walked into his office to find Allison in his arms.

By the time she reached the end of her story, she was in tears. "I didn't want to tell you, Dad. I know you love her, and I know how this must hurt. But I couldn't imagine living here, seeing you every day, and keeping such an awful secret."

He shook his head. "Listen to me, Brianna. I understand what you think you saw. But there are two sides to every story. You saw *what* was happening. But what you didn't see was *why*."

She jerked her hand away from his. "I can't believe this! You're actually taking her side! He was *kissing* her, Dad! Right there in his office! And she was letting him!"

"I don't suppose you gave her a chance to explain."

"No! I ran! I didn't want to hear her lies. I know what I saw!"

He straightened in the chair, wincing with pain. "I told you there are two sides to every story. It's time you heard the rest. Garrett has been helping the Mob get control of my business. They made him some promises, and he was ambitious enough, and naïve enough, to believe them. Allison and I both knew it, but before we could do anything legal to stop them, we needed proof. Allison went to work for Garrett to get that proof. That included pretending to be on his side."

"Like a spy, you mean?" So far, the story sounded pretty far-fetched.

"Yes, like a spy, although I hadn't thought of it in that way. I haven't talked to her since this happened, but I'm guessing she might have been caught searching Garrett's office. Letting him kiss her may have been the only way to protect herself and get out of a bad situation."

"And you really believe that?" Brianna shook her head. "I know what I saw, Dad, and it didn't look like play-acting. What would you do if you found out she was lying—that she and Garrett were having an affair? Would you divorce her?"

Sadness, like a passing shadow, transformed his face for a moment. "If that were true, and if Allison said she was sorry, and meant it, I'd forgive her."

It wasn't what Brianna expected to hear. "You'd forgive your wife for such a terrible thing?" she asked. "How can you be so sure of that?"

His eyes held hers with a tenderness that was almost painful. "Because I did it once before," he said. "And I've never been sorry."

"Once before?" Brianna was stunned. "You mean Allison—?"

"No. Not Allison."

No! The numbness of denial dissolved into a flowing wound that drained her memories of warmth and trust. She would have given anything to have her father take back what he'd just told her. But she realized he'd had no choice. It had been the only way to make her understand.

"It was after your mother lost the baby," he said. "She needed somebody to be there for her. It should have been me. But I failed her. It was as much my fault as hers."

"How . . ." Brianna's voice quivered. "How did you manage to get past it all and stay together?"

"It wasn't easy. But we had you. And we loved each other. In time, we forgave and moved on."

Brianna stared at him, thinking how little she had truly known of her parents and who they were in their private hearts.

"And what about you?" A raw, lingering pain made her bold enough to ask. "I know you spent a lot of time on the road. Were you a faithful husband, Dad?"

"Surprisingly enough, I was," he said. "Oh, I had plenty of chances. But I loved your mother, and I figured that if I slipped up once, there'd be a second time, and a third, and before long, I'd become the kind of man I hated. It was easier not to even start down that path. But you know, Brianna, your mother never asked me what I did on the road—she trusted me that much. And I trust Allison. I don't plan to ask her anything."

As if on cue, they heard the garage door open and the sound of a car driving in. Allison had come home. Brianna jumped to her feet.

"You can stay if you want to," her father said.

"No—I've had enough drama for one day. I'm going up to my room. Tell Allison I'm all right."

Brianna fled up the stairs and down the hall to her bedroom. She could smooth things out with Allison later. Right now she needed to be by herself.

As she closed the door, her gaze fell on the framed photo of her family—her father and Kate, smiling their sun-splashed smiles, as if they'd never known a dark moment in their lives. How human they'd been, how strong. And how safe she'd felt in the little world they'd created for her. As a child, she'd looked at them and seen two perfect people. But now it was time to grow up. It was time to love her parents for who they were and would always be.

She could only wish their kind of love for herself and Liam.

* * *

Allison walked into the living room and collapsed on the sofa next to Burke. "What an afternoon!" she said. "To top it off, I ran out of gas and had to call the auto club. They took forever getting to me. Have you heard from Brianna?"

"She's upstairs," Burke said. "She said to tell you she's all right."

"Thank goodness! I was looking everywhere for her. I was so worried about her." Allison felt the knot in her stomach loosen and unravel. "So she told you what she saw?"

"She did. I managed to calm her down. No need to say another word. I understand."

Absolute trust. That was Burke. Sweet heaven, how she loved the man!

"I brought you a present," she said, taking the phone out of her pocket. After bringing up the photos she'd taken, she handed the phone to Burke.

He took time to study them before he nodded. "Good job. I think we've got the bastards. And I hope to hell you're not going back there again." He laid the phone on the coffee table and leaned back into the cushions. He'd had a long, busy day, and it showed. He looked tired but happy.

"When I was out with Hoagie this afternoon, he took me by the car lot. They'll be delivering a 2013 Camry in the morning. Decent car. It'll do for now."

"So you'll be king of the road again."

"Not quite. But tomorrow, as soon as I've got wheels under me, I'll be taking these photos to the police. Hopefully the evidence will be enough for a criminal case. If not, I'll take them to my lawyer. Much as I'd enjoy putting a few people behind bars, what I really need is to get Edgeway off my back, get rid of Garrett, put Fran back at the front desk, and start renovating the American Heartland."

"But what about the loan?" Allison asked. "Have you heard anything?"

"Oh—with all this excitement, I forgot to tell you. This afternoon, before Hoagie came by, I made a call to the bank. They said they'd reviewed the application and everything looks good. But they want to make sure Edgeway is out of the picture before they issue the funds. We'll be able to do that now. Thanks to you, we've got a weapon to use against those bastards."

He circled Allison with his arm and pulled her close. "You've done a great job. But now that I'm on my feet again, it's time for you to step back and let me take over. Once I've nailed Garrett and his Mob buddies to the wall, I'm going to reorganize the office around the renovation, talk to the contractors, hire a good manager . . ." He bent and kissed her forehead. "You can take it easy."

Allison nestled against him, but she had the vague sense that something wasn't right. Suddenly she knew what it was.

"Maybe I don't want to take it easy," she said. "I've shown you how much help I can be. I've had business experience. Keep me on as your manager— even your partner. Let me work with you."

He frowned, hesitating. "I don't know about that. I didn't marry a business partner. I married a wife. Kate never worked outside the home, and she was perfectly happy. I provided for her. She took care of our daughter and our house, she entertained our friends, shared the boat with me . . ." He stared at Allison's displeased face. "What?"

She rose, turning to face him. "I'm not Kate. And I can't—I *won't*—go back to being your little trophy wife. If you won't make me a part of your business, then I'll go out and find a job somewhere else! And that isn't a threat, Burke. It's a promise."

He'd gone cold, whether with shock or with anger, she couldn't tell. But she wasn't about to back down. She loved her husband. But she was tired of being nothing more than a useless ornament.

This moment, she sensed, was a turning point in their marriage. But where would they go from here? Allison didn't know. She only knew that she'd taken a stand, and there could be no turning back.

"I'm going upstairs to change," she said. "After that I'm going for a walk. If you and Brianna get hungry, there's leftover Chinese in the fridge."

She stalked up the stairs. When she came down a few minutes later, dressed in her running clothes, Burke was nowhere in sight. She could hear the TV from the den, broadcasting what sounded like a football game. She knew he liked it when she watched with him. But this wasn't the time.

Still limping slightly on her twisted ankle, she headed out the back door and down to the path.

CHAPTER 15

Allison lay wide-awake, gazing at the moon through the closed French doors. After a trying day, an hour-long walk, and a stress-filled evening, she was exhausted. But her mind kept replaying the day, over and over, refusing to let her sleep.

Tonight she'd returned from her walk to find Burke still parked in the den with the football game on. Brianna had given her an embarrassingly awkward apology for jumping to conclusions earlier, then ducked out to go to dinner with friends. By the time Brianna returned home, Burke had gone to bed, and Allison had gone to her room.

Restless, she freed her legs from the tangled sheets and swung her feet to the floor. Slipping on her quilted pink satin robe, she opened the French doors and stepped out onto the balcony. A cold night wind rippled the dark waters of the lake and dried a tear on her cheek.

What was she doing in this family? She loved Burke and was growing to love Brianna. But they didn't really want a woman like her. They wanted a motherly earth goddess who could steer a boat, throw a great party, crack a joke, grill a mess of fish, and still give her husband what he needed in bed.

They wanted a woman like Kate.

Allison's hands gripped the wrought-iron rail of the balcony. It wasn't fair. She'd tried so hard. But she couldn't please everyone—not even the man she loved. She wasn't Kate and never would be.

Kate.

Tonight, even the name was like a ghostly whisper on the wind.

A chilling gust whipped her hair across her face and lifted the hem of her robe. Seized by sudden resolve, Allison turned back into the bedroom and closed the French doors against the coming storm. Right or wrong, it was time she learned the rest of Kate's story.

It was time to open the sealed envelope.

Lifting the mattress, she found the packet of letters.

Her fingertips tingled as she held the white, business-size envelope marked *For Burke, to be opened after my death.*

Was she about to make the biggest mistake of her life?

Just do it! she told herself. But she couldn't simply rip it open. She would have to steam it open and glue the flap shut when she'd finished reading what was inside, in case Burke, or anyone else, ever found the letters.

Stop dithering! Just do it!

She shoved the envelope into the deep pocket of her robe, went downstairs to the kitchen, and set a kettle of water to heat on the stove. The house was quiet, but in case Burke or Brianna caught her by surprise, she put a packet of chamomile tea and a cup on the counter.

When steam started rising, she held the sealed envelope over the spout of the kettle. Once the flap was loose, she turned off the stove, turned off the light, and carried the envelope back to her bedroom.

Sitting on the bed, she lifted the flap. Inside she found a smaller envelope, blue, and similar to the ones that had held Kate's other letters. This envelope, too, was sealed.

Allison was preparing for another trip to the kitchen when she turned the envelope over. Her throat jerked tight as she read the single line of Kate's handwriting.

For the woman who marries my husband

There would be no need to steam it open. This, Kate's last letter, was for her.

Allison ran a fingertip under the edge of the flap, trying not to tear it.

With unsteady hands, she lifted the pages out of the blue envelope, unfolded them, and began to read.

> *The doctors have given me just a few more precious weeks. While I can still hold a pen and form words on paper, I want to reach out to you—to welcome you, perhaps, or even to thank you. I understand that sooner or later, after I'm gone, Burke will remarry. Please know that I'm at peace with this. As a man who needs to give and receive love, Burke will be lonely without a companion. I'm grateful that you'll be there to offer him, and our daughter, the love that I can only give them in memory.*

I'm sorry we didn't get a chance to meet—then again, maybe we did. Maybe I stood behind you in the grocery line or watched you jogging on the path that runs below our house. Maybe you're one of the pretty nurses who cared for me at the end of my life. Or maybe you're a stranger from a faraway place. Not that I care whether you're pretty or clever or accomplished. All that matters to me is that you'll be kind to the people I love.

A bit of advice now, if you don't mind.

Being married to Burke wasn't always easy. We were happy in the end, but we had to earn that happiness. We had to learn patience and forgiveness, sometimes the hard way.

Like me, you'll learn as you go. But don't let anyone, not our friends, not even Burke, hold me up as an example. I was the woman Burke needed when he was starting a family, building a business, and raising a daughter. But you're the woman for the man he is now. That's why he chose you. That's why he loves you. Feel free to be that woman.

Here, Kate's handwriting began to waver, as if writing had exhausted what little strength she had left. But still, the letter continued.

Burke can be stubborn and cantankerous. But you'll find that those times are when he needs you the most. And if you show that you need him in return, that can be the greatest gift of all.

Wishing you a lifetime of happiness,
Kate

Allison reread the letter through a blur of tears. When she thought of the dying Kate, her hair gone, her body wasted, writing with love to the woman who would take her place . . .

There were no words.

She lay on her back, holding the letter to her heart. If Burke had given it to her on their wedding day, she would have been touched. But now, knowing what she knew of Kate, reading those words was like opening a vein.

Many things in the letter had struck home. But after clashing with Burke last night and stalking off in a huff, it was the final paragraph that went straight to Allison's heart. Was that what Burke had been trying to tell her when he'd argued against her working—simply that he needed *her*? Not as a business partner, but as a life companion.

And when was the last time she'd let Burke know that she needed him? After the accident, she'd just barged in, taken over and set out to save the day for his business. She'd treated him like a helpless invalid, not like the still powerful man he was. No wonder he'd hated it.

What a fool she'd been.

Sitting up, she swung her legs off the bed, folded Kate's letter and tucked it with the others, under the mattress. Then she walked to the door and turned off the light switch. There were night-lights along the stairs. She could find her way.

Burke's room was dark and cold, the way he liked it for sleep. Slivers of moonlight, shining through the venetian blinds, gave her enough light to see where she needed to go.

Passing a chair, she slipped out of her robe and tossed it over the back. Shivering in her thin silk nightgown, she tiptoed toward the bed. Burke had needed to sleep on his back since the surgery. As she leaned over him, she could hear the low rush of his breathing. How she'd missed that sound and the way it made her feel safe in the night.

Lifting a corner of the covers, she slipped into the warm darkness beside him. She snuggled close, feeling the contours and textures of his naked body and drowning her senses in the rich male aromas of his skin. How could she have forgotten how sweet it was, lying next to him.

He groaned and stirred. "What . . . are you doing here?" he muttered.

"I was lonesome," she whispered in his ear. "Lie still."

She began kissing him and stroking him, her hand moving across his chest and along his belly. By the time her fingers traced the smooth strip of hair that made a path downward from his navel, he was breathing hard and fully ready for her.

With a growl of arousal, he reached for her and pulled her almost roughly on top of him. Hungry with need, she guided him into her and began to move.

Their lovemaking was bittersweet and explosive, sweeping them both away with its intensity, leaving them spent, satisfied, and at peace. Afterward she lay nestled against his side, drifting on the brink of sleep.

"So how soon do you want to sign on as my business partner?" he asked.

"I thought I just did," she teased, laughing. "No, seriously, is this what it took?"

"Don't underestimate me," he said. "I know I gave you a hard time, but my mind was made up before you went stalking out the door. I'd have told you if you'd come into the den and found me. When you didn't I just figured you needed time to cool down."

"You're impossible," she said.

"I know."

"And I wouldn't have you any other way," she said.

"I know that, too." He kissed her with a tenderness that brought tears to her eyes.

CHAPTER 16

Two weeks later

The November day was diamond bright, the waters of Table Rock Lake so clear that Brianna, looking over the stern of the boat, could see all the way down to the rocky ledges that had given the lake its name. The trees along the bank stood bare, but their fallen leaves flashed autumn colors where they drifted on the subtle current.

In happy times past, it had been Brianna's mother who sat in the stern and manned the tiller. Now that honor had fallen to Brianna. She ran the Evinrude E-TEC twenty-five horsepower outboard motor at trolling speed, inching along on a parallel course with the shore, while her father taught the first-timers, Liam and Allison, how to cast for largemouth bass.

"Bass like shelter," Burke was saying. "See those rocks down there? That's a place where they like to hang out and wait for food—worms, minnows, whatever comes their way. But we don't need live bait. These soft plastic lures look enough like the real thing to fool them. Now let's try casting."

Liam went first. Last night at dinner, Brianna had held her breath when he and her father were introduced. But within a few minutes they were hitting it off like buddies, talking about the vintage cars they both prized.

Liam, who'd never fished before, was eager to learn. After a couple of tries, with coaching from Burke, he could cast the line smoothly and accurately. To Brianna, that was no surprise. Liam seemed to do everything well.

Their future was still unsettled. Brianna had been accepted by Missouri State University for the upcoming semester. Liam was applying for jobs in Springfield. He'd had several offers but was taking his time, looking for the right opportunity to build his own business.

Burke had taken a rare day off from supervising the renovation of the American Heartland. Once he'd turned the photos of the forged contract over to his lawyer, the threat of legal action had scared off the Edgeway Group. And Burke had agreed not to press charges against Garrett if his partner would sever all ties with the business and leave town. With Garrett gone and the bank loan in his hands, Burke had made his wife a full partner in the agency and his assistant in the still risky theater project.

"Now it's your turn." Burke handed the rod to Allison and stood behind her, guiding her hands. "Just like I showed Liam. Thumb on the release button and the action smooth, not jerky. That's it . . . up and over . . ."

Allison looked nervous. Clearly she didn't have Liam's natural talent. The line went up and came down tangled, the lure plopping into the water near the boat.

"That's all right," Burke said. "Reel it in and try—"

His words ended in a gasp as the line went taut, arching the rod and almost pulling it out of Allison's hands. "Hang on!" he yelled. "This one's a real lunker. Careful, now, keep the line tight or you'll lose him! Liam, get the net! Have it ready!"

His hands covered Allison's to help her as the big bass cleared the water. Seconds later the fish was in the net. Burke used the club to give it a merciful end. "I'd guesstimate he's about a nine-pounder. There's supper, folks."

Allison looked slightly dazed. "Are you all right?" Liam asked her.

"I think I need to sit down," she said, sinking onto a seat.

Everyone laughed, including Brianna. Her mother would have loved this, she thought.

Brianna had never been sure about the afterlife, but something told her that if her mother's spirit were here, she would be laughing along with them—her favorite people and the loved ones they'd found—all of them happy, as Kate would have wanted them to be.

EPILOGUE

Eighteen months later

"How about unzipping me?" Allison turned her back to her husband, who'd just tossed his tux jacket on a chair. They'd just come home from hosting a big charity event at the American Heartland.

The renovated theater was a true showplace now and had become the hottest ticket in Branson. Burke had called in favors and paid top dollar to get stars from places like Nashville and Las Vegas. His gamble was paying off. He'd already set enough aside to make the loan payments for the rest of the year.

A few months ago, the mayor had approached him about hosting an annual charity show and party at the American Heartland. The event tonight had been a grand success and raised an impressive sum of money for worthy causes. But for Allison, the evening had been exhausting. After three hours in high heels, she could no longer feel her feet.

"Heavens, I hope we don't end up having to do this every year," she said as the gown loosened around her and fell to the floor.

Burke nuzzled the back of her neck. "Especially not if you're pregnant again."

"We agreed that one would be enough," she said as his hand came to rest on the growing bulge of her belly. "I hope you're not having second thoughts."

"Not a one." Burke unfastened her bra. His hands massaged her tired back and shoulders. "With Brianna living in Springfield and engaged to Liam now, I'll be needing a new fishing buddy—besides you, of course."

Allison laughed. "Since I've never gotten the hang of casting, I'll probably just steer the boat."

As his arms went around her, Allison recalled Kate's letter, how she'd wanted to be there to dance at Brianna's wedding and to cuddle her grandchildren. Those pleasures would fall to Allison now.

She would embrace them with joy.

For Kate.

Read on for an excerpt from Janet Dailey's next
Tylers of Texas novel, coming soon.

TEXAS FREE

*She's a woman with a burning need to break
free from her past . . .*

Rose Landro is on the run. Seeking refuge at the
Rimrock Ranch, she is finally ready to claim the
land her granddaddy left her and make a fresh
start. But her return is rife with controversy when
cattle begin disappearing—and a handsome men-
ace named Tanner McCade starts watching Rose a
little too closely. Could the new cowhand be connected to the men she's hiding from? Or is there
another reason the rugged stranger is shadowing
her every move?

He's a man ready to fight boldly for his future . . .

There's a secret in Rose Landro's eyes, a mystery
that Special Ranger Tanner McCade is determined
to uncover. Even if the beauty isn't behind the cattle rustling he's investigating, she's way too skittish,
and all too exquisite for Tanner to just let slide past
his piercing gaze. Then he discovers a vulnerability
in Rose that has him aching to protect her—and
longing to possess her. . . .

Río Seco, Mexico
April 1985

The Mexican village slumbered under the light of a waning crescent moon. In the empty plaza, windblown shadows flickered over the cobblestones. The cantina was closed for the night, its outdoor tables and chairs locked away behind corrugated metal doors. A bat fluttered from the tower of the old adobe church and melted into darkness. A skinny dog foraged for leavings in the deserted marketplace.

The night was almost peaceful. But the stillness was heavy with tension—especially in one small adobe house on a dusty side street. Nothing in Río Seco was the way it had been before the Cabrera cartel took over the town. And for Rose Landro, after tonight, nothing would be the same again.

The click of a boot heel on the tiled patio startled Rose to full alertness. Lying fully dressed in the dark, she checked the impulse to sit up, fling aside the covers, and bolt out of bed. She was a small woman. Face-to-face, she'd be no match for the burly intruder who was stalking her. Her only chance of survival lay in surprise.

The loaded Smith and Wesson .44 was a cold lump under her pillow. As footsteps clicked across the patio, she closed her hand around the grip, cocked the hammer, and slid to the floor. Her free hand bunched the pillows into a semblance of her sleeping body and covered them with the blanket.

She knew who was coming for her. Lucho Cabrera, younger brother of the local cartel boss, was built like a short pile of bricks. He wore high-heeled cowboy boots to make him appear taller. The sound of those boots, clicking across the kitchen, chilled Rose's blood.

Gripping the heavy pistol, she crawled across the floor and pressed upward to stand against the wall, in the shadows behind the door. Her breath came in shallow gasps. Her pulse hammered in her ears.

The cartel would kill anyone who stood against them. They had already murdered Ramón and María Ortega, who'd taken Rose into their home twelve years ago. Rose would have fled for her life before now, but she could not leave without avenging the couple who'd cared for her like their own daughter.

Honor. The Ortegas had lived by that code. Now it was Rose's turn to carry on the tradition.

The footsteps were coming closer. Would Lucho stand in the doorway and fire at the lump in her bed, or did the sadistic pig plan on raping her first, as he'd done two months earlier when he'd caught her walking home alone after dark?

At the memory of his filthy, sweating body, her

finger tightened on the trigger. If ever a man deserved killing, it was Lucho Cabrera. Only his older brother, Refugio, was worse.

The bedroom door creaked open. Rose held her breath as Lucho stepped into the room, his pistol drawn. The faint moonlight, falling through the high, barred window, cast black shadows across his fleshy face. As he neared the bed, he holstered the gun. One hand fumbled with his belt buckle. *Good*. This was almost too easy. She could shoot him now, in the back. But something in her wanted more. She wanted him to see her. When the bullet tore into his body, she wanted him to know who had fired it.

She forgot to breathe. Every muscle was a coiled spring as she waited for the right moment.

"Brujita fea . . ." he muttered. The name, given to Rose because of the birthmark on her face, meant "ugly little witch." Over the years she'd learned to bear it with a measure of pride. Superstitious people tended to fear her, especially some of the men. But that wouldn't stop Lucho. He might even be planning to take a trophy back to his brother—an ear, a hand, or even her head—as proof of his bravery.

Still muttering, he loosened his trousers and jerked back the blanket. That was when he realized he'd been tricked. He spun around, cursing as Rose stepped out of the shadows, the .44 gripped between her hands.

"Muera, pendejo. Die, you bastard," she said, aiming the heavy revolver at his chest.

Lucho had no time to draw his weapon, but in the instant her finger tightened on the trigger, he lunged for her. The pistol roared, but Lucho's move had thrown off her aim. The bullet struck his right shoulder, barely slowing the brute's charge.

Slammed by the recoil, Rose staggered backward. Her feet tangled in the loose rug on the floor. Losing her balance, she went down hard, landing on one arm.

She managed to keep a one-handed grip on the gun, but now he was standing over her, blood streaming down his sleeve. She could hear the hiss of his breath between his teeth as he reached for his holster, then paused, cursing. That was when Rose realized her shot had disabled his shooting arm. The flicker of distraction as he switched to draw with his left hand gave her the only chance she had left.

She cocked the .44 and pulled the trigger.

Connect with Us

Visit us online at
KensingtonBooks.com
to read more from your favorite authors, see books
by series, view reading group guides, and more.

Join us on social media
for sneak peeks, chances to win books and prize packs,
and to share your thoughts with other readers.

facebook.com/kensingtonpublishing
twitter.com/kensingtonbooks

Tell us what you think!
To share your thoughts, submit a review,
or sign up for our eNewsletters, please visit:
KensingtonBooks.com/TellUs.

More from Bestselling Author
JANET DAILEY

Calder Storm	0-8217-7543-X	$7.99US/$10.99CAN
Close to You	1-4201-1714-9	$5.99US/$6.99CAN
Crazy in Love	1-4201-0303-2	$4.99US/$5.99CAN
Dance With Me	1-4201-2213-4	$5.99US/$6.99CAN
Everything	1-4201-2214-2	$5.99US/$6.99CAN
Forever	1-4201-2215-0	$5.99US/$6.99CAN
Green Calder Grass	0-8217-7222-8	$7.99US/$10.99CAN
Heiress	1-4201-0002-5	$6.99US/$7.99CAN
Lone Calder Star	0-8217-7542-1	$7.99US/$10.99CAN
Lover Man	1-4201-0666-X	$4.99US/$5.99CAN
Masquerade	1-4201-0005-X	$6.99US/$8.99CAN
Mistletoe and Molly	1-4201-0041-6	$6.99US/$9.99CAN
Rivals	1-4201-0003-3	$6.99US/$7.99CAN
Santa in a Stetson	1-4201-0664-3	$6.99US/$9.99CAN
Santa in Montana	1-4201-1474-3	$7.99US/$9.99CAN
Searching for Santa	1-4201-0306-7	$6.99US/$9.99CAN
Something More	0-8217-7544-8	$7.99US/$9.99CAN
Stealing Kisses	1-4201-0304-0	$4.99US/$5.99CAN
Tangled Vines	1-4201-0004-1	$6.99US/$8.99CAN
Texas Kiss	1-4201-0665-1	$4.99US/$5.99CAN
That Loving Feeling	1-4201-1713-0	$5.99US/$6.99CAN
To Santa With Love	1-4201-2073-5	$6.99US/$7.99CAN
When You Kiss Me	1-4201-0667-8	$4.99US/$5.99CAN
Yes, I Do	1-4201-0305-9	$4.99US/$5.99CAN

Available Wherever Books Are Sold!

Check out our website at **www.kensingtonbooks.com**.